Movers, Mines and Murder

A Science Fiction Cozy Mystery - Book 2

Katherine Okia

For my darling daughter, Marta
For my supportive husband, Peter

CONTENTS

CHAPTER 1

Coraline Brimble crossed the parking lot of a large convention center at the edge of the city of Tymal. She took her time heading to the front doors, taking in the field of wildflowers flanking the pavement. Wearing a somber gray dress, she'd put her curly brown hair up in a chignon to fit the solemnity of the occasion. She stepped through the large ornate wooden doors and into the entryway, only to be instantly accosted by Hazel Cartwright, a blue-eyed woman with a mass of curly blonde hair. Cora laughed.

"Cora!" Hazel cried as she wrapped her in a tight hug. "I'm so happy you're here."

Cora hugged her with watery eyes as she thought of her friend's pain. Once Hazel let go, she quickly wiped her eyes. Cora blinked a few times, trying to hold back her tears.

"I'm so sorry for your loss," Cora said, noticing Hazel's pale face and strained expression.

Cora was a Feeler who could sense the emotions of others. But now, in a crowd of a few hundred people, she had to shield herself from other people's emotions to keep from becoming overwhelmed. She wished she could lower her shield and sense the depth of Hazel's emotions—she'd helped her like that many times in the past.

"Everything will be alright now that you're here," Hazel said with a lopsided smile.

The funeral was for Hazel's husband, Michael Pendleton, who passed away unexpectedly when he fell down the stairs at the Spring Gala. The Pendleton family hosted this Gala once a year to celebrate the goddess Askae.

In an ancient religion, Askae gave special gifts to certain humans, which were passed down, resulting in Askovians. Their family members were called Askovs. Pendleton Askovians were Movers who could manipulate objects with their minds.

She followed Hazel into one of the enormous rooms that had been prepared for the funeral. A separate private ceremony had taken place earlier for immediate family and very close friends to mourn with the cremated remains. The purpose of this public ceremony was to show the power and prestige of the Pendleton family. The entryway and large conference rooms were traditionally decorated with large paintings in ornate gold frames. It included plush carpets and intricately decorated doors and windows.

"Thank you so much for coming," Hazel said as a look of pure happiness filled her face. "I thought I'd have to endure this on my own."

"Well, you're not alone now. Just point me to the dragons and I'll start the battle," Cora said with her lips in a grim line.

Hazel stifled a laugh. "Don't get me started. You'll get me in trouble."

"You're right," Cora said with a small smile. "I was quoting your favorite poem."

"I know. As much as I appreciate it, the dragons are my parents and I really don't think you'll win," Hazel said.

Cora had become Hazel's big sister and protected her while they were at boarding school. She'd even tried to talk to Hazel's mom about being kinder to Hazel, but had only received a withering glare. After Hazel graduated, her mom had isolated her from all of her friends. Cora didn't meet her again until after her wedding. She met with Hazel a few times after she married and sensed Hazel's increasing unhappiness. Hazel always tried to hide her true feelings, but Cora could always sense them anyway and it made her feel sorry for Hazel.

"How are you really?" Cora asked as the smile faded from her face.

"It's been difficult because of Mom," Hazel said in a muted voice. "I know from experience, I just need to endure her until she gets bored and goes back to ignoring me."

Slowly, the crowd moved to one of the large rooms to start the service. Hazel chose a seat near the back, while her parents sat in the front with the other Pendleton family members.

"Are you sure you're supposed to be here?" Cora asked, with a hint of concern in her voice.

"I don't want to be anywhere near my parents," Hazel said in a tense whisper. "I'm safer back here."

She gave Hazel a sympathetic glance and squeezed her hand.

A somber-looking officiant made his way to the podium and quietly stood next to a gallery of Michael Pendleton's images. Everyone quieted, and the officiant began the service. It started with praise for the accomplishments of the Pendleton family and finally transitioned to Michael Pendleton. The officiant's words included a list of his personal accomplishments, but there weren't many. Then his speech took an unexpected turn.

"Michael Pendleton died unexpectedly in the prime of his life," the officiant said. "In life, many unexpected events occur to test our courage, strength, and resolve. Prepare as much as you can for the unexpected, but also take time to truly enjoy life. Take the time to create meaningful memories, especially with children. Don't dwell on anger and bitterness, and choose to focus on love and happiness."

Cora blinked. The officiant usually reserved these words of encouragement for the private funeral. The surprising turn in the speech contrasted with what should have been a formal second gathering that included extended family and friends.

"Michael left behind a wife, Hazel Cartwright, his mother, Delores Pendleton, a sister, Julia Pendleton, as well as a host of aunts, uncles, and cousins."

A moment of silence elapsed before the officiant continued.

"The head of the Pendleton family and Michael's uncle, Evan Pendleton, is the next to speak," the officiant said.

Evan Pendleton stood and made his way to the podium. He was a sour-looking man with a protruding stomach and graying red hair. He gave an emotional talk about Michael's childhood and included some funny antics. Cora tuned out after that. She noticed Hazel staring out through one window as if she was bored.

After the service, Cora strolled next to Hazel and entered a separate room for refreshments. Askovs filled the new room, and she recognized most of them. Hazel made her way along the wall; almost as if she was trying to avoid someone, while Cora followed.

Suddenly, Winifred, Hazel's mom, appeared out of the crowd with a scowl on her face. She was a striking, slender woman with steel gray hair who looked like an older version of Hazel. Her shadow of a husband appeared just behind her.

"I know you've been trying to avoid me," Winifred hissed at Hazel. "Why didn't you give the speech we discussed? You made us all look bad."

Cora raised her eyebrows, sure no one even noticed. Nobody expected the spouse to make a formal talk at a funeral.

"I'm sorry, Mom. I just couldn't do it," Hazel whispered. "I asked the officiant to remove my name."

"This would've been good exposure for our family," Winifred said in a low voice. "If you weren't going to talk, you should have told me. I would've had your dad do it."

Her parents were both first generation Movers. As a result, Askovs didn't consider Hazel's parents an influential family, and this made them vulnerable. They were especially concerned about their family's only mine. Many Askovs depend on income from Lunar, Martian, and Jovian mines to support lavish lifestyles. Without protection, other Askovs could take their mine by force.

"I told you I really didn't want to. You wouldn't listen," Hazel whispered in a desperate, pleading voice.

"Instead, *that* woman sat where you should've been." Winifred said a little louder. "You had one job, provide an heir. Now there's nothing to tie us to the Pendleton family."

Cora's gaze slid over the surrounding people, and she gently hooked her arm around Hazel's. "We're attracting attention. Maybe you two can continue this conversation later."

Winifred immediately glanced at the people nearby, glared at Hazel, and melted into the crowd.

"Thank you, Cora," she said as her shoulders dropped and she sighed with relief. "Sometimes Mom gets carried away."

Several replies raced through Cora's mind about how cruelly Winifred treated her, but Hazel would never listen. Instead, she guided Hazel to a nearby empty table, and they took their seats. They pressed buttons on a meal crafter, which rearranged food molecules from the kitchen pantry and transported food or drinks to the table. A moment later, juice materialized on the table. A haunted, empty look settled on Hazel's face as she stared into her juice.

"Who's 'that woman' your mom mentioned?" Cora asked.

"Kaye, Michael's girlfriend," Hazel sighed.

"Girlfriend?" Cora raised both eyebrows.

"Kaye's very close with Delores," Hazel said. "She's basically a second daughter. Also, she and Julia are like sisters."

"I think I see," Cora said. "They all wanted Kaye."

"Now, I'm just wondering what Mom has planned next for me," Hazel said with a wan smile. "I know the wheels are already turning."

"Don't you even get time to grieve the loss of your husband?" Cora asked.

"Well... I never loved Michael. I'm not actually a grieving widow," Hazel said, glancing at Cora and turning slightly pink. "I know that sounds bad, but it was an arranged marriage, and he also never made any effort to pretend we were in a real marriage." She sighed. "I'm mostly glad the marriage is over." She gasped. "I don't mean I wish Michael was dead, just that I wasn't happy as his wife."

Worried about a vulnerable mine, the Cartwright's solution to keeping it was to broker an arranged marriage between Michael and Hazel. Michael was part of a lesser Pendleton branch, meaning no one had any special abilities, and thus, they needed income. The marriage gave protection to the Cartwright's mine while funding the poorer Pendleton branch.

"Vivian, Vivian. There're some empty seats here," a woman in a dark-green dress called as she put her hand on a chair opposite Cora and Hazel.

Suddenly, Vivian appeared from the crowd. She was average height with plain brown hair but intelligent blue eyes. She glanced at Cora and Hazel with a frown and turned on her heel and left.

"Vivian, Vivian. Where are you going?" called the dark-green dress woman as she followed Vivian back into the crowd.

The last time she had seen Vivian, she'd called Earth Global Security or EGS, the police force for all Earth. The EGS had arrested Cora because of Vivian's lies.

"Try to ignore Vivian," Hazel said in a whisper. "She never liked me either."

A moment later, Aunt Ferna, Delores, Julia, and a gentleman squeezed through the crowd and took four seats opposite Cora and Hazel. Aunt Ferna was Cora's aunt on her mom's side. She wore a black suit that would have been appropriate for a business lunch as well as a funeral. She shared several features with Cora: the same copper skin tone, curly hair, although hers was gray, and their height. Both women were small, but Cora was slender where Aunt Ferna had filled out with age.

"I think you know my aunt," Cora said, turning to Hazel.

"Of course, Delores's friend," Hazel said as they exchanged nods. "I'm glad you could help arrange this funeral."

Delores had married into the Pendleton family and was a tall, thin woman with short, gray hair. She was reserved and cold whenever Cora met her on her own, but became relaxed and chatty around Aunt Ferna.

"You remember my niece, Dedie?" Aunt Ferna said, selecting a button on the meal crafter. A pale green drink materialized on the table and she took a sip.

"Of course, how are you, dear?" Delores asked as she selected another button on the crafter, producing a small cake slice and a cup of tea.

Aunt Ferna had grown up with Michael's dad and the other Pendleton siblings. When Delores married into the family, Aunt Ferna had taken her under her wing, which meant she'd spent a lot of time with Michael and his sister Julia when they were kids.

"Just fine—" Cora said.

Delores interrupted her when she turned back to Aunt Ferna.

"Oh, my dear, I forgot to tell you about..." Delores said in a lowered voice, and Aunt Ferna leaned closer to her friend. They discussed the latest gossip, swallowing their drinks.

"I think I've been dismissed," Cora said with a quiet chuckle.

"Don't take it personally. Delores is like that to everyone," Hazel said.

Cora wasn't as familiar with her daughter, Julia, who was a tall, slender redhead. Both Julia and Delores had the same pale blue eyes. Julia surveyed the table before taking her seat, and the gentleman sat next to her.

"What are you doing all the way over here? Did the grownups ban you from their table?" Julia asked with a snicker. "The rest of my family has gathered to talk about 'The Fight' over our mine." The Pendletons were considered the second most powerful Askov family after the Spencers. But several months ago, the Spencer family had stolen one of the Pendleton's mines.

Cora raised both eyebrows, surprised at how Julia spoke to Hazel. She glanced between the two women, but Hazel remained silent.

"Hello, Julia. It's been a while since I've seen you," Cora said, trying to diffuse the conversation.

"Yes, we just returned from a trip to visit our mines," Julia said and turned to the man beside her. He was fit, sporting a black jumpsuit and close-cropped hair. "This is Theo Pike. He joined us on our voyage home from Mars."

"It's a pleasure to meet you," Theo said in a somber voice.

Cora nodded her greeting.

"My Theo has a lot of entertaining stories working as mining security for several Askov families," Julia said. "But Hazel met someone on our voyage home, too. Isn't that right?" She added with a sly smile.

Cora wondered why Hazel let Julia talk to her like that.

"What were you saying about a fight over your mine?" Cora asked again, trying to redirect Julia's attention.

"The Spencers launched a small armed force and took over one of our lesser mines," Julia said, leaning forward while warming to the topic. "Unfortunately, Uncle Evan didn't have enough armed protection for that mine. Now, they're trying to figure out how to get it back."

She turned to Hazel. "It's strange they didn't ask your opinion."

"Actually, I've been wondering how you're going to afford your shopping sprees," Hazel said, finally stirring herself. "You used to rely on the income from both your and my family's mines. Now, your income is cut in half." She smirked.

"Don't talk to my daughter like that," Delores said in a loud voice. "You've only married into the family; you don't have any say in the family business." Cora thought this was ironic, given that Delores married into the family as well. Delores turned to Ferna. "Let's go. I want to introduce you to a few friends."

Delores rose and drifted away from the table. Aunt Ferna stood and dithered a little while, glancing from Hazel to her friend. Finally, she shuffled away.

Julia scoffed at Hazel, rose from the table, and stepped into the crowd. Theo followed her.

"Hazel, why do you let them talk to you like that?" Cora asked in a gentle voice.

"It's been six long years," Hazel said while her eyes teared up. "They hate me because I'm not Kaye. They strongly dislike my arranged marriage, because 'I took Michael away from Kaye.'

In the end, they view me as breeding livestock and not worth basic human respect."

Cora leaned over and hugged her friend. This confrontation and her hug felt so familiar. She'd been protecting Hazel since she was eight years old.

"The Pendletons treat you the way your parents treat you," Cora said and squeezed Hazel's hand. "You remember our talk in school? Leave and start your own life. You're still young."

"I can't do it," Hazel said and wiped her eyes with the back of her hands. "I don't have skills like you. I'm not a programmer, doctor, attorney, or anything else. Without the Cartwright mine, I'll starve."

"Hazel, you're a smart woman. You can learn a skill," Cora said, trying to encourage her. "I'll help you."

Hazel pulled her hand away from Cora and shook her head.

"In any case, I owe it to Zach," Hazel said in a very low voice. "If it hadn't been for me..."

Many years ago, Hazel had opened up to Cora, explaining that she'd accidentally caused the death of her eldest brother Zach.

When she was five and Zach thirteen, a little boy had used his Mover ability to push her to the ground. The little boy had then tried to attack Zach, who was a powerful Mover, and he'd retaliated by flinging the little boy into the air.

When the little boy died of his injuries, they had taken him away to an Askovian facility. Her family never saw Zach again, and her mom hated her for taking away her favorite son.

"You were five—it wasn't your fault," Cora said, leaning forward, wishing she could make Hazel see. "Your mom's wrong."

Hazel lowered her head and stared into her lap.

If I could read her emotions while we're having this talk, I might be able to help her get past her fear, Cora thought. *Maybe I'll have a chance later.*

CHAPTER 2

The following afternoon, Cora shielded herself from others' emotions before strolling through the front doors of the Grilled Skewer. The restaurant's decor contained artificial trees and small plants that could hardly be distinguished from the real ones. She inhaled the scents of grilled synthetic beef, chicken, and shrimp and grinned. Specialized factories grew synthetic animal products, seen as cleaner and more ethical alternatives to farming animals.

She was looking forward to seeing Brian in person. She'd missed their frequent lunches where they'd discussed the difficulties of programming her game. After a quick look around, she spotted Brian Farris' blue-gray eyes and broad smile. Cora paced toward him and plopped on a seat opposite.

"It's good to see you," Cora said with a grin.

Years ago, she'd met Brian at a get-together hosted by his uncle, Harold. They hadn't spoken much at the office event, but later that afternoon, they'd run into each other at an art gallery and discovered their mutual love for art.

"I know. I've missed our talks these past few weeks," Brian said with a small smile. "Do you need time to look at the menu?"

"Nope. I want my usual," Cora said, selecting buttons on the meal crafter. A moment later, grilled shrimp and vegetables appeared on a skewer with a small baked potato. A small glass with purple liquid also appeared on the table, and she immediately grasped it, taking several swallows.

"Mm... Love beetroot and carrot juice," she said, glancing at his side of the table. "What did you order?"

"I decided to try the special. It features pork," he said, taking a small bite. "Somehow it tastes like chicken."

They both chuckled. The rumor was that all synthetic meats were grown from the same starter cells, and flavored differently to get the desired meat. Cora, ever the investigator, had taken a tour of the factories. The different meats definitely had different starter cells, but they tended to be seasoned with the same seasonings in restaurants. This made them taste the same.

They ate in silence for a few minutes when Brian finally paused and sighed.

Cora wished she could sense his emotions, but she could tell from his face something bothered him.

"Oh... have you heard about Michael Pendleton?" he asked.

"Yes," she said with a sigh. "I was there when he fell."

"I'm so sorry," he said. "I didn't realize. We could've scheduled for some other time."

"No, no. It happened two weeks ago," she said. "But the funeral was yesterday."

"Do you want to talk about it?" he asked in a gentle tone.

"It was so strange," she said with furrowed eyebrows. "I was standing next to Hazel. You remember her?"

"Your old school friend," Brian nodded.

"The large crowds on and off the dance floor made it difficult to walk," she said in a quiet voice. "Suddenly, the crowd parted, giving me a clear view of Michael's back. He turned for a final wave to someone and stepped forward.

Michael's foot seemed to twist, and he missed the first step. His leg buckled, sending him tumbling headfirst down the stairs."

Brian reached across the table and gave her hand a reassuring squeeze.

"There's something bothering me," she said with a shiver. "What happened to the antigrav safeties?" The safeties were fast acting components that automatically adjusted local gravity to prevent falls. They were most common on stairs, but could be found at the bottom of elevators, immediately outside high-rise buildings, or sidewalks.

"Oh," Brian sat back in his chair, staring at the table. "Maybe they were under repair?"

"Usually, when that happens, they close the stairs," Cora said. "But nobody mentioned it."

"You mean none of them brought this up to you?" Brian leaned forward with a serious expression. "Cora, this could be an accident, but if it is something else, for your own safety, stay out of it."

"I have every intention of staying out of it," Cora said firmly, remembering her investigation into Harold's death. "I'm busy, anyway. Also, the EGS will do their analysis and talk to the Pendleton family. It's not my problem."

"Good to hear," Brian said. "You'd think after dealing with the EGS a few months ago, you'd try to avoid them."

"Unfortunately, Agent Lewis is leading this investigation," Cora said with a smirk. "He's still a jerk."

"Agent Lewis. Too bad," he said with a frown. "This time you're not connected with the family and it looks like an accident. He should leave you alone."

"Let's hope so," she said.

"Did you know Michael Pendleton?" he asked.

"I really didn't know him," she said. "I think I only met him once. I've met his uncle, Evan Pendleton, several times. But I don't really even know *him*." She took a sip of juice.

"I remember her family forced her to marry into the Pendleton clan," he said with a frown.

"I wonder what's going to happen to her now. She never had children with Michael," she sighed.

"Maybe now she can really be free," he said with a small smile.

"Then you don't know her mom," she said. "I'm sure Winifred Cartwright is already planning the next stages of her daughter's future."

"Let's change the topic," Brian said with a broad grin. "How's Mystery Adventures coming along?" Mystery Adventures was an educational puzzle game that allowed users to explore different biomes while using common sense math and science to find treasures or hidden clues.

"It's okay, but my users want more changes and it's getting harder to code them," she said. "Also, I'm still trying to make my launch date."

"So, about the same," he said with a smirk.

Cora chortled, feeling lighter with the change in their conversation. "It seems they want the ability to create groups," she said. "It makes sense. They could have one group against another and race to see who could find the most treasures."

"Sounds like a good idea," he said, taking a sip of water.

"I know, but it's a major rewrite of my entire program," she said. "Not a surface change, but all the mechanics that allow primary features have to be redone. I can do it, but probably not before the launch."

"What if you hold off on that change and promise it a few months from now?" he asked.

"I might have to do that," she said with a lopsided grin.

They chatted about her game for a few more minutes while a lightness spread through her chest as Brian engaged in their conversation.

"So, tell me what's going on with you?" she asked, changing the topic. She enjoyed hearing of the antics of spoiled Askovs that pestered Brian for an early advance on their mine's income.

Brian managed the Albright Corporation, which helped Askov families manage their mines. They handled miner negotiations, raw materials sales, and the quarterly payments to mine owners. These mines were the economic engine of Askov society.

The most profitable mines were located on the moons of Earth, Mars, and Jupiter, which had the highest abundance of alythium. This crystal altered local gravity and was used in almost every aspect of society: hover cars, spaceships, antigrav lifts, meal crafters, and more.

"I think you've heard that the Spencer family basically stole a small mine from the Pendletons," he said as he picked at the food on his plate.

"Yeah, Aunt Ferna told me a few weeks ago," Cora said. "What I can't figure out is why

Spencer Industries took such a tiny mine by force. It doesn't make sense."

"It does if you're Jessica Spencer and absolutely hate Evan Pendleton," Brian said. Jessica headed Spencer Industries, which owned and managed all Spencer family mines. Evan headed Pendleton Mining, which owned mines on four moons and paid out dividends to Pendleton family members. "I wish I understood what's going on between those two, because she's gotten worse over time."

"I wonder if Aunt Ferna has any information," Cora said, raising one eyebrow. "She always seems to know what's really going on in the Askov world."

"Ask her. I would love to know," he said with a sigh.

Cora wished she could sense his emotions. He was clearly down, and she used her ability sometimes to gauge the depth of emotions. She suspected things were worse than he led her to believe.

"Have you spoken to your mom about turning things over to your sis?" she asked.

"Eliza's off-world now and won't be back for a couple of weeks," he said. "She's better suited to dealing with cursing miners, disgruntled traders, and whiny Askovs. Really, it all wears me down, but she revels in it like Uncle Harold." He stared down at the table.

"I miss him too," she said, reaching for his hand and giving it a squeeze. "Wish he was here to guide you."

"I just wish he was here to take over his job," he said. "I shouldn't complain. Dad's been helping, but he doesn't want to get too involved. He was already in retirement when Harold..."

"What about your mom?" she asked.

"She hasn't touched this business since I was a baby," he said. "Things have changed a lot over the past thirty years."

"Well, I hope Eliza can either help more or take over for you," she said, hearing a chime.

Brian glanced at his comm bracelet and frowned.

"I have to go," he said as he stood. He leaned forward and kissed Cora's cheek before marching to the doors.

His sudden departure left Cora bereft. She'd hoped to talk more about her game, but she also worried about him coping with such a stressful job.

CHAPTER 3

Cora rolled onto her back and slowly opened her eyes while she lay in bed. Even though she had a full night's sleep, she felt drained by yesterday afternoon's hours of programming and the constant demands of her users. The thought of another full day of coding made her want to go back to sleep, but she didn't have that luxury.

"Lights," she said, addressing Haley, her home's AI.

She squinted at the bright lights and lowered her feet to the floor as she rubbed her face and ran her hands through her curls. Cora glanced around her room, which resembled a small apartment with a dining table, office table, sofa, and bathroom. It was one of seven bedrooms of her family's home, Brimble House.

"Sonic shower or water shower?" she asked. The sonic shower removed dirt by inaudible sound vibrations.

"Which would you prefer?" Haley asked.

"Water, maybe it will wake me up," she said, dragging herself out of bed and trudging to the bathroom. Although the sonic shower was faster, Cora preferred the coziness of warm water.

She stepped out of the shower, already washed and dried, and picked out casual clothes, which included an orange-yellow top and black pants. She skipped makeup and simply ran her fingers through her curly dark-brown hair as a way to comb it.

Cora sank into a chair at her dining table and selected coffee, synthetic eggs, and toast from the crafter. As soon as she took her first sip, her comm bracelet chimed. She glanced at her bedside table and decided to ignore it while munching on her toast. Her room had a beautiful view of the back garden, and she watched the birds flitting among the blooming flowers, wind rustling through the trees. As she finished her meal, her comm chimed again.

She sighed and paced to her bedside table. Grunting, she pressed a button on her bracelet, and an image of Hazel appeared in a floating screen. She played Hazel's voice message.

"Cora, I'm so sorry to bother you, but I need your help," Hazel said, her face marred with worry. "Something horrible has come up, and I really don't know what to do. I hope I can see you this morning."

Cora sighed. She had a lot of programming ahead of her, but Hazel would never message her unless it was a real emergency. She sent a message telling Hazel she was leaving the house, hoping that the emergency would only take an hour or two.

Cora, flying in her hover car, reached Pendleton Farms, which was a working farm that produced some specialty crops. This was only one of many Pendleton family homes. As her hover car descended, she surveyed the main house, which was a mini-mansion shaped like a pale gray two-story block.

The manor included vast farmland with rows of herbs, vegetables, and fruit-bearing trees maintained by farming robots. It also included a manicured backyard garden and a modest lawn in the front. In the distance toward the Krega mountains, she spotted hiking trails that piqued her interest.

After Cora stepped out of her car, she examined the home's facade. An ornate white trim framed every window and surrounded a heavy decorative wooden door.

As she made it to the front door, it opened, and the home's AI directed her to Hazel's private sitting room.

"I love this room," Cora said with a gentle smile. The room looked as if it could have been in a flower garden. Three large windows filled one wall and had a magnificent view of the backyard. Hazel's room, like Cora's, was also a small apartment within the mini-mansion, but she had walls between the bedroom and the sitting room. "I could sit and stare out of the window all day."

When Cora landed, she shielded herself from unwanted emotions. But now that she was alone with Hazel, she lowered her protection in tiny increments.

"Are you alone in the house?" Cora asked. "I don't sense anyone else."

"Yeah, Mom and the boys had another meeting," Hazel said, tucking a stray blonde curl behind an ear. "Uncle Evan invited all the Pendletons, except me, to his mansion for some sort of meeting." Her lopsided smile couldn't hide the strong current of panic flowing from her. Cora turned to Hazel and held both of her hands.

"Tell me what's going on?" Cora asked, peering at her friend.

Hazel gently pulled her hands from Cora's and stepped toward a floral print sofa which perfectly complemented the room. They both took a seat.

"Let's have some tea," Hazel said, pressing a button on the crafter. Two cups of tea and two small strawberry muffins materialized on the coffee table.

"Your furniture is perfect for this room," Cora said, trying to fill the silence with small talk.

"Yeah, this room and my bedroom were the only rooms I was allowed to decorate," Hazel said, tasting her tea.

"Is this about your marriage?" Cora asked.

"No..." Hazel said and gazed out of the window. "I didn't like Michael. He was a horrible husband."

Cora gasped, imagining the worst.

"No, he was never physically violent," Hazel sighed. "He kept his girlfriend throughout our entire marriage. He split his time between us, staying with her in the Tymal city center and me out on this farm. He even took Kaye to Mars with us. The entire family, except Uncle Evan, treated her like his real wife, making me invisible."

A momentary stab of pain crossed Hazel's face, reminding Cora of Hazel and Michael's wedding. Six years ago Hazel had cried on Cora's shoulder, explaining that she didn't love Michael and didn't want to get married. Also, Michael was in love with Kaye, but Evan refused to allow them to marry. Instead, Winifred and Evan arranged Michael and Hazel's marriage. Cora remembered their conversation from years ago.

"Hazel, please talk to your mom," Cora had said. "Even she wouldn't want you to be so miserable."

"Mom told me I'll make our mine vulnerable if I don't go through with the wedding," Hazel had replied between sobs. "We only have one mine, and if another family steals it, we'll be destitute. I can't do that to my family." Many Askov families obtained their mines by stealing other functioning operations. The Interplanetary Security or IPS was supposed to stop mine jumps, but large corporations who owned their own private forces usually outnumbered any IPS police force.

Now Cora detected new waves of sorrow and reached out to squeeze Hazel's hand.

"I'm sorry you've had to endure this," Cora said in a quiet voice.

Holding Hazel's hand felt so familiar—she remembered countless days where she had comforted and helped Hazel. She felt sorry for her and wished Hazel would leave her family and start living her life.

"Everything changed this morning when I received an anonymous message," Hazel said, activating her comm bracelet. A floating rectangle appeared above her bracelet, filled with text set on an opaque black background. She waved a hand over her bracelet and the floating screen drifted to Cora.

Good Morning Hazel,

This is your friendly neighborhood blackmailer. I stumbled across something very interesting. YOU ARE A MURDERER! I know what you did to your husband, Michael. It doesn't help that you have a boyfriend, which gives you plenty of mo-

tive. For now, I'm withholding my evidence from the EGS. If you want me to continue protecting you, I'll need five thousand credits each month. I'll give you a few days to think about it, then I'm going to the EGS!

"This is unbelievable!" Cora said in a raised voice. "I've known you since we were both in school. You're too sweet to do something that bad. This must be a hoax."

"That's what I thought," Hazel said in a trembling voice. "But if my mom finds out, she'll kill me. I don't know what to do."

Cora sensed Hazel's increased distress and reached for her. Hazel quickly stood and paced to the middle window.

"I think you should turn this in to the EGS," Cora said, following her to the window.

"I can't take that risk! Mom'll find out," Hazel said as her eyes started to water.

"Maybe we can learn something about the sender from this message," Cora said. "Would you send me the original message?"

Hazel nodded and pressed a button on her bracelet. A moment later, Cora's bracelet chimed.

"I'll take a look at the sender information when I get home," Cora said as she turned to the floating message. "This person knows you. It could be any of the Pendletons or a family friend."

"It could be anyone really," Hazel said.

"I don't think so. It's someone who you know," Cora said. "I wonder what type of evidence they're talking about?"

"But I didn't do it. There's no evidence," Hazel sighed.

"It could be something falsified," Cora said thoughtfully.

"Then how would I prove my innocence?" Hazel asked.

"Not sure," Cora shrugged.

"What's this about a boyfriend?" Cora asked and immediately felt Hazel's unease. "Julia also hinted at something like this."

Hazel paced around two small chairs facing away from the windows, past the coffee table and around the back of the sofa.

"Michael took Kaye to Mars. For the one-year journey there, I couldn't escape the two of them," Hazel said and didn't meet Cora's eyes. "We spent a year touring mines. Thankfully, he put Kaye at a hotel, and I stayed in Pendleton's Mars home. It took another year to return to Earth, and I met Sam. He's not Askovian, so Mom would never approve, but he was so sweet. I think he's the first man I've ever been in love with."

Hazel's shy grin and her radiated happiness gave Cora a deeper understanding. Hazel did have a motive. *What if the blackmailer is right?* she thought.

"So who is Sam?" Cora asked in a neutral tone.

"Samuel Iverson," Hazel said. "He helps Askovs invest in mines. His job is to travel to problematic mines and investigate to determine their true value." Hazel walked around the sofa and took a seat. "I want to spend the rest of my life with him."

"Well, I'm glad you're happy," Cora said as a tightness began to form in her chest. *I hope... I know Hazel's innocent,* she thought.

"Sam and I were planning to move in together," Hazel said. "Of course I'll join him on his interplanetary travels."

"But alive, Michael would never have let you out of the marriage," Cora said.

"Michael," Hazel said with a bark of laughter. "I was never worried about him. He would've kept his mistress, and I would still have my love."

"And your mom?" Cora asked.

"Yeah, that was the real problem," Hazel sighed. "Now that Michael's dead, Mom's going to try to marry me off to someone else."

Cora sensed her happiness mixed with despair.

"I suppose you must think I'm callus for gushing about Sam so soon after Michael passed?" Hazel said.

"No. You were unhappy in your arranged marriage," Cora said. "Now, you've found love with Sam."

A smile transformed Hazel's face for a moment before it changed again and settled into a sad expression.

"I'm not sad that Michael's dead," Hazel said matter-of-factly. "He was never mean or harsh toward me. Simply indifferent. A few weeks after we were married, I caught him in bed with Kaye. He explained he never had any plans to get rid of Kaye. I complained to my parents, hoping to get out of the marriage. They refused, explaining that our alliance with the Pendletons was worth more than a marital *inconvenience*."

"So sorry you had to deal with that," she said.

"Well, at least I don't have to deal with Kaye anymore," Hazel sighed. "But the blackmail? What should I do?"

"I already told you," Cora said. "Go to the EGS. They can be confidential."

"No. That's not an option," Hazel said, her mouth set in a straight line.

"Then why did you call me here?" Cora asked as she felt fresh waves of Hazel's fear.

"I heard that you investigated Harold's death," Hazel said. "Rumor has it that without you, the EGS would've never tracked down Oliver."

"First, I had a lot of luck finding Harold's murderer," Cora said. "Second, I nearly died. It's extremely dangerous to track down a killer."

"This is different—it's a blackmailer," Hazel said, leaning forward.

Didn't she hear me? Cora thought. *I nearly died.*

"Look, I think it's Julia," Hazel said. "She tried to blackmail me a few months ago."

"Julia! Why? What was she holding over your head?" Cora asked.

"She claimed that I was cheating on Michael," Hazel said with a mirthless laugh. "Michael met Sam several times and knew about us spending time together. Michael didn't care and continued to treat Kaye as his wife."

"Didn't Julia know that?" Cora asked.

"No. Michael stopped confiding in Julia a long time ago," Hazel said. "She couldn't keep her mouth shut, and it once cost Michael a small business deal. He never forgave her. He also didn't trust his mom for the same reason."

Cora sighed as she mentally sifted through the new information.

"At the time she said she only needed a few hundred credits a month," Hazel said. "I encouraged her to tell Michael, and she never brought it up again."

"What do you think she wanted the credits for?" Cora asked.

"My guess is debt," Hazel said. "I've never seen anyone spend so many credits shopping."

"Okay, I understand better, but maybe Julia is the blackmailer or maybe she isn't," Cora said. "This is someone blackmailing you about a *murder*. They are willing to do something illegal, blackmail, to hide another crime, murder. This person is very dangerous, and I don't want to get involved. Go to the EGS."

Hazel sighed and her whole body seemed to deflate. Cora felt her increasing panic, but she held firm.

"I'm sorry Hazel," Cora said. "I can't get involved."

Later that evening at home, Cora sat at her office desk, examining the blackmailer's message. Even though she'd explained to Hazel she didn't want to be involved, her curiosity got the better of her. One overhead light illuminated her desk, which contained her bracelet and a small tray of tea and half a sandwich.

A screen with a dark background floated over her bracelet and it contained the blackmailer's message. She'd been reading through the message a few times and ran it through a rudimentary word analyzer. There was nothing identifiable about the text.

"Hmm..." Cora said, drinking her tea. "Let's see what you're hiding."

She opened a new floating window, but she filled this one with programming symbols. Using these symbols, she traced the message through the Net, which was the main means of communication. This message had literally traveled through most of the message nodes on Earth. Usually, when someone wanted to obscure the origin of a missive, they sent it through many circuitous routes. She noted, the message's originator was filled with random information.

She started a vidchat with Hazel and took a sip of tea.

"Hey Cora," Hazel said, dressed in a frilly sleeping gown. "Did you find something?"

"Not really," Cora said, placing her teacup back on the tray. "I checked its route through the Net, but it's too complicated for my trackers. I also looked up the originator, but that's filled with junk."

Hazel sighed.

"If we went to the EGS, they'd have better trackers and could put an end to this now," Cora said gently.

Hazel shook her head.

"What should we do now?" Hazel asked.

"If you don't want to go to the EGS, you'll need to wait for the blackmailer to make the next move." Cora said and frowned. "Hazel, I really think you're in danger."

"Mom can't know," Hazel said. "Anyway, thanks for looking into this. Good night."

"Night," Cora said as the vidchat disappeared. She sighed, worried about Hazel's predicament.

CHAPTER 4

Bright and early in the morning, Cora pressed a button on her comm bracelet, activating her Eflector: a high-tech mirror that displayed her 3D image. Scrutinizing her new lavender dress, she made a tiny adjustment to the belt and grinned, thinking of her lunch date with Brian.

Her bracelet chimed, and she frowned at the name announcing an incoming vidchat.

This could only mean one thing, she thought.

"Good morning," Cora said with a forced smile as she viewed Brian's image floating over her bracelet.

"Hey," Brian said with furrowed eyebrows. "I'm sorry to do this to you, but I can't make it for lunch."

"Did something happen?" Cora asked, worry replacing her earlier happiness.

"You could say that." Brian sighed. "It has to do with Jessica Spencer taking that mine from Evan Pendleton. Everyone knows she or Spencer Industries broke the law. But now they want us to generate documents showing that we, Albright Corp, have always managed that mine."

"No. That'll make Albright Corp an accessory after the fact," she said. "I suppose there's really no government body that'll come after them, anyway."

"That's Jessica's reasoning," he said. "She also told me Harold did that in the past when she stole another mine. She really thinks I'm over-reacting, but I just can't do it."

"What does your dad think?" she asked.

"He thinks I'm right," Brian said, rubbing his face. "Dad mentored Harold when he first in-herited his mines, but after a year or two he stayed hands-off, and let Harold make his own decisions."

"Knowing your dad, he must have been disap-pointed to discover Harold complied with the theft," she said.

"Yeah," Brian grimaced. "He seemed more hurt than anything. Dad spent so much time teaching Harold and even Jessica about their moral obligations, but they both seemed to be doing what they want."

"What's your plan now?" she asked.

"I'm going to have breakfast with Mom and Dad. I'll conference in Eliza," he said. "Mom owns Albright Corp now that Harold's passed away, but she doesn't want to run it. Eliza has the temperament to run it, but she's still traveling."

"That doesn't sound good," she said. "They're going to need to put pressure on you to do what Jessica wants. All of us are protected by Spencer Industries, and we could lose our mines if we go against Jessica."

"I know. I know," he huffed. "So you think I *should* create the illegal documents?"

"Of course not," she said. "You shouldn't do something against your basic values." She paused, staring out of the window and into the garden. "You know, if you need moral support, I can show up for the family breakfast."

"Mom would cancel the breakfast," Brian said with a chuckle. "You know she's very intimidated by you." His mom, Nora Albright, was also a Feeler, but she struggled her entire life to shield herself properly from other Askovians.

This made her vulnerable and, as a result, fearful of other Askovians, including Cora.

"I wish she could be comfortable around me," Cora said with a small frown.

"I think if she could spend a little time with you, she'd like you," he said. "Maybe if you came over with Aunt Ferna, but not now."

"Later, when things have calmed down, we can have a family gathering," she said. "What about our lunch? Do you want to try to meet later in the week?"

"I'll let you know," Brian said distractedly.

"Have a good day," Cora said. His image vanished and her face fell.

She considered changing into something more comfortable when her bracelet chimed again. She started the vidchat with Hazel's image.

"Hello," Cora said as her smile began to melt away. She gazed at Hazel's taut face. "Is something wrong?"

"Not wrong, really. Stressful," Hazel sighed. "My mom wants me to make an announcement today to the Pendleton family living at the Farm, basically telling them the Cartwright income is going away."

"Ooooh, that'll make a few people angry," she grimaced.

"Would you mind coming to dinner and holding my hand?" Hazel asked with a hopeful expression.

"I don't understand," Cora said. "Why doesn't your mom make the announcement?"

"She says it'll come better from me," Hazel frowned. "Don't really know what that means." She put her hands together. "Pleeeease."

"You could have told me yesterday," Cora said, mildly irritated.

"I didn't know until late last night," Hazel said. "What if the blackmailer's a member of the Pendleton family? Will the loss of the Cartwright income make him more desperate?"

"Hmm... You have a point," Cora sighed. "Okay. Message the time and directions to me. I'll be there."

"Thank you, thank you," Hazel bobbed up and down in her chair.

Cora smiled as she caught a glimpse of the young girl she'd gone to school with.

"I'll see you in a few hours," Cora said and ended the vidchat. She tried to anticipate who would give Hazel the most trouble. Julia? Delores? She hoped the evening would go well but suspected it wouldn't.

At seven in the evening, Cora made her way to the Pendleton Farm and shielded herself as she stepped toward the front door. She still wore the lavender dress from this morning and hoped it would be appropriate for the evening dinner. The door opened automatically.

"Welcome Ms. Brimble," the home's AI said. "Please follow the signals to the dining room."

Cora followed the soft lighting in the floor and made her way through two hallways. Framed in dark wooden paneling, she strolled past images of Pendleton ancestors. Stepping through the dining room doors, she was pleased to see a modern light space with white walls softened with images of flowers.

She relaxed to see that her lavender dress fit in perfectly with everyone's casual clothes. Hazel stood and raced to Cora's side.

"Thank you so much for coming," Hazel whispered. She turned to the others at the table. "I think everyone remembers Cora." Hazel escorted Cora to an oval table with eight seats on each side. The center of the table contained four flower vases that each helped camouflage a food processor. Hazel placed Cora in a seat right next to hers.

"Cora, this is Remy, Michael's uncle," Hazel said while gesturing across the table to a tall thin man with gray hair and blue eyes.

"Pleased to meet you," Remy said.

Cora nodded.

"You know, Delores," Hazel said, pointing out the tall thin woman sitting next to Remy. She nodded stiffly.

"That is Oscar, Michael's assistant," Hazel said, indicating a bland young man sitting on Remy's left side. He was the sort of man who would easily blend into a crowd.

"It's a pleasure to meet you," Oscar said in a welcoming tone.

"Evening," Cora said. "How are you doing?"

"Well... Considering I've been let go, not too bad," Oscar said with a twinkle in his eyes.

"Oh, no. Did you get notice?" Hazel asked.

"Yes, but it was expected," Oscar said. "I don't have a boss."

Delores sniffled.

Silence fell across the table.

"Julia's not here, but I think we should start eating," Hazel said, glancing around the table. "I'm not sure when she'll be back."

Remy, Delores, and Oscar began activating the meal crafters closest to them.

Cora selected her meal from a menu with items that included beef sauteed with broccoli and roasted rosemary chicken. She made her selection and slices of synthetic roasted chicken, a baked potato, and crystallized vegetables materialized on her plate. The vegetables were cooked in a sonic oven that encouraged the minerals already in the vegetables to crystallize, making them crunchy.

"So, how long have you known each other?" Remy asked genially.

"I think I was ten, and you were eight," Cora said with a quizzical look.

"That's right. My mom sent me to a different school at first, and then moved me later," Hazel said.

"So the answer is twenty years," Cora said, turning to Remy.

"Admirable. I have a handful of friends that I've known for forty years," Remy said wistfully. "They're the best friends I've ever had."

"Good evening, everyone," Julia said, entering the dining room as her long auburn hair hung loose behind her. She took a seat next to her mom, Delores. Theo sat next to her.

"Hello," Cora said, addressing both of them.

"What's for dinner?" Julia asked, ignoring Cora and turning to her mom.

"Umm... beef and chicken," Delores glanced at Cora, a little embarrassed by her daughter's behavior.

"Good evening, Cora," Theo said, standing and stepping to shake her hand.

Julia frowned at Theo and then selected food from the crafter.

"We're so sorry, we were late," Theo said, taking his seat next to Julia. "Got side-tracked riding down one of the trails.

"Horseback?" Cora asked with a delighted smile. "I haven't ridden a horse since I graduated."

"Oh, you should come with us some time," Theo said, pressing buttons on the crafter.

"I'm surprised you ride," Julia said, jumping into the conversation. "Hazel never rides."

"Really?" Cora said. "She's an excellent rider."

All eyes turned to Hazel, who turned a little pink.

"What are you having, Theo?" Hazel asked.

Why is Hazel hiding her horseback riding awards? Cora thought.

"Beef," Theo said.

The chatter at the table quieted down as everyone ate.

"The chicken is very good. I especially liked the crystallized vegetables," Cora said as she finished her food.

"I never could stand vegetables prepared that way," Delores said. "I think they must be an acquired taste."

"Let's be honest, Dedie," Remy said. "You never liked vegetables prepared in any way."

Julia chuckled, with Remy joining in.

Delores set her mouth in a grim line and ignored Remy.

"Hazel, dear, why have you called us here?" Delores asked.

"Yes, we should get started," Hazel said, clearing her throat and glancing at Cora.

Knowing what Hazel was about to say made Cora think back to the first time she'd met Winifred Cartwright. Cora was heading toward Hazel's bedroom at their boarding school when she heard screaming. She sensed a small stream of Hazel's dread, but she was almost overpowered by waves of anger rolling toward her even through Hazel's closed door. She quickly shielded herself so that she wouldn't be overwhelmed by the emotions.

"You're not Askovian," Winifred yelled. "No abilities means you have to settle for one of the lesser Askov families."

"Mom, I would like to marry for love," Hazel said in a quiet voice.

Winifred scoffed.

About half of the kids, including Cora, sent to Heliton Boarding School needed training to control their special powers. The other half had no special abilities and were sent to make political and social connections that would help the family after graduation. Hazel was in the second group. Heliton was a city, like Tymal, populated by Askovians.

"I'm sorry to interrupt," Cora said, trembling a little. She was terrified of Winifred, but she just couldn't leave Hazel alone with her horrible mom. "We have a class, Ms. Cartwright. I came to help Hazel get ready."

Winifred glared for a few seconds, glanced at her husband, and stridden out of the room.

Now, it was twenty years later, and instead of screaming from Winifred, Hazel was likely to face it from Julia, Delores, and Remy.

"Right now you all receive income from the Pendleton and Cartwright mines," Hazel said.

"My dear, the Pendleton mine income will stop in a few months now that the Spencers have taken it by force," Remy said.

"Yes, I'm due to start transferring Michael's documents to Evan's assistant in a few days," Oscar said.

"Well, my hope is that Evan will siphon some credits from the remaining Pendleton mines for you," Hazel said.

"Then you don't know Evan very well," Remy said with a dry laugh. "My brother can be mean and vindictive—he's the reason I *had* work as a doctor. My brother Jon also earned a living as a doctor. We live well enough, but we could've lived in luxury."

"I know, and I'm very sorry," Hazel glanced at Cora, who nodded her support.

"Oh, just spit it out," Julia said. "You're so slow."

"Julia, that's uncalled for," Delores said in a stern tone.

Hazel set her mouth in a thin line, but Julia rolled her eyes.

"The income from the Cartwright mine will end in about six months," Hazel said, glaring at Julia.

"What? Why? You're still part of the family," Delores said.

"Your mom's going to sell you to the highest bidder, isn't she?" Julia guffawed. "Does Sam know?"

"Julia, stop or leave the table," Delores said in a raised voice.

Julia crossed her arms, beaming daggers at Hazel.

"I'm not really part of the family since Michael passed away," Hazel said.

"That's not true," Delores said. "I think we didn't get a chance to know you."

"To be fair, it's been six years," Remy said. "We had plenty of time to get to know her."

"Most of you wanted Michael to marry Kaye," Hazel said. "I don't blame you—Uncle Evan wouldn't let Michael and Kaye marry. Because of the arranged marriage, I'm only good for credits and children."

A moment of silence settled over the table. Delores turned slightly pink, and Theo shifted uncomfortably in his seat.

Cora reached out and squeezed Hazel's hand.

"What? Are we supposed to feel sorry for you?" Julia spat out, jumping to her feet. "You're still wealthy and the three of us are now poor." She stormed out of the room.

Surprisingly, Theo kept his seat and exchanged looks with Delores and Remy.

"Please excuse my headstrong daughter," Delores said. "She sometimes says things without thinking through her words."

"Don't worry," Oscar said with a smirk. "She's rude to me all the time."

Delores glared at him, and Oscar turned away.

"Can you explain to your parents that we need the Cartwright mine because of the recent skirmish?" Remy asked with a serious expression.

"I already have," Hazel said in a gentle tone. "They won't budge."

"Is there something I could do to help?" Theo said with a worried look.

"Not unless you could go back in time and stop the Spencers from taking our mine," Remy said.

"I'm so very sorry," Theo said, shaking his head.

"What doesn't make sense is that mine will run out of Alythium in around fifty years," Hazel said. "Mining reports show it wasn't that valuable, and I can't believe Spencer Industries would expend that many resources on a tiny mine."

"This has more to do with a disagreement between Evan and Jessica Spencer," Remy said. "Nobody knows the details, but it's been going on for ten or fifteen years."

"We had a family meeting yesterday," Delores said in a condescending tone. "Evan hinted that he's going to counter sue and force IPS to take action against Spencer Industries."

"Evan can try, but it won't work," Remy said and chuckled. "That government body has no teeth. Evan also stole a mine from that other family. Do you remember their name?"

Delores shook her head.

"Well, nothing happened to him either," Remy said.

"So, for the next few months, we can rely on the residual income from the Cartwright mine," Delores said. "I'll talk to Evan in the coming months about an alternate plan."

"I'm sorry it's come to this," Hazel said. "Let me know if I can do something to help."

"I'll go and check on Julia," Theo said, standing up. "Thanks for letting us know."

"I'll be in my room," Delores said as she pushed away from the table.

"I'm going to run an errand," Oscar said, standing. "I should be back in an hour or so."

After Oscar left the room, Cora wondered about the disagreement between Evan and Jessica. *Did Aunt Ferna know more about it?* she thought.

"Do you know what your plans, or rather your parents' plans, are for you?" Remy said with a sad smile.

"Not specifically," Hazel said. "I'm sure they're planning something, though. I'm afraid to see what they'll come up with."

"Well, remember you're not alone," Cora said in a gentle voice. "We can weather your parents together."

CHAPTER 5

"I can't meet you three days in a row," Cora said, pulling her hair in a ponytail and adjusting a coral top as she peered at Hazel's image in a floating screen. "I've got a deadline for a new release of my game."

"I know, and I'm sorry," Hazel said as she hugged her knees to her teal blouse. She looked small in her cushioned chair. "My mom is flying in this afternoon to give me a 'talk.' Cora, you know what she's like."

"I know," Cora sighed, eyeing her empty coffee cup and considering a second.

"Also, Sam will be here this afternoon," Hazel said. "He was doing some work for Uncle Evan, and I already told him he could stay here."

"If you want to hide Sam from your mom, just ask him not to come," Cora said, moving from the dining table to the office desk in her room as the floating screen followed her. "But they're going to have to meet sometime. Might as well get it over with now."

Hazel whimpered.

"Look, your mom is going to hate Sam," Cora said in a serious tone. "Think through what she'll do and if you can live with her actions."

"Okay, that's too complicated," Hazel said. "Please come this afternoon. I'm planning a game of Oroes out back with lots of drinks."

Cora shook her head.

"You can work on your game this morning and arrive around one in the afternoon," Hazel said, placing her feet on the floor with a lopsided smile. "It's only for a couple of hours and then you can go back to work."

"A couple of hours?" Cora asked, dubious of the time.

"Yeah, I only need you here long enough for the 'talk,'" Hazel said. "After that, Mom will leave, and I can spend time with Sam, and you can go back to work."

"Well…" Cora's voice trailed off, torn between protecting her friend and meeting work obligations.

"Thank you, thank you," Hazel said.

"I'm just warning you, I'm leaving after a couple of hours," Cora said with her arms crossed.

"Of course, of course," Hazel said with a grin. "This won't take much time at all."

Hazel's image disappeared, and Cora felt she had agreed to something that would definitely take longer than two hours.

Around one in the afternoon, Cora's hover car began its descent to Pendleton Farm. She was flying from the office park where she'd worked feverishly through the morning, trying to implement features requested by her users. Sitting on one of the u-shaped cushions in her car, she finished a small snack and cleaned the table as the car prepared to land. A moment later, it floated over the lawn and came to a suspended stop next to another hover car she didn't recognize.

Automatic steps extended to the ground, and Cora stepped toward the house and reached the door.

"Welcome Cora Brimble," the home's AI said as one of the ornate wooden double doors swung open. "Please come in."

Cora took a couple of steps into the dark wood paneled entryway and paused. Normally, she would follow lights to meet Hazel, but she saw none as she glanced around. As she was about to open her mouth, she heard a noise.

"Cora, I'm so glad you're here," Hazel said with red rimmed blue eyes. She smiled, but it didn't reach her eyes. Just behind her followed her mom, Winifred, who wore a well-tailored navy jumpsuit and a frilly cream blouse. She looked as if she was ready to captain a ship.

Cora hugged her friend tightly, sensing oceans of despair. *Something's happened*, she thought.

"Are you alright?" Cora asked with a frown.

"Good afternoon," Winifred said, interrupting any reply Hazel could have given.

"Hello, Ms. Cartwright," Cora said, sensing waves of triumph from Winifred. *I wonder what she did to Hazel*, she thought.

"I'll be in my room catching up on some work," Winifred said as she leaned her cheek close for Hazel to kiss it. "We'll talk again when I'm done."

Cora and Hazel made their way further into the mini-mansion, following winding hallways. Paneled in dark wood and featuring images of flowers and Pendleton ancestors, the halls also contained doorways leading to other parts of the house. They linked arms as they walked, and Hazel led the way through to the back and out on to the patio.

A magnificent view of a manicured backyard filled with flowers, birds, and the occasional bee acted as a backdrop. They sat at a large oval table surrounded by chairs. Cora selected tea from the crafter while Hazel selected a slice of vanilla cake with lime green swirls.

"Okay, tell me everything," Cora said, studying Hazel. "I thought she was arriving later this afternoon."

"She got here an hour ago because the blackmailer asked her to review the security video," Hazel said in a quiet voice. "He explained if you look closely, there's something wrong with the way Michael fell. His leg bent at an angle that made it seem as if he ran into something, and then he tumbled down the steps."

"Ran into something?" Cora asked. "Sounds like a Mover, but that's impossible."

"Of course," Hazel said, nodding.

"Did you see the vid?" Cora asked.

"Yeah, I see what they mean, but I can't explain it," Hazel said.

"What did the autopsy show?" Cora asked.

"Nothing unusual," Hazel said. "His injuries are consistent with a fall."

"I still think this blackmailing is a job for the EGS," Cora said. "They've got advanced algorithms that can simulate all possible falls and determine exactly why Michael's leg bent at an unexpected angle. That would remove all the guessing."

"My mom is dead set against going to the EGS," Hazel said in a tense voice. "She wants to protect the family's reputation." She said the latter in a sing-song voice.

"Actually, I wouldn't be surprised if the EGS has already created a model of the accident," Cora said. "Otherwise, how would they know it really was an accident?"

"So, Mom and I watched the vid of Michael falling down the stairs," Hazel shivered. "There's no one anywhere near him, but the person closest to him is Mom. Most Movers have to be closer than that to manipulate objects."

"What about your brothers?" Cora asked thoughtfully.

"Mom thinks it's important that the black-mailer didn't send them a message," Hazel said with a resigned expression. "She said the black-mailer's 'proof' will probably show it couldn't be them."

"Does your mom seriously think it's you?" Cora asked.

"No, of course not," Hazel said with a dry laugh. "She thinks this blackmailer only wanted a victim too weak to defend themselves. In other words, me."

Cora sensed Hazel's... amusement? She wasn't sure because it lasted for less than a second before she returned to her usual trickle of intense sadness. Cora reached out and squeezed her hand.

"Cora, please help me find the blackmail-er," Hazel asked desperately. "If the blackmailer turns their information into the EGS and embarrasses Mom, she'll kill me. I only have seven days, otherwise my family will have to pay out five thousand credits a month."

"Seven days?" Cora asked. "Did the blackmail-er say that?"

Hazel nodded. "And she's extra mad at me for trying to hide the blackmail from her."

Cora held Hazel's hand while waves of her despair slowly filled the room. Cora considered shielding herself.

"At the end of our talk, she ordered me to send Sam away."

"I'm so sorry," Cora said with a frown. "Would you like me to try to talk to your mom?"

"That never goes well," Hazel said. "Would you stay for the week and help me find the black-mailer?"

"No Hazel," Cora said in a raised voice. "This is really dangerous. We should get EGS involved."

Hazel deflated as she exhaled.

"I really hate my mom," Hazel said. "I know in the end this is about her blaming me for what happened to Zach."

Cora sensed Hazel's despair.

"Please Cora. I really need you," Hazel sniffled. "If you find the blackmailer, I'll tell Mom, and she'll handle it."

"I really don't know..." Cora's voice trailed off.

"You and I would be safe," Hazel said. "No one would dare harm Mom. She's a powerful Mover."

They turned as the door to the patio opened.

"There you are," Sam said as he strolled toward her and gave her a peck on the cheek.

Cora turned and saw a tall man with copper colored skin and brown hair.

They hugged while Cora turned to the flowers in the garden.

"When did you get here?" Hazel asked with a broad smile.

"Just now," Sam said, as his smile faded. "Are you alright?"

"This is Cora," Hazel said, hurriedly avoiding Sam's question.

Sam peered at her for a moment before turning to Cora.

"How do you do?" Sam said as a greeting to Cora.

"Afternoon. It's good to finally meet you," Cora said with a smile.

"I was just going to say the same thing," Sam said and chuckled.

Hazel guided him to a third chair near hers.

"Want something?" Hazel asked.

"No, I'm fine," he said, surveying Hazel. "My guess is things went very badly with your mom?"

"You guessed correctly," Hazel said with a lopsided smile.

"Does she want you to end things with me?" Sam asked.

"Yes, again. Mom is very angry with me," Hazel said as she leaned toward him and relayed her entire conversation with her mom.

The three of them sat in silence for a few minutes.

"Okay, the way I see it, we have at least seven days before I have to leave," Sam said.

"But Mom—" Hazel said.

"I know," Sam interrupted her. "I think I can reason with her to let me help you for the next seven days. We can talk more later."

Hazel frowned.

"Have you talked to Winifred before?" Cora asked.

"No, but I have experience with difficult Askovians," Sam said with a grin. "Trust me." He turned to the yard, gesturing at an open space of grass. "That's the Oroes court?"

"Y-Yes," Hazel said, glancing at the court. "But I don't think—"

"Let's play Oroes and try to figure out who the blackmailer is," Sam said with a twinkle in his eyes as he stood.

"I think we should go to the EGS," Cora said. "The blackmailer could be dangerous."

"If we find solid evidence, we'll take it to the EGS," Sam said, glancing between Cora and Hazel.

"No—" Hazel said.

"We can send it to them anonymously," Cora said, interrupting Hazel. "It's the only way I'll agree to help you."

A worried expression marred Hazel's face, but she nodded.

"You know, I haven't played this game since we were in school," Cora said. "Would you run through the rules again?"

"Sure. It takes place within a square," Hazel said unenthusiastically, pointing at an illuminated square on the grass. "Each player gets ten holographic mountains about ten centimeters high, which are color coded, and have the name of one of the Oroes gods. Then we all get a set of balls and try to land them in the middle of the other players' mountains. This causes the mountains to disappear. The last mountain left wins."

"Cora? Which god do you want to be?" Hazel asked.

"I'll be Nysos," Cora said. "She was the great thinker."

Ten bright blue mountains appeared randomly within the illuminated square.

"Sam and I will be Tymal and Kithar," Hazel shyly smiled at Sam as ten green mountains and ten yellow mountains also appeared in the illuminated square.

"The lovers?" Cora said with a raised eyebrow.

"Quiet," Hazel said.

Cora sensed her lighter mood and thought the game was a good idea.

They all gathered their balls from a small outdoor cabinet.

"Who should go first?" Cora asked, tossing a ball from one hand to another.

"I'll go," Hazel said and tossed her ball. It landed on one of Sam's yellow mountains, which winked out a second later. The score displayed for several seconds above the square before fading away.

"Good shot," Sam said. "I think the blackmailer lives in this house with you."

"Unfortunately, I think you're right," Hazel said as the smile melted off her face. "That could be Delores, Remy, Julia, Theo, and Oscar." She turned to Cora. "You're next."

"What about your family?" Cora asked. "They're not here full time, but frequently enough."

"I think we should consider them too," Sam said with a thoughtful frown.

Cora threw her ball, which just missed one of Hazel's illuminated green mountains, and then it rolled out of the square.

"I was always terrible at this game," Cora said with a smirk, and she turned to Hazel. "Earlier you said you thought it could be Julia."

"Yeah, she already tried to blackmail me," Hazel said. "Also, I heard her mom scolding her for her high debt?"

"Do you know how much she owes?" Sam asked and tossed one of his balls, which missed Hazel's mountain and rolled onto one of Cora's blue mountains. The mountain faded away, and the score displayed above the playing square.

"No, but I could find out," Hazel shook her head.

"Who else needs credits?" Sam asked.

"All of them. I heard them all ask Michael for extra credits every few weeks because they'd all exceeded their budgets," Hazel said.

"If you think about everyone living here, who would you say is the most desperate for credits?" Cora asked.

"Oh, that's easy, Oscar," Hazel said, stepping forward and throwing her ball, which landed in the middle of one of Cora's blue mountains. It winked out of the game.

"You two are ganging up on me," Cora said, putting her hands on her hips with a half-smile.

"Sorry, it was an accident," Hazel said, trying to stifle her laughter.

"So, what happened with Oscar?" Cora asked.

"The day before Michael passed, the rest of us were in the sitting room waiting for Michael to start a game," Hazel said. "We all heard Michael and Oscar shouting at each other. It seems Oscar was in a lot of debt and helped himself to some of Michael's funds."

"Wait... Why was Oscar at the Spring Gala?" Cora said.

"They seemed to patch things up," Hazel said. "Michael never told me about the fight, but my guess is Oscar promised to pay him back. They'd been friends since school."

"A simple promise, and Michael forgave him?" Cora asked.

"Also, Oscar plans a lot of events for Kaye," Hazel said. "I have a feeling she influenced Michael's decision."

"Okay, so somehow Michael forgave him," Sam said. "There were enough good feelings that Oscar attended the Gala. I don't see how that means he'd blackmail you."

"We're clearly missing some information," Cora said.

They continued for half an hour throwing balls as the game progressed.

After several rounds, it was Sam's turn to throw a ball. He tossed it over the playing square, and it halted in mid-air.

Cora and Sam gasped, but Hazel's face became set and her entire demeanor stiffened. Cora sensed Hazel's... rage? She wasn't sure because it only lasted for a second.

All the balls on the lawn floated off the lawn, gathered into a large mid-air cluster, and sorted themselves into an organized pile near the patio.

Slow dawning made Cora realize there must be a Mover nearby. *Why can't I sense the Mover?* she thought.

Everyone turned, following the motion of the balls.

"Mom," Hazel said in a flat voice. "I didn't know you were here."

"Obviously," Winifred said, peering at Sam. "Would you introduce me to your friend?"

"This is Sam Iverson," Hazel said, linking her arm through Sam's.

Winifred's steely blue-eyed glint made Cora shiver. She'd seen her crush her daughter so many times. Hazel usually tried to stand firm against her mom in the beginning, but Winifred always won in the end.

"Please stay for the week," Hazel whispered to Cora.

Cora sensed Hazel's desperation and a spark of Winifred's animosity. In a weak moment, she nodded and whispered, "Yes."

"It's a pleasure to meet you," Winifred said with a smile that looked as if she could devour Sam.

"Good afternoon. It's good to meet you, finally," Sam said and cleared his throat.

"Tell me, how long have you known Hazel?" Winifred asked, stepping on to the lawn.

"Nearly a year," Sam said. "We met on the voyage home from Mars."

"Of course you create those mining reports," Winifred said in a measured tone. "I purchased one of them for my mine, but I never thought I'd meet the author."

"I hope it was helpful," Sam said as he pulled his arm out of the link with Hazel and took a step aside.

Winifred stepped between Hazel and Sam, intertwined her arm with Hazel's, and took small steps toward the house.

"It was quite informative. You do good work," Winifred said over her shoulder. "Hazel, I think it's time to continue our talk."

Hazel paced beside her mom, not making a sound. She glanced once at Cora, who frowned.

Once Hazel and Winifred entered the house, Cora and Sam exchanged glances.

"I suppose the game is over?" Cora asked.

"I'll turn it off," Sam said, heading for the patio. "I've never seen a Mover manipulate objects," Sam said. "It was a bit intimidating."

"Well, that was the point," she said, stepping toward the patio. "At the Spring Gala, Hazel's mom expertly delivered presents to the Pendleton family members sitting at the high-table. She even made them do a little dance before they landed."

"I would've loved to have seen that," he said with a small smile.

"Askovians like Winifred need to make sure everyone else knows how important or powerful they are. Frankly, she does wield a lot of political, financial, and social influence. Be very careful of her."

"Don't worry, Hazel warned me about her."

They both glanced into the dark house.

I hope Hazel's okay, Cora thought.

CHAPTER 6

Cora stepped into the dining room of Brimble House much earlier in the morning than she expected. Brian had sent an urgent message last night asking to meet her and they decided on breakfast.

"Good morning, Aunt," Cora said. The room always reminded her of her mom with its repeating leafy patterned white ceiling, light sage green walls, and colorful garden images.

Aunt Ferna lived in one of the home's beautiful bedrooms with the best view of the gardens. "Morning Dear," she said, selecting a chocolate muffin and tea from the crafters lining the center of the table. She always looked elegant, even in her simple coral dress.

"Morning," Brian said with a grin. "I was afraid I was going to have to wake you." He wore an expensive jumpsuit suitable for an office.

"This isn't my favorite time of day," Cora said with a loud yawn as she plopped onto a chair and began selecting coffee. She'd managed to pull her hair into a ponytail and wore a simple long-sleeved pale blue top with matching striped blue and white pants.

"Well, I appreciate you making an exception for me," Brian said, as his smile faded.

Aunt Ferna chewed on her muffin, Cora sipped her coffee, while Brian pushed scrambled eggs around his plate.

Cora sensed Aunt Ferna's worry and Brian's deep-seated despair—she decided to get the conversation started.

"What happened with the family meeting a couple of days ago?" Cora asked.

"When Harold and my mom started the Albright Corporation," Brian said. "They agreed to split everything sixty percent to Mom and forty percent to Harold. Even though they were brother and sister, my mom had more credits. But Harold could schmooze with other Askovs, win their trust, and get them to let him manage their mines. However, as more powerful families joined, they demanded part ownership of the Albright Corp, and Harold gave it to them."

"What's the ownership split now?" Cora asked.

"Mom has fifty percent," Brian said. "Spencer Industries demanded some from her." He leaned back in his chair, thinking. "I inherited Harold's ten percent, and the rest is primarily owned by the Spencers and other members."

"You have the controlling interest," Aunt Ferna said. "If you side with Nora, the two of you control the direction of Albright. I'm sure the Spencers don't like that."

"Yes, but we're split on this," Brian said. "She wants to give the Spencers the illegal documents showing the Spencers' management over that mine they stole."

"Why do they even care?" Cora asked. "The IPS won't do anything to Spencer Industries."

"They're facing a bit of backlash," Brian said, pushing away his plate. "Many of our members are now terrified Spencer Industries will steal their mines as well."

"Are they putting pressure on you to give up your remaining shares?" Cora asked.

"Mom wants me to sell my shares," Brian said in a defeated voice. "But I feel I'll let Harold down."

"Yes, of course," Aunt Ferna said. "As soon as they get control, they'll kick you out, hire a replacement, and create their illegal documents."

"The thing is, if Harold was alive, he'd give them their illegal documents," Cora said. "Why do you think Harold would be disappointed?"

Cora felt Brian's sharp stab of pain as his eyes teared. He quickly wiped his eyes and cleared his throat.

"Over the years, Harold trained me to be his replacement," Brian spoke in a low voice. "I felt I was the next to take the reins. My dad trained Harold, and Harold trained me. I thought I would train my son in the future."

"Did you know about Harold's... questionable deals?" Aunt Ferna asked.

"No. Of course not," Brian said with an edge in his voice.

"Then he didn't really train you... Or didn't complete his training," Cora said. "Would you have stayed if you'd known about his illegal activities?"

"No. Not for a moment," Brian said, crossing his arms. "When I worked as an attorney, if I'd done business like Harold, I would've lost the few clients I used to have."

"Well, my dear, I think Cora is right," Aunt Ferna said. "You were never the right replacement for Harold. It would have been worse if you worked with him for a decade or more and then discovered these illegal activities."

"My guess is Harold never told you about his illegal dealings because he knew he'd lose you," Cora said in a gentle voice.

"I'm sure Nora'd never give your legacy away," Aunt Ferna said, placing her teacup on the table. "My guess is she'll ask you to give your ten percent to Eliza. That way, she retains controlling interest."

"Also, my sister is furious with me," Brian said with a frown. "Eliza's afraid we'll lose Spencer Industries and their protection."

"I'll talk to Nora," Aunt Ferna said. "She gets easily stressed, and I'm sure she could use some support right now."

"I'm so glad to hear you say that," Brian said with a sad smile. "Dad is putting pressure on her to do the morally right thing, but that could mean the end of our family business. It'd also make us vulnerable to attacks from other Askov families."

"I'll visit this morning," Aunt Ferna said. "I was always able to calm her in the past."

"What do you think the Albright Corporation should do?" Cora asked.

"I think Eliza should do what Jessica wants," Brian said. "I just don't want to be involved."

"When will Eliza return?" Aunt Ferna asked.

"In about ten days," Brian said. "But it depends on when her current deal is done."

"You really have a few options, if you think about it," Cora said. "You could create the illegal documents or wait for Eliza and continue to stall Jessica. Another option is to join with the Pendletons in their lawsuit against Spencer Industries. Finally, you could disband Albright Corp and rebrand as something else."

"I don't like any option related to the Pendletons," Aunt Ferna said, her mouth set in a grim line. "Evan is a tyrant. Jessica is also controlling, but Evan is worse."

Cora frowned.

"I've been meaning to ask. What sparked the war between Evan and Jessica?"

"Well, that's a much longer and tragic story," Aunt Ferna said and turned to Cora. "What are your plans today?"

"Oh, sorry Aunt. I forgot to tell you," Cora said. "I went to meet Hazel at the Pendleton Farm, and she asked me to stay for the week."

"The week? Why?" Brian asked.

Cora hesitated, unsure if she should tell them about Hazel.

"Hazel's mom is visiting her now," Cora said. "You've met her before." She turned to Aunt Ferna. "She can be a bit... difficult."

"Difficult! She's a bully," Aunt Ferna said. "I always find it interesting that the Askovians with the most powers tend to abuse those around them the most. Winifred and Evan are powerful Movers and their families are terrified of them both." She made a tutting sound.

"I agreed to be moral support while her mom is there," Cora said, shifting uncomfortably in her seat. She always felt uneasy not telling Aunt Ferna the whole truth, which included the blackmail.

"I've heard you talk about Hazel many times," Brian said. "I always have the feeling you're trying to rescue her. But she's an adult and needs to learn to stand on her own."

"Yeah, I know," Cora said.

"Also, Winifred is not safe to be around," Aunt Ferna said with a worried expression. "There've been a few rumors. Please be careful."

She heard these rumors and spent time with Winifred. Although she could be unpleasant, Cora never felt unsafe.

"Do you want to come over and save me?" Cora said with a half-smile. "Maybe tomorrow or the day after, you can come to Pendleton Farm and visit with Delores?

"I was going to check on Dedie anyway," Aunt Ferna said. "Maybe tomorrow?"

"Sounds good," Cora said. "Look forward to seeing you there."

Later that morning, Cora walked with Hazel through the manicured flower beds in the back gardens of Pendleton Farm. These gardens represented the best in outdoor design. They displayed geometric raised beds, floating tea lights, real and artificial plants. Many Askov families vied for popularity by hosting tea parties.

This garden had no features to focus the design, but it didn't need it. Cora still enjoyed the quiet and shade from the established trees.

"I could stay out here all day," Cora said. "It's lovely."

Cora sensed Hazel's increasing anxiety.

"What's wrong?" Cora asked, placing a hand on Hazel's arm.

"Nothing new," Hazel said. "I'm worried. How are you going to find the blackmailer?"

"Oh, that..." Cora turned and continued their stroll. "I usually just ask questions while I'm sensing their emotions. I can usually tell if they're lying and evading a question."

"Do you have any questions prepared?" Hazel asked in a tense voice. "Maybe we should prepare together."

"No, it has to appear natural," Cora said. "Otherwise no one would open up to me."

"Oh... I see what you mean," Hazel said.

"What are you worried about?" Cora asked.

"You might be in danger," Hazel said with a worried expression.

"Now, you're worried I'll be in danger," Cora smirked. "I've been saying all week we need to involve the EGS."

"No—" Hazel said with finality.

"Okay, let me do this my way," Cora said.

Hazel nodded.

"Where's Sam?" Cora asked. "Have you spoken to your mom about him staying?"

Hazel sighed.

"Is it that bad?" Cora asked and gave Hazel a hug.

"Sam and I tried talking to her at dinner," Hazel said. "But she cut the conversation short and went to her room. Right now, he's catching up on some work."

"Does that mean he can stay?" Cora asked.

Hazel shrugged, and they continued their walk in silence while Cora listened to the birds singing in the garden.

"So, as far as I can tell, there are five possible suspects," Cora said. "Oscar is the most suspicious because of the fight before Michael died. Julia's next because she's already tried to blackmail you. Delores and Remy seem unlikely, but I'll look into them, anyway. On the other hand, I'm not sure what to think of Theo and Sam."

"Sam?" Hazel said, coming to an abrupt stop. "He would never do anything to harm me. No, it's not him. You can drop him from your list."

"Sure. He's an unlikely suspect anyway," Cora said and resumed their amble through the garden. "The real issue is I can't see a motive for

Theo or Sam whereas, I can see one for the remaining Pendletons living here at the Farm."

"I agree," Hazel said in a firm voice. "I think we should start with Julia."

Cora felt a spike of Hazel's anger, which quickly disappeared.

Hazel never had that kind of control in school, she thought. *Did she learn to shield her emotions after I left?*

———————— ✿ ————————

Several minutes later, the two women walked through the home's front door and immediately ran into Oscar, dressed in a professional brown jumpsuit, rushing down the main hallway. Cora felt his agitation.

"Oscar," Hazel called. "Are you alright?"

He turned and stared at her for a moment without recognition.

"I'm sorry to interrupt you, but you seemed upset," she said.

"Afternoon. Sorry, I'm trying to fix a problem with access to the Net," Oscar's face changed from a frown to a small smile.

"Oh, then Cora might be able to help you," Hazel said. "She does that for a living, you know."

Not exactly true, but close enough, Cora thought.

"Umm... Yeah. What's the problem?" Cora asked, glancing between Hazel and Oscar.

He dithered from foot to foot while glancing between Hazel and Cora.

"Okay, let me show you," Oscar said, taking two steps to a door closest to him, which slid open with a whoosh. He stepped inside and Cora followed.

"I'll catch up with you two later," Hazel said, continuing down the hallway.

Cora stepped into a surprisingly modern office with views of rows of lavender plants blowing in the breeze. One wall contained two very large windows, the other two were covered with pale red, blue, and yellow geometric patterns. A large black desk dominated the center of the room.

"This is... was Michael's office," Oscar said, taking a seat in what looked like the primary office chair. "One of the Pendleton accountants contacted me and asked me to prepare some files to transfer Michael's office to them. The problem is, I can't access the files, and I also can't access the Net."

Cora sensed the barely controlled panic underlying Oscar's words and wondered how a simple access problem could be this upsetting.

"Show me how you normally access his files," Cora said, leaning over the desk.

Oscar swiped a hand over the desk, which chimed.

"Hmm... You've never seen it chime like this before?" Cora asked.

"No, I've been trying to gain access for several days now," Oscar said. "I was hoping to get this one thing right before I had to find a job."

Cora sensed his lie and wondered why he was really upset.

"Let me sit down, and I'll see what I can do," she said, sitting on the chair while Oscar stood over her.

"I only want to try a top-level scan," Cora said as she pressed a button on her comm bracelet, which caused a floating screen to appear at arm's length. She filled the screen with coding symbols. After rearranging a few, she started her scan.

"This tracer is a top-level search for data centers in this room," she said. "I won't be able to look at the data, but I may be able to help you with access after the scan." She gestured to a chair. "Take a seat."

Oscar grabbed a thinly padded chair from the wall and moved it next to Cora.

"Probably a lot of what you do is confidential," Cora said. "But can you tell me, in general terms, what you are trying to do?"

"I'm trying to close out Michael's office," Oscar said with a sigh. "My fear is he removed my access codes before he passed. That could mean no one has access."

"I heard rumors of a fight between you and Michael before he passed away," Cora said. "What was that about?"

"Like you said, much of what I do is confidential," Oscar said, as his eyes darted to the ceiling. "It was really a misunderstanding. If he'd lived longer, we could have cleared it up."

"Of course, of course," Cora said and checked the progress of her tracer program. "Can you tell me a little about Michael? What was he like? Was he similar to his Uncle Evan?"

"They were nothing alike," Oscar said and sighed. "Evan could be cold and unforgiving if you made a mistake. But Michael was warm and friendly. Most people do business with

Evan because of the power he wields as head of Pendleton Mining. But Michael created new business deals by being easy-going and friendly. I've been working for Michael since the two of us graduated years ago.

"Do some family members oppose Evan?" she asked.

"Yeah, Michael was a classic example," he said. "He married Hazel, but kept his relationship with Kaye."

"But Evan wouldn't care about Michael's girlfriends," she said. "How is that defiance?"

"Evan wanted Michael and Hazel to have babies," he snorted. "But Michael kept putting it off. Also, since Michael had Kaye, Hazel found Sam on the voyage home from Mars."

Cora checked her scanner's progress and returned to the conversation.

"Did you notice anything strange on the trip to and from Mars?" she asked.

"Strange like what?" he asked.

She sensed his slightly elevated tension and thought quickly for a way to calm him.

"I was thinking in terms of someone shady hanging around," she said.

"No. The entire trip was carefully choreographed," he said, relaxing into his seat. "The miners steered us away from anything questionable and kept us focused on the parts of the mines working well."

"Almost sounds like a wasted trip," she said, glancing at her scanner that had just completed its analysis.

"Well, yes and no," he said. "Michael learned a lot based on what they wouldn't show us. Then Hazel's new friend, Sam, helped Michael with some of his mining reports."

"That sounds awkward," Cora said with one raised eyebrow.

"Not really. They sent messages to each other and never met in person," he said. "Sam probably made a few credits, and Michael learned a few things that helped his uncle."

"Well, the scan has finished," she said with a lopsided smile. "I know why you can't access Michael's files any longer."

"Can you fix it?" he asked.

"No, it's not possible," she said. "There're no storage units left in this office. Someone, or possibly one of Evan's robots, removed all storage devices. The good news is you don't have to do anything else."

Oscar's face fell and Cora felt his skyrocketing panic.

"No, no, no…" he said, as his voice trailed away. "Are you sure?"

"Yes. What's the matter?" Cora asked.

Oscar shot to his feet, quickly glanced around the room as if he expected someone to attack him, and bolted out the door.

"What's going on?" Cora called after him. But he was gone.

CHAPTER 7

Cora sat in Hazel's sunny and cheerful private sitting room. An hour earlier, she'd moved into Pendleton Farm for the week. She surveyed the garden through a large window as she drank her coffee and munched on toast. Hazel sat next to her on the sofa, staring out the window, but she hadn't touched her tea or raspberry muffin from the crafter.

Cora sensed her unease, but struggled to determine if it was more or less than normal for Hazel. Finally, she decided to ask.

"Did something happen last night?" Cora said, placing her coffee on the table. "I went to my room early to catch up on some work and grabbed dinner from the crafter."

"I was trying to wait until you had some breakfast," Hazel said, turning to Cora.

"Spill. What's going on?" Cora asked.

"Well, Oscar disappeared sometime last night," Hazel said. "He left everything behind. Mom doesn't want to alert the EGS, but I'm scared something happened to him."

"I didn't get a chance to tell you about it yesterday," Cora said, and recounted the events in Michael's office.

"Oh, I see," Hazel said. "Mom may be right. She thinks he could be the blackmailer."

"He panicked when I explained all of Michael's storage units had been removed," Cora said. "Maybe they contained some sort of proof."

"Uncle Evan sent me a message that he wanted Michael's office moved to the main house," Hazel said. "I assumed they'd already talked to Oscar since he was Michael's secretary, but obviously not."

"I can see why they'd want control of his business deals, mining contracts, or whatever else he may have been working on," Cora said.

"Strange Evan never contacted Oscar," Hazel said.

"I still think we should contact the EGS," Cora said.

Hazel opened her mouth to protest while Cora sensed a spike of panic that quickly disappeared.

"Hear me out," Cora said, raising both hands. "If Oscar is the blackmailer, he knows something about Michael's death. Based on what you know about him, would he bring that to the EGS's attention immediately? Hold on to that information and blackmail you? Sell it to the highest bidder? Something else?"

"Oscar and Michael were very good friends," Hazel said. "I know they thought of each other as brothers. He would have turned in any information he had if he thought it would help catch Michael's killer." Hazel crossed her arms. "But Mom still won't budge on this. If either of us goes to the EGS and somehow this falls on the Cartwright family, she'll kill me!"

"I told you if I find any evidence, I'll take it to the EGS," Cora said in a stern voice. "Do you still want me to continue?"

"Yes, yes," Hazel said, deflating a little. "You're right. But you don't have evidence yet, so we don't need to get them involved."

"Well, we don't really know what Oscar is thinking," Cora said. "If he's desperate enough, he can still blackmail you. It's still not safe for you."

"I know," Hazel said. "But let's keep looking for clues. If we have definitive proof, my mom will have to agree to go to the EGS."

Cora nodded. *But this isn't the best plan,* she thought.

A couple of hours later, Cora stepped through the house to the patio and spotted Aunt Ferna, Delores, and Remy sitting at a large oval table.

"Aunt, I didn't know you were here," Cora said, and kissed her aunt on the cheek. She nodded to Delores and Remy.

"Yes, Dedie and I both had a free day," Aunt Ferna said, wearing a floral print dress that complimented her curves.

"Well, you're always welcome," Delores said. Like Aunt Ferna, she also wore a floral print dress, but it didn't hang properly on her thin frame. "We're also expecting Winifred, but she has to wrap something up."

"Is anyone else coming?" Cora asked.

"No, Hazel has a headache, Sam is working, and Julia went riding with Theo," Delores said. "It's just us unless Winifred joins us. Also, I don't think her sons have been here for a couple of days."

They took turns selecting a meal from the crafter and began to eat. After a moment, Cora stopped to taste her bubbly mango juice.

"Hmm. This is good," Cora said, eyeing the yellow bubbles. "I thought all mango bubble juice was the same."

"No, the mangoes are fresh from the green house," Remy said, with a small smile. "One of the many advantages of living on the farm."

A moment of silence spread over the table as they were lost in thought.

"So, how did you enjoy the voyage to Mars and back?" Cora asked, trying to change the topic toward finding the blackmailer. "I've always wanted to go."

"It was alright," Delores said, and turned to Aunt Ferna. "Ferna, I should tell you about the fashions in Mar's capital, Anteros. They have some sort of collar that covers the neck and restricts head movement."

"Sounds inconvenient," Aunt Ferna said, and snickered with Delores.

"Well, I found it quite educational," Remy said, after giving Delores a disapproving shake of his head. "It's important to understand the source of your income. Since Evan doesn't like to share the throne, most of the family has no idea what it takes to mine, how vulnerable we are to miners, how minerals or crystals are exchanged for credits, and so on. Michael and I learned a lot from our mines and Hazel's Sam Iverson."

At the sound of Michael's name, Delores became quiet and stared down at her lap. Aunt Ferna patted her hand.

"It sounds like you two bonded over that?" Cora said, in a gentle tone addressing Remy, who blinked back tears.

"I never had any children, and Michael..." Remy said, and cleared his throat. "But you're right, we also bonded over learning about our mines."

Cora sensed a deep well of his sadness.

"How terrible for you and Dedie when Michael passed," Aunt Ferna said, while squeezing Delores' hand.

"I'm truly sorry for your loss," Cora said.

"We heard from the EGS yesterday," Delores said, wiping her eyes. "After their preliminary analysis, they determined it was an accident."

Cora sensed Delores' growing sadness, but luckily, Aunt Ferna and Remy both had their emotions in check. Otherwise, she would have needed to shield herself.

"I suppose there are no doubts about the EGS's analysis," Cora said, wondering what the blackmailer had on Hazel.

"No doubts," Remy said, his pale blue eyes boring into Cora. "Is there something you're trying to say?"

Cora felt a wave of his hostility.

"I feel awkward bringing this up, but what happened to the stair antigrav safeties?" Cora said. Those safeties should have immediately changed local gravity to cushion any fall down the stairs. "I assumed the EGS would've addressed this."

"The EGS did address this," Remy said in a quiet voice. "You are not family and are not privileged to have any information about my nephew."

Cora paused, unsure what to do, as waves of anger washed over her.

"You're right. It's none of my business," Cora said back peddling. "I really didn't mean to upset you."

Delores patted Remy's hand.

"It's just that it's still so fresh for us," Delores said. "We're satisfied by the EGS's preliminary findings."

"Of course. I apologize again," Cora said, her own guilt causing a heaviness to settle in her chest. She'd really been fishing for information about the circumstances of Michael's death.

"Hello, hello," Julia cried in a loud voice. "Have we missed lunch again?"

"Excuse me, there's some work I want to catch up on," Remy stood and paced into the house.

Julia plopped into Remy's chair and Theo grabbed the one next to her.

"Where did you go, my dear?" Delores asked with a forced smile.

"We rode on the forest trail through the north side of the property," Julia said, and chuckled. "Theo fell off."

"I ran into a tree branch," Theo said, as his face turned pink. "But the antigrav safeties saved me from a hard bump."

"Theo, I haven't had to use the safeties since I was a child," Julia said with a chortle.

Theo chuckled, but Cora sensed embarrassment and something... *What was he afraid of?* she thought. After that, she shielded herself to avoid being overwhelmed by too many emotions.

"I love horseback riding," Cora said. "I'd love to come with you when it's convenient." She braced herself for more of Julia's surly behavior.

"Of course. Come with me tomorrow morning," Julia said in a cheerful voice. "Theo has some tiring work to do, and I love to ride with others."

"I'll be there," Cora said, wondering at the change in her attitude.

"So, have you heard the juicy news?" Julia asked with a sparkle in her eyes.

"Julia, no," Delores said, frowning.

"Mom, Cora is Hazel's best friend, which makes her family," Julia said. "Anyway, first Michael and Oscar have a screaming match about credits, then he suddenly disappears. He's running from the EGS. We should turn him in."

"No EGS," Winifred said, from the doorway. Dressed in a taupe jumpsuit that complimented her gray hair, she looked as if she could command a spaceship or a large corporation. "I've personally dealt with them, and they have every possibility of harming as helping. If we need to find Oscar, we'll hire a private agency."

"What do you mean, *if* we need to find Oscar?" Julia asked in a raised voice. "Of course, we need to find him. He stole from us."

"Do you think a man like that still has your credits?" Winifred said, as she took a seat opposite Julia.

"That's why we need the EGS," Julia said. "They can trace the credits through the Net."

"No. That type of trace is very expensive and the EGS will only do that for extremely large sums of credits," Winifred said. "Also, they'll hold any left-over credits, only releasing them after they've withdrawn their fees."

"What do you suggest we do instead?" Delores said, trying to side with her daughter. "Simply let him go?"

"Yes," Winifred said. "People like that always get in their own way. Let the universe take care of him."

"I didn't realize you were religious," Aunt Ferna said with a chuckle.

"I'm not religious," Winifred said, scowling. "I'm trying to save you from the EGS. Nothing good will come from working with them."

Winifred knew first-hand how unfair the EGS could be to Askovians. Even Cora had to deal with questionable behavior from Agent Lewis.

"Wait, do you have your own small army to take care of people like Oscar?" Julia asked eagerly.

Winifred hesitated, and Cora desperately wished she could lower her shield.

"Cartwright Mining does have a small army, but it's deployed around our solitary mine," Winifred said, as her eyes bored into Julia's. "Which leads me to our current dilemma? Your Uncle has lost a mine to Spencer Industries, and because he can't recapture it, he is showing weakness. Do any of you understand the mining industry? Are you aware of how vulnerable you are right now? Why are you wasting energy on Oscar when you could become destitute in a few months?"

A heavy blanket of silence settled over their gathering.

Curiosity overcame Cora, and she lowered her shield for a second. Waves of Winifred's anger washed over her and threatened to drown her. She immediately raised her shield and carefully scrutinized Winifred, who appeared only a little annoyed but somehow managed to hide that level of fury. Cora also sensed heightened levels of Winifred's fear, which surprised her. *That mine battle must be more important than I realized,* she thought.

CHAPTER 8

The following morning, Cora woke before the sun to try to get some work done. Hazel had placed her in a room similar to her own, as it had a bed and side table on one side, a small dining room in the center, a desk next to the window, and opposite a door to the bathroom.

Her room faced the barn, and she kept an eye out for Julia while she created new code. The enhanced feature would allow her users to form groups and communicate with each other. This was the tedious part of her new program which required creating new symbols and testing them with the existing symbols. Later, she could enjoy the fun part, entering the virtual world and experiencing her new code.

Suddenly, Cora saw movement from the corner of her eyes and smirked.

Time to get started with Operation Julia, she thought.

She closed her coding window and sprinted out the door, trying to catch her quarry. She raced down the hall, one flight of steps, and out the side door toward the barn. As she rounded the corner, she spotted Julia and, much to her surprise, Kaye.

"Oh," Cora said, a little out of breath.

"Hello. Did you want something?" Julia said with a broad smile.

"Well, yes... I was just a little surprised to see Kaye," Cora said. "How are you both?"

Kaye nodded. She was a curvy woman a little older than Cora with striking emerald green eyes. She glared at Cora, who felt her irritation, anger, and something else wash over her. She guessed she had interrupted a private conversation, but then remembered there was a blackmailer to unearth.

"We are both in good health," Julia said. "I invited Kaye. I didn't want her to be alone."

"So what do you want?" Kaye said, with an edge to her voice.

"I've been looking forward to riding again ever since I heard the Farm has horses," Cora said, ignoring Kaye's increasing waves of anger. "Would you mind if I rode with you?"

Kaye turned and stalked into the barn.

"Join us," Julia said with a soft smile. "The more the merrier."

Cora sensed Julia's relief, guessing spending time alone with Michael's grieving girlfriend would be difficult as the mourning sister.

"I recently found out you became the head of Brimble Mining, after your sister's death," Julia said. "I know you'll understand my grief now."

Cora finally understood why Julia's attitude changed toward her. It had nothing to do with their shared grief and everything to do with credits. She would eventually ask for something.

Cora followed Julia and Kaye further into the barn. Old-fashioned dark wooden planks encased the barn's exterior, but the inside resembled a high-tech hospital ward with machines to groom, feed, exercise, and entertain the horses. Many robots floated around the barn tending to the horses, some of whom walked on treadmills for exercise, others socialized with each other round bales of hay.

"Do you have a preference?" Julia asked, gesturing at the horses.

"Something gentle and slow," Cora said, wide eyed. "I haven't ridden in more than ten years."

"Of course," Julia chuckled, pressing a button on her comm bracelet and selecting a few options on the resulting floating screen. "It'll take a moment."

"Where are we going today?" Cora asked, eyeing one set of robots preparing an older full-figured gray mare who seemed reluctant to leave her feed. Another set of robots prepared a younger black muscular gelding and young spirited chestnut mare. Eventually, the robots led all three horses outside with Cora, Kaye, and Julia.

"Scout's my favorite," Julia said, gently rubbing the gelding's neck and shoulders. The horse turned toward her, clearly enjoying her company. "Kaye always rides Rain, and yours is Willow."

"Hello Willow," Cora said, gingerly rubbing her shoulders. Willow wasn't irritated, but seemed uninterested, and instead continued turning to the grass a few meters further from the barn. "I think that's as cordial as she'll get."

"Give her some time," Julia said, chortling. Using her bracelet, she caused a set of mounting blocks materialized beside Scout, Rain, and

Willow. Similar to the meal crafter tech, much of a horse's tack and even the mounting blocks appeared from a storage area beside the barn.

Several minutes later, Julia led the way on Scout, and Kaye followed closely behind on Rain. Cora brought up the rear, riding Willow. They took a path through the forest Cora had seen earlier on one side of the Farm.

Kaye followed in stony silence, while Julia chattered away about her limited budget now that the Cartwright income was going away. She also complained about how Uncle Evan never tried to understand her point of view. She whined about needing a larger income so that she could buy the latest fashions in order to fit in with other Askovs.

Cora's horse, Willow, followed much slower while stopping repeatedly to munch on clumps of grass. She'd continue for a few more steps once Cora gently urged her to get going but would stop again at another clump of grass.

"Willow's really taking her time," Julia said, after noticing the gap between the three horses.

"I know," Cora sighed. "I think it might be faster if I got off and walked. At least I could reduce the frequent stops."

"No, you just don't know how to control your horse," Julia said, jumping off her horse. "I'll ride her. Can you get down?"

Cora jumped off her horse and walked to Scout. She rubbed his sides, but he pulled away.

"No, it won't work," Julia said, eyeing Scout. "I'm afraid he's attached to me."

"I'm sorry Julia," Cora said. "I'm holding you and Kaye up. Why don't you two go on and I'll return to the barn."

Cora sensed a tiny spike of Julia's panic. She really didn't want to be left alone with Kaye.

"No, it's alright," Julia said, returning to Scout and rubbing his sides while whispering something to him. "Let's walk to the clearing. It's my favorite spot on this whole farm."

Kaye grumbled something under her breath, and Cora sensed her increasing irritation.

Julia led the way on foot, while Kaye and Cora followed. Cora managed to stop Willow from reaching for grass clumps so frequently while they followed the trail. The clearing was at the top of a gently sloping hill, and it took about thirty minutes to make it to the top.

Cora gasped. The view was spectacular. The Krega mountains appeared closer and more majestic. She watched the entire farm, including the robots tending to rows of cultured flowers, vegetables, and fruits. At the edge of the property sat the Pendleton's mini-mansion, acting like an entrance to the entire property.

Cora sensed Julia's deep contentment while Kaye's irritation decreased and finally disappeared. She glanced at Kaye, wondering how the view could cause such a huge change.

"Is this where you come when you're with Theo?" Cora asked with a small smile as she sat on the grass.

"Yeah, it's so easy to spend time with him," Julia said, with a wistful look joining Cora.

"Michael brought me here on our first real date," Kaye said in a quiet voice.

Cora now felt her waves of sadness. She considered shielding herself, but decided to wait.

Julia patted the ground next to her.

"Come and sit with us," Julia said. "We're all still grieving."

Kaye sat and began to wipe tears from her eyes.

"Sorry, I don't mean to be so down," Kaye said, while Julia leaned in to hug her.

"It's only been a few weeks since..." Julia said. "Of course you're still down."

"What did you do on your first date?" Cora asked, hoping to change to a pleasant conversation.

"He had the robots create an outdoor dining room," Kaye said with a small smile. "The crafters created an amazing meal. We ate and talked for hours."

"That sounds so romantic," Julia sighed. "I wish Theo was romantic like that."

"How did you and Michael meet?" Cora asked.

"My mom was Alice Spencer, the middle of the three Spencer sisters," Kaye said, as her hand brushed the sparse grass. "I had to attend a conference in Lunar City representing the Spencers, even though my last name is Stone. My mom had passed away a few months before the conference, my brother had traveled Earthside, and the Spencers looked down on my dad." She paused and surveyed the Krega mountains lost in thought. "Anyway, Michael was at the conference. We met and hit it off. We had to be careful. The Spencers and Pendletons aren't exactly friends."

Julia rubbed Kaye's shoulders while they all sat without talking for a few minutes.

"We were going to have children and start a family," Kaye said in a strained voice. "Why did he have to die?"

"I don't know, dear," Julia said in a hoarse voice. "I miss him too."

Several minutes later, Julia chuckled. "You must think we're a sad, pitiful bunch," she said to Cora.

"Of course not. You're in mourning," Cora said. "This is exactly what you're supposed to do."

"I wonder what's going to happen to Hazel," Julia said. "Her mom is already shopping her around like last year's formal wear."

"I don't care," Kaye said, with an explosion of hatred. "I wish she'd died instead."

Cora didn't expect her outburst, but she did expect her sentiment.

"Kaye, this is Hazel's best friend," Julia said, nervously eyeing Cora.

Shooting to her feet, Kaye stomped away from Julia and Cora, ending up beside her horse, Rain. A second later, she mounted the mare.

"I'll see you at the barn," Kaye shouted, and she urged her horse down the gently sloping hill.

"Should we go after her?" Cora asked. "Make sure she's safe."

"No, Kaye is a hothead," Julia said. "She needs time to cool off."

"I didn't realize she was part of the Spencer family," Cora said as the birds chirped nearby.

"Yeah, Mabel, Alice, and Jessica inherited after their dad passed," Julia said. "Mabel throws those afternoon teas for Askovs and Jessica controls Spencer Industries. Unfortunately, Alice, who was Kaye's mom, passed away a few years ago."

"Is Kaye a Reader like her mom?" Cora asked.

"No, her older brother, Henry," Julia said, while standing. "Maybe it's time to head back."

"That's fine," Cora said, getting to her feet. "I think I'll walk Willow back—it'll be faster," she smirked.

Julia chuckled and said, "I'll walk with you."

They gathered their horses and started the trek back to the barn.

"So, tell me about Theo. You met him on the journey home from Mars, right?" Cora asked.

"He was in uniform, having just completed some sort of maneuver," Julia said with a fond smile. "He looked magnificent."

Cora gently guided Willow away from another clump of grass as she rubbed her sides, trying to reassure her. Cora wished she could read the horse's emotions, but decided based on the horse's behavior, it may be for the best.

"So, you've been together for about a year now?" Cora asked.

"I asked Michael if I could marry him," Julia sighed. "I'm not in love with him, but he's rich and he could support me."

Cora took a minute to digest Julia's words—she'd expected her to mention love. Parents decided who their children should marry in about half of all Askov families. Interestingly, arranged marriages seemed standard in the Pendleton family but were non-existent in her own.

"What did Michael say?" Cora asked.

"No. Uncle Evan would never approve," Julia sighed.

"Does Theo know you could never marry him?" Cora asked.

"Of course, I wouldn't lie about something that important," Julia said, as disapproval laced her voice. "Our plan was to move into a home of our own when the timing was right. But then Michael..."

"I'm sure you must miss him," Cora said, watching for anything that seemed like deception. But Julia was one of the few Pendletons whose spoken emotions always matched the transmitted ones. "I hope in a few weeks or months you'll be able to find a place and move."

Julia slowed with Scout, allowing Cora and Willow to catch up.

"Next time, let's get a younger horse for you," Julia said. "You've hardly done any riding."

"It's okay," Cora said. "I still got some time outside and a little exercise."

Julia walked in silence for a moment.

"Michael's accident was truly unfortunate," Cora said, trying to think of a way to steer the conversation. "Have you thought about the antigrav safeties?"

"Yes, the EGS mentioned them," Julia said in a quiet voice. "As far as they could tell, they malfunctioned, but they're still doing their investigation."

Cora continued their trek in silence, thinking of the strange coincidence of the malfunctioning safeties.

"Sometimes I have nightmares about it," Julia said in a somber tone. "I see him tumbling down the stairs and there's nothing I can do."

"I'm so sorry," Cora said, as she sensed Julia's waves of grief. They continued in silence while the wind rustled the leaves on the nearby trees.

Cora reflected on their conversation. Neither Julia nor Kaye had tried to deceive her when she broached the topic of Michael, which made them unlikely blackmailers.

A few hours later, Cora sat with Hazel in her private sitting room. The view out of the window was a little subdued, as the sun would set in a couple of hours. Cora took a sip of tea while Hazel bit into one of the tiny lemon cakes served with the tea.

Cora leaned on a cushion, sensing Hazel's muted emotions.

"So what are you thinking about?" Cora asked, placing her teacup on the coffee table.

"I don't know," Hazel said, as she pulled herself away from the window and turned to Cora. "I guess, I'm wondering what Sam's doing and when he'll be free."

Restraining herself from a gasp, Cora instead held her breath and let it out in slow increments. *Why is Hazel lying?* she thought. Cora still didn't know what she was thinking about and wondered if she could get her to confess.

"So far, I've had a chance to talk to Delores, Remy, Julia, and Kaye," Cora said, carefully sensing Hazel's feelings.

"What did you learn?" Hazel asked, focused completely on Cora.

"They all believe Michael died by accident," Cora said. "I don't see how they'd blackmail you if there was no crime."

"They could've made fake evidence," Hazel said. "Maybe..."

"I just can't see Delores, Julia, or even Kaye doing that," Cora said. "They're very straightforward people. They're pretty clear about what they like and don't like."

Hazel chuckled. "You are so right about that."

Cora patted her hand.

"Maybe you can leave this family soon, since your mom is here," Cora said.

Hazel's face fell.

"I'm sorry. I shouldn't have reminded you of that," Cora said.

"It's okay. Mom has been working for days to find another match for me," Hazel said with a sigh. "I know my days of freedom are numbered."

"I'm pretty sure Remy also thinks Michael died by accident," Cora said. "The only reason I'm not completely sure is he got angry so quickly I wasn't able to read him as well."

"Yeah, I don't think it's any of them," Hazel said. "I think Oscar is the only real option."

"Only option for what?" Winifred asked as she paced into Hazel's room.

"Mom," Hazel said as she shot to her feet. She gestured at the chairs across from the sofa and Winifred lowered like royalty expecting to be waited on.

Cora sensed no emotions from Winifred—she'd shielded her feelings well.

Hazel selected a button on her bracelet, creating a new tea setting with a small lemon cake.

"Cora and I were talking about the possibility of Oscar being the blackmailer," Hazel said, as she took her place next to Cora.

"Why him?" Winifred asked, swallowing her tea.

"He needed the credits," Hazel said.

"Lots of people need credits, but it doesn't mean they'll resort to blackmail," Winifred said.

"True..." Hazel said, turning to Cora.

"He had access to all of Michael's finances, business connections, and legal documents," Cora said. "We already know he stole from Michael."

"The theft is hearsay. We don't really know what they fought about," Winifred said. "In the end, Michael still invited him to the Spring Gala. The fight couldn't have been that bad. On the other hand, there's a strong possibility you're right."

"So far we've talked to Delores, Julia, Kaye, and Remy," Hazel said, glancing at Cora. "We don't think any of them could be the blackmailer."

Winifred's gaze switched from Hazel to Cora and back to Hazel.

"How did you determine they couldn't be guilty?" Winifred asked.

"Umm... Well, it's really Cora," Hazel said, and turned to Cora.

"I suspect you've been doing the real work," Winifred said. "How did you do it?"

Cora glanced at Hazel, detecting her embarrassment.

"Well, sensing someone's emotions while they're talking to me helps me figure out if they're lying," Cora said.

"Does this work all the time?" Winifred asked, all her attention now focused on Cora.

"No. If an Askovian is shielding, I can't observe their feelings," Cora said. "I also struggle if their emotions are too strong or change too quickly."

"Is there someone else you plan to investigate?" Winifred asked with a serious expression.

"Yes, Theo and Sam," Cora said.

"Sam! Why Sam?" Hazel asked in a raised voice.

"Umm—" Cora said.

"Because Theo and Sam both benefited from Michael's death," Winifred said, interrupting Cora.

"Evan may still stop Julia from moving in with Theo," Cora said. "And I may be wrong, but I had the impression you were planning a new husband for Hazel. Sam is probably not an option for Hazel."

"Well..." Winifred paused, glancing around the room. "I don't think Evan cares for Julia as much as he did Michael. She may be able to marry Theo," she shifted uncomfortably in her chair. "I'm finding it difficult to find families here on Earth open to an arranged marriage. Those two still may benefit."

As the conversation devolved into small talk, Cora thought, *I wish she could be kinder to Hazel. Maybe she could finally get away from her mom.*

CHAPTER 9

"What did your mom say before leaving this morning?" Cora asked, turning away from the birds flitting from flower to flower. With the window behind her, Cora stood in Hazel's sitting room, drinking coffee. Her casual top and black pants contrasted with Hazel's soft, off-white dress. She sensed Hazel's steady stream of sadness that always intensified after one of her talks with Winifred.

"Well, first she started with the usual," Hazel said, quickly wiping her eyes. "She's so disappointed in me. I should've had a child by now. I should've helped my brothers. And so on..."

Cora stepped to the sofa, placed her coffee cup on the table, sat next to Hazel, and hugged her.

"I'm so sorry your mom is... that way," Cora said, squeezing her arm.

Hazel produced a watery smile.

"I suppose this scolding was worse than normal?" Cora asked.

"Yeah, I'm a failure for not finding the blackmailer," Hazel said. "Then she kind of complimented me by saying at least I know enough to get help from a friend."

"You know you're intelligent," Cora said in a stern voice.

"Yeah, I know," Hazel said with a half-smile. "She's been subtly calling me stupid my entire life, but then she sent me to school. At school I always got praised by teachers and other students." She sighed. "I just wish she didn't hate me so much."

"I wish you would break away from her," Cora said. "You're an adult. You have more than enough credits to fund a higher degree."

Hazel shook her head, pulled her hands out of Cora's grasp, and took a sip of tea.

Maybe if I say it enough, she'll break away from her mom's control, Cora thought.

In the early afternoon, Cora sat cross-legged at her desk wearing her gaming glasses. She walked through a brand-new forest checking for glitches. A few hours slid by as she patched her world, hoping to make it as authentic and realistic as possible. A chime on her bracelet interrupted her work, and she considered ignoring it, but changed her mind.

Removing her gaming glasses, she turned to her bracelet and started a vidchat from Hazel.

"Would you come down to the living room?" Hazel asked, her face pinched with tension.

"Oh, I didn't know you were home. What's going on?" Cora asked.

"Vivian Pendleton requested a family meeting," Hazel said. "These never go well."

"Are you sure I should go?" Cora asked. "I'm not really family."

"I need you there," Hazel said, wide eyed. "Please come to my sitting room. We can walk down together."

"I'll be there in a minute," Cora said. She shut down her coding windows, checked her casual light blue top and pants set for lunch food stains, then pulled her hair into a ponytail.

A few minutes later, Cora followed Hazel into the formal living room near the front of the home. Covered in an ornate dark wood design, the ceiling was the most arresting and oppressive part of the living room. The rest of the room contained dark red sofas and chairs with brass trim, several dark paintings of Pendleton ancestors, and bookcases filled with actual books.

Cora shielded herself as she entered to find Delores and Remy on one sofa while Theo and Julia occupied the second sofa. Sam stood when Hazel entered and they sat on two chairs nestled together opposite one of the sofas. Kaye sat in one of two armchairs and gestured to the second for Cora. On the remaining sofa sat Vivian Pendleton, who glared at Cora for a moment before turning to the rest of the room.

"Hello, Councilor," Cora said in a cordial tone. "Pleasure to see you again." The last time the two had met, Vivian had lied to the EGS and got Cora arrested.

"What are you doing here?" Vivian asked with an edge to her voice. Her straight brown hair rested on her shoulders, and she was dressed in a business jumpsuit similar to Winifred's, but in a dusty pink color. She worked as a diplomat to the Lunar City Council, acting as the face of the Pendleton political arm.

"I wanted her here for support," Hazel said while holding Sam's hand.

"Seems to me you have enough support," Vivian said as her eyes darted between Hazel and Sam.

"I can leave if you'd be more comfortable," Cora said with a bland face, knowing that implying she had any control over Vivian would irk her.

"It doesn't matter," Vivian said, and turned to everyone else. "I understand before he passed, Michael explained that your income would be affected by the scuffle with one of our mines. Since Spencer Industries captured that mine, we've had no income from it. As a result, you'll all receive your final quarterly credits in about three weeks."

"What do you mean by final?" Remy asked as his thin frame tensed.

"I mean that you won't receive any more income from any Pendleton mines after three weeks from now," Vivian said matter-of-factly. "I know this is sudden, and I apologize. It took Evan a while to consult with the family accountants to realize how bad things are."

"I thought we had several more months," Julia said in a raised voice. "I've made plans."

"You'll simply have to unmake those plans," Vivian said. "There's nothing to be done at this point. The only purpose for that mine was to provide income for this branch of the family."

"How are we expected to live?" Delores asked.

"I don't understand the problem," Vivian said. "You have income from the Cartwright mine."

"Actually, no," Hazel said. "That income is going away in about six months."

"What? Why didn't you inform Evan?" Vivian asked with raised eyebrows.

"My mom... I mean Winifred did contact Evan," Hazel said a little defensively. "I was in the room when the conversation took place."

"I see," Vivian said, pursing her lips. "He never mentioned it to me."

"I would imagine my brother is overwhelmed right now," Remy said with a sympathetic smile. "He simply forgot."

"You're still married into the Pendleton family. Why are they removing the income?" Vivian asked.

"It-It's intended for my next husband," Hazel said in a quiet voice. All eyes turned to Sam, who shifted uncomfortably in his chair.

"Very well," Vivian said, glancing at the ceiling. "This will require some discussion with Evan. However, I think there's a simple answer."

"Delores and Julia can move back to the main house in Heliton," Vivian said, glancing at the two women. Heliton was a mountainous city on the other side of Earth, from Tymal. It was known for the Heliton Boarding School, where Cora attended. Vivian turned to Remy. "You have your pension."

"What!? I can't be expected to live on that paltry amount," Remy said, almost shouting. "My brother is a selfish monster!"

"We never received a proper allowance under Evan's roof," Delores said. "He makes us justify every single expense."

"He never understands," Julia said. "It takes credits to dress properly for influential parties and chat with other Askovs."

"I know Evan can be... stingy," Vivian said in a softer voice. "I also have my problems with him. But there's nothing we can do now. There isn't enough income for all of us to continue living the way we're used to."

"I promise you there are enough credits," Remy said, popping to his feet. "My brother is sitting on them and won't share. You tell my brother to go to hell." He stormed out of the room.

Cora was grateful she'd been shielded during the discussion. Theo whispered something to Julia, who smiled and hugged him. Cora could only guess what they talked about.

"Well, I'm very sorry to be the bearer of bad news," Vivian said. "I'll send you more information as Evan makes up his mind."

"Can we talk to Evan directly?" Delores asked.

"Of course," Vivian said. "Maybe you can reach a separate understanding with him." She glanced at her comm bracelet. "And now I need to leave if I'm to make my next appointment."

After Vivian left, Kaye stood, glancing at Julia.

"It's been a long day. I'll be going now, Julia," Kaye said. "Let me know if you want to visit the city. You always have a bedroom."

"I'll walk you out," Julia stood. She and Theo followed Kaye to the door.

"Does Kaye get an income from the Pendleton mine?" Cora asked.

"No, but everyone considers her family," Hazel said. "Rumor is she's heading back to Lunar City. Her family lives there."

"I suppose she'll have to wait for the all-clear from the EGS," Cora said thoughtfully.

"Yeah, we all do," Hazel said and turned to Sam. "Do you want to get going?"

Sam nodded, stood, and followed Hazel to the door.

"I think I'm going to my room now," Delores said, standing and pacing to the door.

Now Cora was the last person in the room. She thought through what she'd learned about each of the family members before turning toward the door and heading to her room.

Stepping out of the dining room, she headed up the stairs, which opened to a landing. Around the corner from the top step was an alcove where she clearly heard Theo and Julia.

"Maybe in the future we could discuss marriage..." Theo said as his voice lowered, making it difficult to hear him any longer.

"Uncle Evan... final..." Julia said in a low voice, making it difficult to hear the rest of the words.

Cora decided to continue to her room, since it was none of her business.

That evening, Cora ate alone in her room. She wanted time to think about the meeting with Vivian. Afterwards, she continued making changes to her game. She'd completed a walk-through of a brand-new field when her bracelet chimed. She sighed, taking off her gaming glasses.

"Hey Brian," Cora said, answering the new vid-chat.

"How's it going?" Brian said, tension marring his face.

"It's fine here, but you don't look good. What's going on?" she asked.

"Oh... I just had a screaming match with Eliza," Brian said. "She thinks because she's older, she can boss me around."

"Why did your sister scream at you?" Cora asked, even though she thought she knew.

"The new Spencer mine," Brian sighed. "I'm so sick of that mine. I refused to do anything illegal, and I thought my reasoning would have been obvious, but..."

"The few times I met Eliza, she reminded me of Harold," Cora said. "They're not inherently bad, only they feel 'the ends justify the means' sometimes."

"Exactly," Brian said in a harsher voice. "She thought if she shouted at me long enough, I'd cave, but that only worked when we were kids.

I've been running my own businesses for well over a decade."

"What did you do while she shouted?" Cora asked with furrowed eyebrows.

"I kept my cool and responded to her with logic," Brian chuckled. "She hates that. She wants an emotional response, and I give her only logic."

"Only a brother could wind up a sister like that," Cora said with a small smile.

"Anyway, enough about my fun," Brian said. "Are you any closer to finding the blackmailer?"

"Not really," Cora said. "The most likely suspect is Oscar, and he's disappeared."

"Want me to dig around and see what I can find out?" Brian asked.

"Well, it wouldn't hurt," Cora said thoughtfully. "I've been thinking it may be time to search his bedroom. Maybe I'll ask Hazel to help."

"What about the others?" Brian asked. "Why do you think they're innocent?"

"I see a motive for all of them," Cora said. "They all seem to need credits. But I can't figure out what evidence they'd have, real or falsified. I'm kind of stuck."

"Well, you'll figure it out," Brian said. "You always do."

A moment of comfortable silence settled over their conversation.

"I miss our lunches," Brian said. "With any luck, Eliza will come back early and I can run from this disaster."

"When do you think she'll be back again?" Cora asked.

"In about a week," Brian said. "It looks like she's wrapping things up early."

"I'll be here a few more days," Cora said with a gentle smile. "Maybe we can have lunch then."

"Sleep well," Brian said and ended the vidchat.

I miss our lunches too, Cora thought.

CHAPTER 10

The next day, after lunch, Cora followed Sam, Theo, and Remy to the patio and into the garden.

"Let's see," Remy said. "I think the Hammer Ball set is here." He opened the outdoor cabinet and pulled out four clubs that looked like mallets with elongated handles.

"Which color would you like?" Remy asked, turning to Cora.

"I'll try yellow," Cora said, grabbing the yellow club and a set of six yellow balls.

Sam took red, Theo blue, and Remy green.

Remy selected a button on his comm bracelet and a floating screen appeared over the bracelet. He set the playing area, which was a large square of grass, and chose a path that resembled a simple snake trailing back and forth over the playing area.

"I've never played this before," Theo said. "What are the rules?"

Cora felt a sharp spike of Remy's contempt.

"Of course, let me explain," Remy said with a smile. "The goal is to hit your color ball through all the hoops spaced out along the path. You get a point for each hoop your ball goes under." Remy paused and gazed at Theo, who nodded. "You're allowed to knock other player's balls off the snaking passageways. And if you knock another player's ball off the path, that player has to choose a new ball and start over. The first to make it to the end wins."

Cora had met people like Remy, whose detected emotions didn't match their facial expressions. It usually meant something wasn't right with them.

"Good. Who goes first?" Theo asked with a grin.

"I'll go," Sam said with a chuckle. "I used to play this game with my family all the time." He walked to the start of the course, placed his red ball under the starting hoop, and knocked it down under two hoops. A score illuminated above the playing field showing everyone's score before blinking out.

"Sam, how did you and Hazel meet?" Cora asked.

"I wish it were a romantic story, but it was so mundane," Sam said, shaking his head. "We were on the cruise home from Mars when I entered the dining room to discover every table taken. The robotic matre'd asked if I minded sharing a table with someone. I said if the other person agreed, then I didn't mind. We just seemed to hit it off right away."

"I don't know," Cora said. "It sounds like the beginning of a great romance."

Sam blushed.

"I think I'd like juice," Remy said. "Anyone else interested?"

Sam hurried after him as if trying to hide his embarrassment.

"I'll go next," Theo said as he grabbed his blue ball and placed it at the start. He hammered his ball, which zoomed past Sam's but ended up going out of bounds of the playing square. "Too hard?"

"Well, it takes practice," Cora said. "I'll go next. So, Theo, how did you meet Julia?"

Cora cued her yellow ball at the start and gently tapped. It rolled past the first two hoops, stopping beside Sam's.

Sam and Theo clapped.

Grinning, Cora stepped onto the patio and selected a cold juice from the crafter on the patio table. "Well..." she asked expectantly.

"She stalked me!" Theo said with a chuckle while Sam and Remy joined in.

"What?" Cora said. "There has to be more to the story."

Remy took a sip of his drink, but it wasn't juice. The amber colored liquid looked like a type of whiskey she'd seen Harold drink in the past.

"I think it's my turn now," Remy said, placing his glass on the patio table and stepping to the starting hoop. He placed his green ball and gave it a whack. It whizzed past Cora and Sam's balls and didn't stop until it reached hoop five.

Cora, Sam, and Theo clapped while Remy chuckled.

"How did my disobedient niece stalk you?" Remy asked in a boisterous voice with slightly slurred words.

"I got in the habit of running laps for my daily exercises," Theo said, trying to stifle his laughter. "According to her, it took me a solid week before I noticed she always ran into me and struck up a conversation. Once I did notice, I asked her out. We've been inseparable since."

"I think you said you work security on Mars?" Cora asked.

"Yeah, I recently retired," Theo said, glancing at the patio. "I think I'll get a drink too."

Cora sensed Theo's mild deception, but couldn't tell if it was from his discomfort with the game or his recent retirement.

"Sam, Hazel mentioned you're a consultant for Askov families," Cora said. "I understand you investigate mines. How did you get started?"

"I had a mentor who taught me everything I know," Sam said. "He helped me launch my consultant business and helped me get my first clients. He's passed away now, but I owe him everything."

The four continued their play while talking and drinking. The sun lowered in the clear sky—they had been playing for a few hours.

"I think it's my turn now," Remy said, slurring his words. He moved to one of his green balls and gave it a gentle tap. It veered around Sam's red ball and ended by rolling across the last hoop. "Ha! I won."

Cora, Sam, and Theo clapped.

All four returned to the patio for new drinks.

"Should we play another round?" Remy asked, holding a new amber drink.

"Not all of us are retired," Sam said with a chuckle. "I need to catch up on some work."

Cora, Theo, and Remy settled into chairs with fresh drinks while Sam stepped into the house.

"You're a retired doctor," Cora said. "How did you enjoy the journey to Mars and back?"

"I've noticed a lot of questions from you?" Remy said. "What's this all about?"

"I thought I was getting to know you all," Cora said, while probing his emotions. "I don't want to pry."

Why is he angry? What is he hiding? she thought.

"Actually, Julia said you asked a lot of questions about how Michael died," Theo said. "What was that about?"

"Oh, that's unfortunate," Cora said, warming to her lie. "Someone told Hazel's mom that Michael died under mysterious circumstances."

"That's ridiculous," Theo said with his mouth in a grim line. "That's someone's sick joke."

"I think you all know Winifred Cartwright," Cora said, leaning closer and lowering her voice.

The other gentlemen nodded.

"She's making Hazel's life hell until we find who started the rumor," Cora said.

"Poor Hazel," Theo said.

"So, I gather you think Michael died of natural causes," Cora said.

"Of course he did," Theo said, nodding. "The EGS ran a full investigation on his death. It was definitely an accident."

Cora sensed no deception from Theo.

"What do you think?" Cora asked, turning to Remy.

"That's slander!" Remy shouted as he shot to his feet. "No one here had any motive to kill Michael except Oscar." He leaned toward Cora, but had to steady himself on the table. "We needed Michael alive to keep the family credits flowing. Oscar, on the other hand, was stealing, and when Michael found out, he was heading to jail." He slammed his drink on the table and continued his rant. "Michael tripped, and no one was near him when it happened! Tell Winifred to stop looking into the rumor or the Pendleton family will sue her."

Remy spun on his heel and stormed into the house.

"Did I miss something?" Theo asked. "Why did he become so irate?"

"I don't know," Cora said, slowly rising to her feet. "I'm confused too."

Theo and Cora walked into the house. At the top of the stairs, he turned into a nearby doorway while Cora continued to her room.

Cora continued to mull over Remy's emotions and his behavior. The only thing she was sure about was he lied about something. *Did he lie about Michael tripping or no one near the body? Why did he emphasize Oscar had a motive to kill Michael? What was he trying to hide?* His emotions were a jumbled mess, and she couldn't untangle them.

Cora sat in her room at Pendleton Farm later that evening. She'd finished her evening meal by herself. As it turned out, none of the family ate in the dining room downstairs. She'd just finished a butter cookie and still had crumbs on her shirt while drinking hot tea.

Her eyebrows furrowed while manipulating the symbols for her game. She worked on implementing a feature that allowed her players to share tools. This change would allow gamers to excavate into mountains or defend themselves against wild animals. They could cooperate on a mission with other players. After working for a couple of hours, a knock at the door interrupted her focus. Glancing at the door, she wondered if she should tell the home's AI to send the person away or open.

After a moment of deliberation, she closed her coding window, stood while dusting crumbs off of her shirt, and paced to the door of her room. It opened automatically and revealed Julia framed in the doorway with a broad smile on her face.

"Julia, I wasn't expecting to see you again tonight," Cora said. "Is there something I can help you with?"

Cora sensed her nervousness mixed with fear, which piqued her interest.

"Well, yes you can," Julia said. "Would you mind if I come in? I need to speak to you about something kind of urgent."

"Of course, of course," Cora gestured toward the sofa in her room.

"Would you like some tea?" Cora asked.

Julia nodded.

A second later, two cups of hot tea appeared on the coffee table beside the sofa. They both took a sip and Cora placed her cup on the table and leaned into the sofa, waiting for Julia to begin talking.

"I'm not blaming you for anything," Julia said cautiously. "I've had a chance to talk to Theo and Kaye. And we're wondering why you keep asking about Michael's death."

That's why she's so nervous, she thought. Leaning forward, she relied on the lie she had told Theo earlier in the afternoon.

"Here's my problem," Cora said. "Winifred Cartwright heard a rumor that there are some inconsistencies in the way that Michael passed away."

"That's absurd," Julia raised her voice and crossed her arms. "I've seen the EGS preliminary analysis. He broke his neck and back when he fell down the stairs."

"The EGS released their preliminary findings to everyone?" Cora asked.

"No. Uncle Evan sent us a copy," Julia said, relaxing her arms. "Me, Theo, and Kaye pored over it. Everything is completely consistent with a fall."

"I'm guessing Winifred hasn't seen the report," Cora said with a small smile. "I might be able to wrap this up by showing it to her."

"What exactly were you supposed to do?" Julia asked as her blue eyes examined Cora's.

"I promised to see if anybody here at the farm noticed anything odd about how Michael fell," Cora said. "However, everybody thinks he died of natural causes. When I told Winifred, she wouldn't let things go. She wanted me to continue looking into the source of that rumor. She's afraid it reflects badly on the Cartwrights because most of the family was closer to Michael before he fell. Specifically, she wants to know who started it."

"No one thinks there's anything unusual about Michael's fall," Julia said with raised eyebrows. "Also, you might never find that person."

"I know," Cora sighed. "But I'm hoping that if she sees the report, she'll let it go. A vicious rumor won't stand up against an official EGS investigation." She hesitated. "Would you mind if I take a look at their document?"

"Of course not," Julia said. She pressed a button on her comm bracelet, creating a floating window. It was a privacy window, so Cora couldn't see into it. But Julia maneuvered something on the screen, and a second later Cora's bracelet chimed.

"Thank you," Cora said, looking down at the notification on her bracelet. "I'll read through this and send it to Winifred. Hopefully, this puts her mind at ease."

"Well..." Julia hesitated. "Would you mind talking to Kaye? She's very upset about your questions."

"Of course not," Cora said. "Why don't we create a vidchat right now and talk to her?"

Julia, using her existing window, arranged something else on her screen. A moment later, Cora heard Kaye's voice.

"Hello, Julia. What's going on?" Kaye asked. Julia adjusted something on the screen, and now Cora could see Kaye.

Kaye's demeanor immediately changed once she spotted Cora. Her mouth became tight and her green eyes glared at Cora.

"What do you want?" Kaye asked.

"Kaye," Julia said. "I've talked to Cora about her questions. Would you like to hear from her, or would you rather stay angry?"

Kaye rolled her eyes. "Yeah, well out with it."

A knot in Cora's chest unwound with relief not to be experiencing Kaye's anger in person. She decided to ignore her rude response, keeping in mind she was still grieving for Michael. But it didn't change the fact that she was beginning to dislike her.

"So, a few days ago, somebody sent a message to Winifred Cartwright," Cora said. "Hazel's mom—"

"I know who Hazel's mom is," Kaye said in a clipped tone.

"Of course, of course," Cora took a deep breath, willing herself to remain polite. "The message explained that Michael died under mysterious circumstances."

"That woman's stupid," Kaye said in a raised voice.

"No, it's more that she's afraid," Cora said, warming to her lie. "The Cartwright mine is in a very vulnerable location, on Phobos, one of the moons of Mars. If the Cartwright family angers another Askov family, it could lead to a battle and they could lose that mine."

"So this is more of a defense move," Kaye exhaled, leaning back into her chair. "Well, that woman is only stirring up trouble."

"You're right," Cora said. "But she's also trying to keep her mine and the income safe."

"So, what were you trying to do?" Kaye asked.

"She wanted me to try to figure out who would've sent that message," Cora said. "Talking things over with Hazel, we decided if someone tried to kill Michael, it must be somebody who was at the Gala. There's no real motive for one of the friends to do it, but a family member might be tempted."

"That's the stupidest thing you've said so far," Kaye spat out. "Everyone in this family need- ed Michael alive to continue receiving income. Now that he's gone—no credits."

"I don't mean to upset you, but you're not de- pendent on Pendleton credits," Cora said. "Julia would like to marry Theo, but Michael wouldn't agree. Even Hazel would be better off without Michael because she might have Sam. Delores and Remy are the only two who wouldn't bene- fit from Michael's death."

Kaye wiped her eyes several times while turn- ing away from the screen.

"What's your theory about why I'd kill Michael?" Kaye asked, then cleared her throat.

"Michael might've finally agreed to go along with his uncle and start a family with Hazel," Cora said. Ever since Kaye mentioned starting a family during their horseback ride, Cora sus- pected it wasn't true.

Kaye covered her face and wept silently.

"Kaye dear, should we continue later?" Julia said in a sympathetic tone of voice.

"No, it's okay," Kaye said. "How did you know?"

"I know Evan," Cora said. "If Michael had even hinted at starting a family with you, he'd have felt Evan's wrath."

"Michael told me a few days before the Spring Gala we would have to break up," Kaye said with a sniffle. "We couldn't disrupt the Gala, so we continued as if everything was fine. He explained he was ready to do what his uncle wanted and create children with..."

"Oh, Kaye," Julia said. "Why didn't you tell me? I would've talked to him for you."

"I was going to after the Gala, but then he..." Kaye said, wiping her eyes again.

"Are you going to be okay tonight?" Julia asked in a worried tone of voice.

"I think I want to be alone tonight," Kaye turned to Cora. "What're your next steps?"

"I'll read through the report and send it to Winifred," Cora said. "I hope this ends my investigation."

Kaye and Julia said their goodbyes, but somehow Cora still felt uneasy. *There is still a blackmailer, and someone wanted Michael dead,* she thought. *Why?*

CHAPTER 11

"I'm meeting Brian and his family for lunch," Cora said, worried. "I hope I can help them."

"Is that why you're so dressed up?" Hazel said, taking a sip of tea and gesturing to Cora's floral dress. She wore a playful ensemble that included a pink top with orange shorts. However, Hazel's expression was anything but playful as she stared out of the window of her sitting room into the beautiful flower gardens.

Cora turned a little pink.

"Brian, huh?" Hazel said with a half-smile.

"I wanted to explain that I finished working on my investigation," Cora said, trying to change the conversation. "As far as I can tell, nobody related to the family could have harmed Michael. I really don't have enough information to confirm what the blackmailer is saying."

Hazel glared at Cora for a moment, crossed her arms, and stared out of the windows.

"Look, Hazel. I'm really sorry about this," Cora said. "I know you need to have some answers for your mom. But all I've got right now is the EGS record detailing their analysis, which I forwarded to you and your mom. I looked it over carefully last night. It clearly shows that the damage done to Michael's body is consistent with the fall."

"What am I going to tell Mom?" Hazel asked as Cora sensed her increasing agitation.

"Has she contacted you about the EGS findings?" Cora asked, standing and pacing to the window.

"Not yet," Hazel sighed.

"I can't imagine she'd have too much to say," Cora said. "She may even be open to going to the EGS, since the blackmailers have no evidence."

Hazel chuckled.

"I know wishful thinking," Cora said with a small smile. "Your mom hates the EGS. But to summarize, I have spoken to every single person in this house and used my abilities to gauge if they were lying. Every single one of them, including Oscar, felt Michael died from the fall."

"I believe you, I'm only worried about Mom," Hazel said from the sofa.

Cora paused as she tried to decide if she wanted to mention something else.

"What is it?" Hazel asked. "If you're trying to tell me something gently, don't. Just tell me everything."

"Okay, there's something unusual about Remy," Cora said with furrowed eyebrows. "I was never able to get a completely clear emotional reading on him. He always became upset, and I wasn't able to clearly decipher his emotions. That doesn't mean he's guilty or anything."

"Remy?" Hazel said, standing and strolling to the window.

"It always happened whenever I brought up anything related to Michael's passing," Cora said.

"Oh, yeah, it's true. Remy and Michael were very close," Hazel said. "They probably got closer after Michael's dad died. Remy was very close to Michael's dad and was devastated when he passed. Afterwards, Remy grew close to Michael. So, it makes sense he'd be very emotional, and you'd have trouble detecting his emotions."

They stood at the window in silence, thinking.

"This is what you can do if you want to continue the investigation yourself," Cora said. "Ask the blackmailer to send you proof. It could be a vidchat or secret package. Once you see the proof, that could tell you something about who is blackmailing you."

"Hmm..." Hazel said. "That's a good idea."

"I still think you should get EGS involved," Cora said in earnest. "Think about it. Now that the EGS's findings are available, they'll be on your side."

"The last time we got the EGS involved in something, they took Zach away," Hazel said. "I don't trust them, and Mom hates them."

"Not that I'm trying to defend them," Cora said. "They feel their job is to protect people without abilities. That's what makes them tricky to work with."

"I know you think the blackmailer could be dangerous," Hazel said with a gentle smile. "But I'll be careful."

"Well, I can't force you to call them," Cora said. "On another topic, what do you think about inviting your parents to the Albright Corporation?"

"Why would you do that?" Hazel asked with raised eyebrows.

"Well..." Cora stammered, not expecting her response. "It's just an idea—I haven't spoken to anybody. I thought we could ask your mom and dad to join the Albright Corporation for a few shares of ownership and then ask them to vote in favor of doing things legally. They would be voting against the Spencer family, but in favor of everybody else."

Hazel smirked

"Cora. You've known my mom for twenty years," Hazel said. "Mom doesn't do allegiance. Her focus is always to keep the family mine safe and profitable. You could ask her to join Albright and vote against the Spencer's. But if the Spencers offer her a more lucrative deal, she won't remain loyal to you."

"I know. You're right," Cora said and exhaled. "I guess I was just so desperate. I'll try to think of something else that might be a better fit for the Albright Corporation."

"I don't want to say it couldn't work," Hazel said with a thoughtful expression. "But Mom can be... unpredictable."

"So, what do you have planned for the rest of today?" Cora said.

"I'm going horseback riding," Hazel said.

"Oh, with Julia?" Cora asked, wishing she could join them.

"Absolutely not," Hazel said with a frown. "She's good friends with Kaye, and the two of them have made my life miserable."

Cora sensed Hazel's anger, but it faded as she spoke.

"There is no way I'd spend my free time with her," Hazel said. "I was hoping to talk Sam into horseback riding and maybe a picnic. He's working, but he should be free in a few hours." She grinned.

"Sounds like a wonderful afternoon," Cora said with a small smile. "I'd change my plans and join you, but I have a feeling I'd be in the way."

Several hours later, Cora walked into the Farris's home. She had not been in this home for a few years. But she and Brian had decided to have lunch in his house in the hopes that possibly she could convince Nora Albright, Brian's mom, to join them. Unfortunately, Nora felt intimidated by Cora's Feeler abilities, which meant that Nora always refused to meet her. But even lunch with Brian alone would still be productive.

Brian's family home was a modest size sandwiched onto a tiny city lot. On the other hand, the style was in the latest fashion, that included a blend of modern and ornate. A flourish of decorative curved wooden white trim under and over the windows seemed ornate, but the walls were a pale gray. The window trim contrasted with the straight, stark white lines on the roof, complimenting the home's plain white front door.

As Cora stepped to the front door, it opened automatically

"Welcome Coraline Brimble," the Farris home's AI said. "Please follow the signal lighting to the dining room."

"Thank you," Cora said as she stepped into the entryway. Unlike Pendleton Farm, this one had bright white walls and was flooded with lots of light for the street facing windows. Strategically placed flowers softened the hard surfaces and made it feel homey.

She followed the floor lighting and, in a few steps, emerged into the dining room. Painted a pale yellow and flooded with light from the skylights, this room left Cora with a cheerful smile.

"Ah, it's so good to see you in person," Brian chuckled, took a few steps forward, and kissed her on the cheek.

"Have a seat," Brian said as they both sat at the large rectangular dining room table.

Cora hadn't shielded herself, hoping to sense Nora. Instead, she felt Brian's obvious pleasure mixed with fear and anxiety.

"My father might join us a little later on," Brian said and continued with a slight frown. "My mom refuses to meet you. Of course,"

Cora had hoped to meet Nora, but she was momentarily distracted that he didn't mention her dress.

I'm being silly, she thought. *It's just a dress.*

They made their lunch selection from the meal crafter. Cora selected herb salmon on couscous with crystallized asparagus, and Brian selected a steak and mashed potatoes with corn mix. They ate in silence for a few minutes.

"So, how's your game coming along?" he asked.

"I have my good days and my bad days," Cora said with a small smile. "I think I've almost finished implementing the group function so that everybody can share tools or weapons. But it really needs a lot of testing. So I think I'll disable that option on launch day, but at least it gives me peace of mind that it's essentially ready."

"Excellent," Brian said. "I knew you could do it, even though it was a lot of coding. You've been at it for months now. Right?"

Cora nodded while she chewed on some asparagus.

"Well, well. Who do we have here?" Benjamin Farris said as he entered the room. He was a gray-haired distinguished gentleman who had the same blue-gray eyes as his son.

"Good afternoon," Cora said with a grin. "I don't think I've seen you for several months."

"Yes, I believe you're right," Benjamin said with a small chuckle. "I'm sorry I'm late for lunch. Nora and I had an early lunch at a friend's house. She's still there, but I came back to try to catch up with you. I want to discuss this Spencer mess."

He grabbed a seat and then selected water from the meal crafter. Cora finished her plate and put it through the recycling. Brian did so next.

"What do you think about the Spencers stealing that mine?" Benjamin asked with a scowl.

"I think it's terrible. But what surprised me the most is this has happened before. And Harold brushed it under the rug. This is against everything I taught that boy."

"Dad," Brian said, interrupting Benjamin. "I already told Cora all of this."

"Yes, well. I just can't believe it," Benjamin huffed. "This is also against everything I ever taught Jessica. I already went to her house and gave her a piece of my mind, but she laughed in my face. I turned around and left."

"Now Dad, don't rile yourself up," Brian said. "We're here to focus on solutions."

"Well, there is no solution," Benjamin scoffed. "The only thing to do is disband Albright Corporation. We can't have this stain on our family name."

"It won't be that simple," Brian said. "Mom is set on helping the Spencers. In any case, we already have a stain based on what Harold did."

Benjamin grumbled under his breath.

Cora sensed Benjamin's irritation and Brian's resignation, while she dithered on whether to float her idea.

"Well, there is one possible long shot," Cora said and waited for both sets of eyes to turn her way. "My idea comes with a lot of danger, but if it works, you could regain control of Albright Corp."

"What's your long shot?" Benjamin asked with furrowed eyebrows.

"The Cartwright family has a lone mine," Cora said in a steady voice. "It's under the Pendleton family's protection. What if we ask the Cartwrights to join the Albright Corp? They'll get Spencer family protection, but we'll ask them to vote to keep things legal."

"I can't see Winifred biting the hand that feeds her," Brian said with a small shake of his head. "She'll be asking the Spencers for protection and then voting against something the Spencers want or really need."

"But Feelers can tell if someone is telling the truth," Benjamin said. "Brian, Nora, and I will make an appointment with Winifred and her husband."

Brian nodded.

"Nora will be there to check if Winifred or her husband are lying," Benjamin said with a small smile.

Cora sensed his elation. He really thought this could work.

"Feelers can't get an emotional read on someone who is shielded," Cora said. "Winifred is usually shielded, and I doubt she'd let her husband anywhere near the negotiations. If the meeting has other people, like assistants who understand the negotiations but aren't shielded, Nora might be able to determine if something's not right."

"Sounds like so many things could go wrong," Brian said.

"The thing is, being able to figure out if somebody's telling the truth or not is more of an art. It requires a lot of experience," Cora turned to Benjamin. "Nora seems to spend more time among people she knows well. I wonder if she'd be comfortable with this."

"Are you trying to tell me my wife is incompetent?" Benjamin said in a casual voice, but Cora sensed his unease.

"No, of course not," Cora said, pausing to choose her words with care. "Lie detection is not taught in schools. Instead, it's an intuitive ability that has to be exercised regularly. Usually, you practice on several different types of people for years."

"Dad. You know, Cora has a point," Brian said. "Mom's a bit of a recluse. She might struggle with this skill."

"Well, I don't know about that," Benjamin said. "I'll ask Nora what she thinks."

"We could bring Cora with us to visit the Cartwrights," Brian said. "She has years of experience."

"No, she's not a member of Albright management," Benjamin said. "She's a client and part owner. We'll discuss this with the management team and let you know the outcome."

Benjamin finished the rest of his water, stood, and sauntered out of the room.

Cora turned to Brian with a lopsided grin. He chortled in turn.

"That went well," she said, her voice laced with sarcasm.

Ten minutes later, Cora stood outside of the Farris home and on a very quiet residential street. She always liked this part of town, but she needed to get back to work. She considered requesting the family hover car to pick her up or walking fifteen minutes to Tymal's city center.

She felt the need for a break and began her trek downtown, eventually reaching her favorite coffee shop on the bustling main street. As she stepped inside, the strong smells of coffee and the wide array of pastries brought a smile to her face.

Cora spotted Kaye alone at a table and her face fell. She nearly turned around, but Kaye spotted her and beckoned her over.

"Hello Cora. What are you doing in this part of town?" Kaye asked with a broad grin.

"I'm basically playing hooky," Cora said, taking a seat. "I have a lot of work to do, but I don't feel like it. So, what are you doing here?"

"Well, I'm glad you asked," Kaye said. "But first, how much longer are you staying at Pendleton Farm?"

"Leaving tomorrow," Cora said. "Why do you ask?"

"Have you finished your investigation?" Kaye asked, ignoring Cora's question.

"I got as far as I could and I sent the EGS analysis to Winifred," Cora said, selecting a black coffee from the crafter.

Kaye selected a small ginger nut cake as she'd already ordered tea. Once the dessert appeared on the table, she quickly glanced around the cafe as if she had a juicy secret.

"I did some investigation of my own," Kaye said with a sly smile.

Cora had already shielded herself before she entered the coffee shop. She considered lowering it for a moment to gauge Kaye's emotions, but immediately changed her mind.

"What did you discover?" Cora asked, carefully surveying Kaye's behavior.

"Sam was in a neighboring restaurant during the Spring Gala," Kaye said with a smirk.

"How did you find out?" Cora said, now feeling more interested despite her dislike for Kaye.

"I happen to be talking to a friend of a friend," Kaye said. "He mentioned that a mutual friend of ours met with Sam in the lobby of the restaurant. It was a short business meeting which would have given Sam time to harm Michael."

"Interesting. I wonder why Sam never mentioned that," Cora said thoughtfully.

"I just wonder if the EGS knows he was so close by," Kaye said, as glee made her green eyes twinkle. "I think I should let them know about this."

Kaye wants to get Sam in trouble to hurt Hazel, she thought.

"I think you should tell the EGS," Cora said in a solemn tone of voice.

"Oh—oh yes," Kaye said as she blinked in confusion. "I thought you'd try to talk me out of it."

"No, I've felt from the beginning they should be involved," Cora said.

"I suppose they won't be interested anyway," Kaye said. "They feel Michael's death was an accident."

"It's completely up to you," Cora said, standing and dumping half a cup of coffee into the recycling. "Do what makes you feel comfortable."

"I'll be leaving for Lunar City in a few days," Kaye said. "So I may not see you again."

"Safe trip," Cora said, turning to leave the coffee shop.

Kaye's dislike of Hazel seemed to border on obsession. It was one of the reasons Cora really didn't care for her.

CHAPTER 12

The following afternoon Cora stood on the patio of Pendleton Farm with a cool drink of fizzy mango juice. A faint flower fragrance wafted from the gardens as she chatted with Hazel and Sam.

"What are your plans for next week?" Cora asked and swallowed her juice. She wore a breezy yellow summer dress.

"I have a couple of meetings with some potential clients," Sam said. He wore a pale green shirt and loose-fitting matching pants. "And then my plan is to convince Hazel to join me on a trip to Lunar City. It's for a couple of weeks." His lips formed a lopsided smile.

"I thought we were going to keep that a secret," Hazel said, glancing at Delores, Aunt Ferna, and Remy, who sat around an oval table quietly chatting. She wore an afternoon tea dress covered in pale blue tropical flowers.

"At some point—" Sam started to say.

"I don't want to irritate my mom ahead of time," Hazel interrupted him. "It'd be better if we boarded the Lunar Shuttle and told her after we got there."

"I know it would be easier," Sam said. "But at some point, you have to stand up for yourself."

"Says the man who's never had to go toe-to-toe with the Cartwright matriarch," Hazel scoffed. "Even my dad doesn't cross her."

Sam glanced at Julia and Theo as if gathering his thoughts. They stood on the grass sipping green bubbly drinks while holding hammer ball clubs. The game wasn't actually set up yet. Clearly, they had started chatting and forgotten all about it.

"I understand all of that," Sam said, turning back to Hazel and Cora. "Your mom is tough, and your dad and everyone else in the family are completely cowed by her. But that doesn't mean that she can continue to rule your life."

Hazel rolled her eyes and turned to Cora as if to say, 'can you believe what he's saying?'

Cora agreed with Sam, but thought it was better to change the topic.

"So Hazel, outside of going to Lunar City, do you have any plans?" Cora asked. "More horseback riding? The theater? Anything like that?"

"As a matter of fact, Sam and I are going to the Alinac Gallery tomorrow," Hazel said. "There's a new Jupiter image exhibit."

"It's been done before, but this is supposed to be spectacular," Sam said, savoring a layered red and orange drink with a small smile.

"So, what's on the plate for you?" Hazel asked.

"My game should launch in a few more weeks," Cora said. "I'll be busy until then, but maybe I'll visit the Alinac afterwards."

"I still want to try out your game," Hazel said. "I told Sam all about it."

"No, that's alright," Cora said. "I really only want players who are actually interested in investigative adventure games because I'm really looking for feedback."

Delores, Aunt Ferna, and Remy, suddenly burst out laughing. They chatted in a quiet voice so Cora couldn't understand them. She noticed that Delores seemed less of a shadow these days. She clearly wasn't the same since the death of her son, but she always got better when Aunt Ferna was around.

Remy took a swallow of his amber drink, leaned back in the chair, and closed his eyes. He appeared to ignore the two women, but Cora thought he was paying close attention. Delores and Aunt Ferna looked like a pair of gossiping schoolgirls as they leaned toward each other whispering.

"Cora, Sam. Want to play hammer ball?" Julia called from the grass.

Cora noticed Julia trying to exclude Hazel again.

"I'll sit this one out," Cora replied.

"Come," Sam said, placing a hand on Hazel's elbow and gently guiding her toward Julia and Theo.

Julia's face fell, and she raised her arm to select a button on her comm bracelet. The Hammer Ball playing square and a trail of hoops appeared on the grass.

Julia, Theo, and Sam gathered around the square while Hazel went to the outdoor cabinet, grabbed balls for everybody, and brought them to the game's start point. Everybody took turns grabbing colored balls.

Sam went first and placed his yellow ball at the start. He tapped the ball, and it rolled under three hoops. He grinned while the remaining three clapped.

Cora smiled and turned to join Aunt Ferna, Delores, and Remy at the table. When she sat down, the two women turned to her, chuckling at a joke.

"Sorry, I had a last-minute meeting," Winifred strolled toward the table in a green flowered afternoon tea dress. She lowered herself into an empty chair. "Have I missed much?"

"No, Julia has started a hammer ball game," Aunt Ferna said, turning to Cora. "Why aren't you joining the game?"

"I wasn't up for it," Cora said. "And I wanted to say my goodbyes. I'll be leaving today."

"Well, we enjoyed having you," Delores said.

Cora almost raised an eyebrow at that because Delores had essentially ignored her most of the time she'd been on the Farm.

"I have a lot of programming to do," Cora said.

"Hazel mentioned your new game," Winifred said. "Tell me about it."

Cora paused, unsure where to start, "It's a puzzle adventure game set in a virtual world."

Remy sat up, opened his eyes, and took another drink.

"You have a launch coming up, right?" Remy asked.

"Yeah, the date's fast approaching," Cora said, taking a sip of her fizzy mango juice.

"Unfortunately, I've never enjoyed those virtual games," Remy said. "Best of luck." He raised his glass and swallowed.

"I agree," Winifred said. "Those games always felt like a vast waste of time."

Cora narrowed her eyes, irritated at Winifred's comment. Suddenly, Julia stepped up onto the patio.

"Oh, Cora, you're not leaving now," Julia said, grabbing the chair next to her.

"Yeah, I was going to talk to you and Theo next," Cora said.

"But we have so much to discuss," Julia said, leaning a little closer. "Mom and I were thinking of moving in with some friends. You know, so we don't have to live with Uncle Evan. He's always bossing us around."

"Who were you thinking of asking?" Cora asked, but she already knew the answer.

"Well..." Julia said, exchanging a glance with Delores. "One of our options is to stay with you, if you'll have us." Her lips spread into a small smile.

So that's what she wanted, Cora thought. *I knew there was a reason she was suddenly nice to me.*

"I'm sorry Dedie, Julia," Aunt Ferna replied for Cora. "That is simply out of the question. I can't allow my niece to support you. Especially when you have family that can afford to do that."

"Well, we're not asking her to pay us an allowance," Dedie said in a huffy voice. "We only wanted a place to sleep. We have enough income for any shopping that we might need to do." She turned to Cora. "It's just that you're in such a central location."

This is not about a place to sleep, Cora thought. *They need income.*

"No," Aunt Ferna said. "It's Cora's house and her decision, but since you're my friend, I feel that I need to make sure she doesn't feel obligated in any way."

Winifred chuckled softly, drawing everyone's attention.

"So, what do you think, Cora?" Aunt Ferna asked, turning to Cora.

Cora raised both eyebrows, surprised her aunt supported her and shocked she asked her opinion.

"I agree with my aunt," Cora said gently.

Delores glared at Cora, but didn't reply.

"Of course, we thought we'd ask you in case you might be open to it," Julia replied in clipped tones. She stood and returned to Theo's side.

"Well played, Ferna," Winifred said, leaning toward the crafter to select a drink.

Delores stood and hiked onto the grass toward Julia. This caused Remy to chuckle.

"Mmm... The fizzy mango is delicious," Winifred said, examining the glass.

A few minutes later, Hazel stepped onto the patio.

"Is something wrong?" Hazel asked. "Julia seems... angry."

"I want to clear the air with Dedie," Aunt Ferna pursed her lips and followed Delores.

Cora had seen that determined look on her aunt's face before and she felt a little sorry for Delores.

"There's nothing wrong that Ferna can't set right," Remy said as he struggled to his feet. He finished his glass and stepped onto the grass, but he strolled further into the garden and soon disappeared among the bushes and trees.

"Is someone going to tell me what's going on?" Hazel asked.

Cora explained the conversation with Julia and Delores.

Several minutes later, Delores, with her nose in the air, and Aunt Ferna, with a grim expression, returned to the patio and strode into the house.

Hazel, Winifred, and Cora exchanged glances.

"I don't know if I should feel sorry for Delores or Ferna," Hazel said and chuckled. "I need to make a vidchat to dad. It's his birthday and there's a communication window coming up."

"Comm window? Where's he going?" Cora asked.

"The rest of the family left late last night for our home on Mars," Winifred said.

"The EGS gave them permission?" Cora asked with raised eyebrows.

"They don't dictate what happens in our family," Winifred said condescendingly as she stood and turned to Hazel. "Send him my birthday wishes. I'll call later." She stepped toward the path leading into the garden.

Hazel shrugged and strolled into the house.

Worry etched Cora's face as Winifred's back disappeared among the foliage. Then she turned to watch Julia place her blue ball on the grassy field and tap it. It rolled under two hoops.

"I am a bit bored of this game," Julia said, turning to Theo. "I think I'd rather go horseback riding."

"Let's go," Theo said with a broad grin.

They collected the hammer clubs and their balls and placed them in the outdoor cabinet on the patios. Julia whispered something to Theo, and they disappeared down a small trail leading toward the barn.

Sam strolled to the outdoor cabinet and placed his hammer club and balls inside.

"I'm curious to see the barn, but I don't know if Julia and Theo want to be alone," Sam said.

"I think it's okay for you to take a peek," Cora said. "I don't think they'll remain in the barn, anyway. They'll probably ride to one of the beautiful spots here on the Farm."

Sam turned and headed down the trail to the barn.

This left Cora alone on the patio, and she decided to go to her room to think over Winifred's words and finish packing.

Once Cora finished packing her belongings into a small bag, she ambled to the window facing the trail to the barn where she'd seen Julia strolling a few days ago.

She peered at Sam walking back from the barn toward the house and wondered if he'd seen Julia. Cora picked up her bag and went downstairs, leaving it in the entryway.

Suddenly, she heard shouts from the backyard.

"Help! Help!" Sam yelled. "Somebody help me!"

As Cora rushed toward the patio, she almost ran into Hazel, who'd stopped in the middle of the hall.

"Come on," Cora said, dragging Hazel by the arm as they both sprinted to the patio.

The sight sent chills down Cora's spine. Remy lay face down in the grass and Sam knelt next to him in the process of rolling him over.

"Do you have a medipad?" Sam shouted.

"Yes, I'll be right back," Hazel turned and scampered into the house.

"What's going on?" Cora demanded as tightness gripped her chest.

"I think he's dead," Sam said in a panicked voice. "He's not breathing."

Cora felt waves of Sam's panic, fear, and desperation. As she surveyed Remy, she felt absolutely nothing. He was gone. A few seconds later, Hazel rushed from the house with the floating medipad, her face pinched with panic. She frantically selected a few buttons, and it started to unpack itself. The medipad extended its arms with probes on the end and scanned Remy.

"Clear the body," a mechanical voice from the medipad called. Everyone scooted or stepped away from Remy's body. It applied an electric shock to start his heart three times and examined his head with another probe.

Cora studied the screen. It showed zero heartbeats, unresponsive brain waves, and no breathing. After a moment of staring at the screen. Cora's senses were confirmed—Remy was dead.

Aunt Ferna and Delores stepped out of the house, and Cora could feel their tidal waves of emotions. She shielded herself so that she wouldn't be overwhelmed.

"What's going on?" Delores asked. "I heard shouting... Remy!" She raced onto the lawn and fell on Remy's body with loud, wracking sobs. Aunt Ferna followed and hugged Delores as she wiped her own tears. Sam remained kneeling next to the body and Hazel joined him, silently weeping.

The medipad withdrew its probes and repacked itself into a floating oval.

"Subject is deceased," the mechanical voice of the medipad said.

Only Cora remained standing as she activated her comm bracelet

"Emergency. We have an emergency," Cora said. "Please send the EGS."

"What is the nature of your emergency?" a mechanical voice replied.

"Remy Pendleton has passed away in the backyard. We're at Pendleton Farm.

"We're sending units at this moment," the mechanical voice said. "Please ensure the environment around the body is disturbed as little as possible."

Cora looked down at Remy, whose body had been rolled over and whom Delores was weeping on. She thought about coaxing Delores from his body, but she didn't have the heart to pull her away.

"What's going on?" Winifred asked, emerging from the foliage at the edge of the lawn.

Sam explained in a wobbly voice how he'd found Remy.

"Must've been a heart attack," Winifred said in a solemn tone.

About fifteen minutes later, Agent Lewis, followed by three other EGS agents, streamed onto the patio. He wore a brown jumpsuit and his pale blue eyes scanned the scene, finally settling on Cora.

"Please stand away from the body," Agent Lewis commanded. He whispered something to a middle-aged woman with black hair speckled with white.

She approached Delores and Aunt Ferna.

"Hello, I'm Agent Tuck," she said in a gentle voice. "I'm truly sorry for your loss, but we need to investigate. Let me help you."

Agent Tuck bent and wrapped an arm under Delores's shoulder, while Aunt Ferna did the same with the other shoulder. They both gently lifted Delores off Remy's body and helped her to a chair on the patio. Aunt Ferna sat beside Delores, while Agent Tuck sat on her other side. Winifred followed and chose a seat across from the trio.

"Are you going to try to revive him?" Sam asked in a thick voice.

"I'm sorry, no," Agent Lewis said. "We had the data from your medipad before we arrived. This is now an investigation."

"Oh..." Sam coughed or sobbed. Cora couldn't decide.

"Is anyone else on the property?" Agent Lewis asked Sam.

Cora thought this was strange because Hazel actually lived on the Farm and Agent Lewis should have addressed her instead.

"Yes, Julia Pendleton and Theo Pike," Sam said, turning to Hazel. "Did I miss anyone?"

Hazel shook her head, her face pinched and white.

"Where are they now?" Agent Lewis asked.

"We're not sure," Hazel replied. "They left to go riding earlier."

"Agent Vance will get your statement," Agent Lewis said, gesturing to Cora. He turned to Agent Vance. "Take her inside the house and don't let her talk to anyone for now."

Cora bristled at being dismissed so easily and didn't move.

"Agent Welby will get your statement," Agent Lewis said, turning to Hazel. "Take her inside, but keep her isolated until you get her statement."

Hazel stepped toward the house with Cora close behind. The two agents scurried after them, trying to keep them apart. Before they entered the house, Cora heard the beginning of Sam's interview.

"Would you tell me what happened?" Agent Lewis asked as he began to take his statement.

"I was coming from the barn," Sam said, but Cora didn't hear the rest.

After her interview, Cora entered the living room to find Delores and Aunt Ferna chatting in a low voice. Winifred sat a little apart, studying a floating screen.

"I suppose Agent Lewis deposits us here after our interviews," Cora scoffed.

A few minutes later, Hazel joined them. They sat around for another thirty minutes before Julia entered, still sniffling, followed by Theo with a stony face.

Cora tried to distract herself by surveying the ornate, dark wood design on the ceiling. If it had felt oppressive before, it felt positively suffocating now. She wondered if it was the dark color, old-fashioned design, or simply the fact that there was so much of it.

"Sorry for keeping you waiting," Agent Lewis said, strolling into the living room. "We've completed our preliminary scan of the body and the surrounding grounds."

"He's not a body," Delores said in a wobbly voice. "He was..."

"We all know how close you two were," Aunt Ferna said. "Agent Lewis is relaying important information about his investigation. Wouldn't you like to know what happened to him?"

Delores nodded.

"We've taken the... Dr. Pendleton away," Agent Lewis said. "But I have a few questions."

"Excuse me," Hazel said. "Where's Sam?"

"He has an urgent appointment this afternoon," Agent Lewis said. "We let him go."

"But he was..." Hazel said as her voice trailed off. "Sorry, please continue."

"This is part of Sam Iverson's statement," Agent Lewis began. "I was walking from the barn." He looked about the room. "Did anyone see him?"

"Yes, I saw him as I was packing," Cora said. "When I glanced out the window, I saw him walk by."

Agent Lewis took notes on his private floating window and continued. "As I rounded the corner, I saw Remy fall to the ground. I ran to him and called for help." Agent Lewis glanced around the room again. "Which of you heard his call for help and where were you?"

"Dedie and I heard him and we were in her little parlor," Aunt Ferna said.

"I heard him, and I was in the hallway leading to the patio," Hazel said.

"I was in the front entryway, dropping off my bag," Cora said.

Agent Lewis took a few minutes to add more notes to his floating screen.

"Julia and Theo seem to be the first to leave your afternoon get together," Agent Lewis said. "Did anyone see them return prior to Dr. Pendleton's demise?"

Everyone glanced at each other, but no one replied.

Agent Lewis nodded while taking notes.

"Let's see. Hazel Cartwright went to her room to make a vidchat," Agent Lewis said under his breath. "Verified."

"When can we leave?" Winifred asked.

"You took a walk around the grounds?" Agent Lewis asked. "Did you see anyone?"

She shook her head.

Agent Lewis turned to the gathering. "Did anyone see Ms. Cartwright?"

The room remained quiet.

"Very well, Ms. Brimble. Did anyone see you go to your bedroom to pack?" Agent Lewis asked.

"No," she said.

"Yes. I have a little sitting room with a perfect view of the stairs," Delores said. "Ferna and I saw her going up the stairs just behind Hazel. Cora brought her bag down a little later."

Nodding, Agent Lewis made notes.

"Did you see Ms. Pendleton or Ms. Robertson in the sitting room?" Agent Lewis asked.

"I'm sorry no," Cora said. "I wasn't paying attention."

"Thank you for your time," Agent Lewis said. "You're all free to leave, but do not leave Tymal. We'll contact you when you can leave the city."

Everyone started to exit the living room, but as Cora reached the door, Agent Lewis detained her. They both took a seat on a nearby sofa. He started questioning her once the room was empty.

"I only wanted to know why you're here," Agent Lewis said with an edge to his voice. "This is the second death you've been mixed up in. Is there something you want to tell me?"

Since it was the two of them, Cora lowered her shield in small increments to see if she could sense any of his emotions. As usual, he wore a neurowall that blocked Readers and Feelers. She exhaled as the events of the days weighed on her.

"I'm here as Hazel's guest," Cora said. "That's why I was at the Spring Gala and why I was here this afternoon."

"When Dr. Pendleton was alive, he helped bring many Askovians to justice," Agent Lewis said. "More than a few threatened him. It seems odd, you were at the deaths of your sister and brother-in-law and now at the death of two more people."

"I didn't know about Dr. Pendleton's past," she said, ignoring Agent Lewis's insinuation. "How did he help the EGS?"

"I can't answer that," he said. "What about you being at the scene of two crimes?"

Cora paused, wondering what to say. "You don't know it yet, but you have a very serious problem," she said, examining Agent Lewis's reactions. She still couldn't tell what he was feeling. "Somebody is blackmailing Hazel." His eyebrows shot up at that.

"Nobody mentioned that," he said. "In fact, I don't quite believe you."

"Very well. Is there anything else?" Cora asked, standing.

He shook his head, his mouth set in a grim line.

Cora glided out of the room.

He never asked questions about the blackmail, she thought. *I'm not going to force them to do their job.*

CHAPTER 13

Cora sat in the formal sitting room of her home used for guests. She held her coffee while sitting posed with a straight back on the large sofa. She glanced across the coffee table at Hazel, who perched on the edge of her seat, arms crossed, and an angry glint in her eye.

Hazel broadcast waves of terror and anxiety, which she covered with anger. Cora sensed all of Hazel's emotions and received her in this stiff, formal room, which served as a visual barricade against Hazel's ire. She knew exactly why Hazel was so upset that she'd flown from Pendleton Farm at the last minute.

Taking a sip, Cora considered starting the conversation. Fortunately, she remembered from their days in school that it would be best to wait until Hazel calmed down enough to talk rationally.

"Why did you tell the EGS someone was blackmailing me?" Hazel asked in a loud, tense voice. "I didn't give you permission to tell them."

"True. You did not," Cora said, placing her coffee cup on the table. "Have you noticed that two people in the same family have passed away in two weeks? That's extremely dangerous Hazel."

"I told you not to tell them!" Hazel yelled.

"I know you're terrified of your mom," Cora said with rising frustration. "But people are dying! I can't stand by hiding something as serious as blackmail."

"That still doesn't give you the right to tell the EGS," Hazel scowled.

Cora tilted her head, thinking for a moment.

"You're absolutely right," Cora said in a level tone. "You didn't give me permission, and I'm sorry I broke your trust. Probably it would've been better if I had told you ahead of time and then gone to the EGS to tell them. But to be clear—I was going to tell them no matter what."

Hazel scoffed and shot to her feet. She stomped to the back of her chair and then paced the room.

"I can't believe you did that," Hazel said.

"When did you find out?" Cora asked, anticipating Winifred at her door next.

"This morning," Hazel said in a curt tone. "The only thing that saved me from Mom's wrath was that Agent Lewis was completely unconcerned, and won't do anything with the new information. He thinks the blackmail was a hoax, or it was Oscar who nobody can find right now. He doesn't think it's in any way related to the murders."

"I agree it's better for you that your mom hasn't found out," Cora said with furrowed eyebrows.

Why isn't he doing his job? Cora thought.

"But I disagree with Agent Lewis," she continued after a moment's pause. "A blackmailer is trying to extract credits from you about the death of your husband. It is definitely connected."

"Agent Lewis says you're wrong," Hazel smirked. "And I agree with him."

"I wonder why he thinks it's not connected," Cora said in a worried tone. "The blackmailer approached you and then your mom." Cora stood and ambled to one of the Martian paintings on her wall, pursing her lips in thought. "Something's going on with him."

"Well, I don't care," Hazel said, letting her arms flop to her side. "As long as he leaves Mom alone."

"Actually, there's something off about both deaths," Cora turned to Hazel, concern etched on her face. "Why didn't the antigrav safeties stop Michael's fall, who was the blackmailer, and why did Remy drop dead? If he had heart problems, a meditab under his skin would've released medication keeping him alive."

"Remy didn't have heart problems," Hazel said. "But he did drink too much, especially after retiring. He didn't know what to do with his time."

Cora sensed her waves of anger diminish and sorrow take their place.

"There's something very important we're all missing here," Cora strolled to another painting of daffodils growing on Ganymede, thinking. "You or anybody living at Pendleton Farm could still be in danger. If only Agent Lewis would take this seriously."

Hazel returned to her chair and huffed as she sat.

"I still can't reach Sam," Hazel said in a quiet voice.

"Really?" Cora asked, turning from the painting. "That's odd. Did he go off-world?"

"Agent Lewis knows where Sam is, but refuses to tell me," Hazel said.

"Hmm... I wonder if that's even true," Cora said. "It feels as if Agent Lewis is putting in the least amount of work he can get away with."

"What do you mean?" Hazel asked, peering at her.

"Agent Lewis could've lost contact with him," Cora said, gauging Hazel's emotions. "Sam could be with clients or even off-world."

"Why would he leave?" Hazel asked. "And how am I going to reach Sam now?"

"I don't know why," Cora said thoughtfully. "Something's wrong, but I can't tell what it is."

"Do you think Sam could be in trouble?" Hazel asked in a tense voice.

"Don't know..." she said slowly. "Sometimes Brian meets new clients and remains unreachable for a day or two while they hammer out a contract," Cora paced toward the sofa. "Sam also meets new clients. Do you know any of his friends or business acquaintances?"

"No. I've never met any of them," Hazel sighed.

"Don't you think that's strange?" Cora asked, "What if Sam is actually the murderer? He was the first person to find the body."

"What are you talking about?" Hazel shot to her feet and said in a raised voice. "Sam could never harm anybody—he's sweet and gentle."

"Well, you know him better," Cora said. "If you don't hear from him in a couple of days, then we should bring this to the EGS."

Hazel nodded.

Cora perceived Hazel's emotions change from defensive to angry, and settle into a steady stream of sadness.

"You know what's really strange?" Cora asked. "Sam is the second person to go missing after Oscar."

"Sam and Oscar are unreachable for different reasons," Hazel said. "Sam is probably working, and Oscar is running from the law."

"Do you know if the EGS is doing anything to locate Oscar or Sam?" Cora asked.

"Uncle Evan told me they're looking for Oscar," Hazel said.

"These look like two different disappearances," Cora said. "But I feel they're related. Has the EGS looked through Oscar's belongings?"

"They didn't come to the house," Hazel said. "I checked the logs and spoke to Delores and..."

Cora now sensed Hazel's increasing despair, but it was tinged with something... Fear?

"I wish I knew what happened to Sam," Hazel said. "I miss him."

"I know you gave the EGS your statement," Cora said, trying to distract her away from Sam. "What did you tell them?"

"Oh, you and I left the patio at the same time," Hazel said. "You continued to your room, and I went to my room for a vidchat with my dad—his birthday's coming up. I returned to the patio, and I was in the hallway when I heard Sam shouting. I also ran into you, and we both made it to the patio..." Hazel frowned. "You know the rest."

"What did you say in your statement?" Hazel asked.

"Almost the same as you, except I went to my room to pack," Cora said, wondering who could have killed Remy while everyone was away.

The following morning, Cora stood at her window, staring at her garden. She'd already dressed in a comfortable pink and purple top with matching pants and had plans to go to her office and test her game.

Before Hazel left yesterday, they'd made up. However, Cora had felt Hazel hiding something from her. She knew from experience confronting her wouldn't work. For now, she'd play nice until she unearthed more clues.

Cora pressed a button on her bracelet and opened a floating window to start a vidchat.

"Cora? How's it going?" Hazel yawned. "It's a bit early."

"I know, and I'm sorry about that," Cora said. "Something about Michael and Remy's deaths is still bothering me. Would you let me into Oscar's room? I want to look around and see if I can find anything."

"Oscar... Why would you bother finding Oscar? He's a thief?" Hazel asked.

"I don't know. I feel I'm grasping around in the dark," Cora said. "It shouldn't take long."

"Well... It's okay, I'll be ready in half an hour," Hazel said.

"Thanks, I'll be there shortly," Cora said, ending the vidchat.

An hour later, Cora and Hazel stood in the middle of Oscar's room.

"Well, he was certainly very neat and organized," Cora said. "It doesn't look as if anybody lived here."

"Yeah," Hazel said, looking around. "He used to keep his office super neat like this." She flopped onto the bed. "I think this is a waste of time, Cora."

"Maybe," Cora said, taking a few steps to the closet. As she approached, it automatically opened, and she viewed nicely hung jumpsuits in various shades of black, gray, and brown.

"Why would he leave all of his clothes?" Cora asked. "What if Oscar's dead and not hiding?"

Hazel guffawed.

"You have an active imagination," Hazel said.

Cora slowly spun around the room and spotted his desk. She tried to open some drawers and found them locked.

"Do you have access to this?" Cora asked.

"No," Hazel said, pressing a button and shaking her head.

Cora huffed in frustration.

"Okay, I'll try something else," Cora said. "I wonder what I can find about him on the Net?" She created a floating window with her comm. "Just a moment while I take a quick look."

Scrolling through the Net, Cora found information on Oscar Dalton. She found his previous workplaces as well as an old girlfriend, Zara Ingham. Cora reused an old tracking bot she'd created months ago and had it monitor Oscar's old girlfriend's apartment. She also decided to monitor two of his old workplaces.

"I'll let that run for a few days," Cora said. "I suppose I've finished here."

"I told you this was a waste of time," Hazel said irritably.

Cora felt her returning sadness, but she masked it.

"Well, thank you for letting me look through Oscar's things," Cora said. "You're probably right, and this is nothing. I think I'll head over to my office and get some work done."

Sensing somebody coming, Cora tried to decipher the range of emotions. They were happy, or even giddy emotions, but she couldn't figure out who was coming.

The bedroom door slid open and Kaye stalked into the room.

Hazel crossed her arms and glared at Kaye with a pinched face.

"What are you doing here?" Hazel said in a surly voice.

Kaye ignored Hazel and turned to Cora.

"Guess where I've been?" Kaye asked. "I've been talking to that cute Agent Lewis about Sam."

Lowering her arms, Hazel surveyed Kaye as a worried expression settled over her face.

"What did you tell them?" Hazel asked.

Kaye didn't turn to Hazel, but continued addressing Cora.

"I told them about my theory that Sam is the murderer," Kaye smirked. "He was in a perfect position to start rumors about Hazel murdering Michael. He was nearby when Michael passed, and he was the first person to reach Remy. The EGS have it all on vids."

"Why did you say that?" Hazel yelled. "You have no right to ruin a man's life!" She stomped toward Kaye.

Kaye backed away, chuckling.

"Hazel, calm down," Cora said. "There's no motive."

"You have no idea what you've done," Hazel turned to Kaye, replying in a low, menacing voice. "I'll get even with you." She spun on her heel and stormed out of the room.

"It's obvious you did all that only to get a reaction from her," Cora said. "So you got your reaction. Was there something else you needed?"

"If you'll remember, I never addressed her," Kaye smirked. "How was I to know she'd get so upset? Anyway, I came to pick up one or two things I left in my room." She turned and flounced out of the room, heading toward one of the larger bedrooms.

Cora didn't want to get in the middle of a fight between Kaye and Hazel, so she decided to leave.

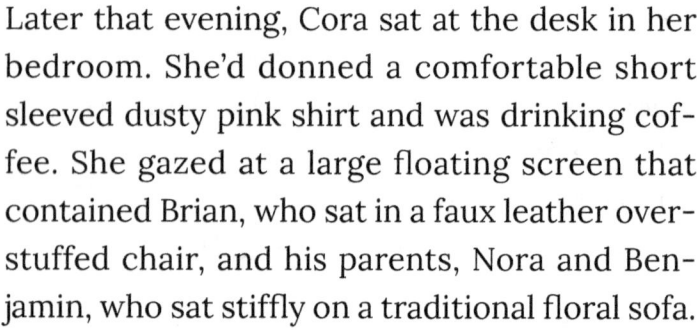

Later that evening, Cora sat at the desk in her bedroom. She'd donned a comfortable short sleeved dusty pink shirt and was drinking coffee. She gazed at a large floating screen that contained Brian, who sat in a faux leather overstuffed chair, and his parents, Nora and Benjamin, who sat stiffly on a traditional floral sofa.

"I think we should invite the Cartwright family to vote with us," Brian said with an edge of desperation in his voice. "Voting against the Spencers may be the best way to combat their insistence on doing something illegal."

"It doesn't matter if this is illegal or not," Nora said in a clipped tone of voice while narrowing her green eyes. "Between the Spencer and Pendleton families, there really is no law on interplanetary mining. Maybe in a few years, IPS will develop their own armed guards and actually enforce the law, but the time isn't now."

"Legalities do matter," Benjamin said in a loud voice. "It's a question of character and being able to look at yourself in the mirror. Obviously, Spencer Industries is going to force this issue, but that doesn't also mean Brian has to compromise his values."

"You can shout as much as you want, but this doesn't change cold hard facts," Nora said in a steady but menacing tone. "If we go against Spencer Industries, we and most of our clients will lose their protection. All of us depend on the income from those mines."

"I want to jump in here," Cora said, raising her voice, causing all three to turn to the vid screen. She continued in a quieter voice. "Even if we invite the Cartwright family to join Albright Corp, we can't guarantee they'll vote with us. Winifred votes for her own family's interests, and the best we can hope is their interests align with ours."

"What do you mean our?" Nora spat out. "I'm the majority holder in Albright Corp and I do *not* want the Cartwright family invited!"

"Nora, it won't hurt to at least talk to her," Benjamin said. "You're right and you have the controlling vote, but it's by a slim margin. Jessica Spencer could talk one of our smaller clients to her side."

Nora glared at Benjamin. A few seconds elapsed before she turned to Cora, "Okay, let's hear her out."

"I've already spoken to her, but in general terms," Cora said. "Wait while I conference her in."

Cora created a new window and Winifred Cartwright appeared on her screen.

"Hello, Winifred," Cora said. "I'm calling about your family joining Albright Corp. Can you talk now?"

"Of course," Winifred said. "How does this work?"

"I'm going to conference you into a vidchat with Brian and Benjamin Farris. I think you know Benjamin."

"I've known Ben since we were children," Winifred said. "I've met his wife Nora a few times as well."

"Good, this should be easier," Cora said. "Nora will be in on the call as well."

Cora made more adjustments to her screen and altered the vidchat to include Winifred.

"Winifred, I'm not sure if you know Brian Farris," Cora said tentatively.

"We've never met, but you look almost exactly like your dad," Winifred said with a half-smile. "Good evening, Brian, Ben, Nora." Everyone nodded to each other.

"Ms. Cartwright," Brian said. "We know you're under the protection of the Pendleton family and we wouldn't want to do anything to jeopardize the safety of your mine."

"First, call me Winifred," she said in a gentle tone that clashed with her steel gray chignon. "We're all friends here. Second, you're right, I'll do whatever's necessary to keep our family mine safe."

"Would you consider joining the Albright Corporation?" Brian asked.

"Why?" Winifred asked. "The Spencers are the dominant family in your management company. But the Pendletons protect our mine. The two families aren't on friendly terms, and we don't want to anger either one."

"Yes, but we're not asking you to join with the Spencers," Brian said. "We're asking you to join with our other clients and my mom. We're trying to prevent Spencer Industries from using us to create illegal documents."

Winifred chuckled. Even laughing, Winifred's smile didn't reach her eyes, adding a touch of menace to her severe appearance.

"I finally see what's happening," Winifred said, her amusement dying down. "Jessica Spencer needs to make sure the theft of that mine from Evan Pendleton appears as a legal transfer. You don't want to generate those documents. Are you afraid you'll be an accessory to fraud?"

"I told you this was a bad idea!" Nora said in a raised voice. "All she has to do is run back to Evan and tell him what's going on at Albright. He could sue and take everything."

"Hold on there, Nora," Winifred said with a genial smile that left Cora cold. "My goal is not to cause any more damage. I have no incentive to spark a new skirmish between Jessica and Evan. That's going to distract Evan and could result in his redeploying security from our Cartwright mine to one of Evan's more valuable mines."

Nora sat back in her chair, mollified for the moment.

"May I ask a question?" Winifred asked.

Nora and Benjamin nodded.

"Hasn't this happened before?" Winifred asked. "Jessica has stolen countless mines in the past while Albright Corp managed them. What's different now?"

"In the past, Harold Albright handled things," Brian said. "I didn't realize he broke the law for Jessica on multiple occasions. I just can't bring myself to do the same."

"Of course, of course," Winifred said. "So, what would you like me to do?"

"We would like you to join the Albright Corporation," Brian said. "But vote against Jessica so that the Spencers have to create their illegal documents. That way, we won't be liable."

"Walk me through the steps," Winifred said. "What would happen if Cartwright Mining joined?"

"I don't think we should answer this," Nora said in a raised voice. "We'll be giving her too much information."

"There's no other way," Benjamin said in a heated voice. "She doesn't really know enough to make a decision."

"Actually, since tempers are high, it's best to table things," Cora said, trying to avoid a screaming match which might really divulge too much to Winifred. "Let's meet again when everyone is calm."

"I agree with Cora," Winifred said with the same genial smile. "I would like some time to think things over in any case. I think we should meet again to talk further."

"Have a good evening," Cora said in a rush, anxious to end the conference.

Winifred nodded and her screen went dark.

Nora and Benjamin started bickering.

"Cora, thanks for setting things up," Brian said, trying to talk over his parents.

"Good evening," Cora said with furrowed eyebrows.

I hope everything's okay at their home, she thought.

Chapter 14

The following morning, Cora sat bolt upright in her bed. She glanced out at the dark window, wondering if it was late at night or early in the morning. Turning to her bedside clock, she realized it was about an hour before sunrise. She pulled the covers off her legs and stood slowly, raising her arms above her head to stretch and yawn.

As she paced to the dark window, that nagging feeling resettled in her chest.

If I don't do something, someone else is going to die, she thought.

She paced back past her office desk, dining table, and sofa, stopping at her bed. All the while, she let thoughts cascade through her mind.

Remy was the first person to reach Michael's body, she thought. *And Sam was the first person* to reach Remy's body. *Does that mean Sam is actually in danger?*

She turned and paced in circles.

I have to find Sam, she thought. *Either he knows something or somebody is going to try to harm him. Or both.*

She scampered to her chair and plopped down in front of her desk. Pressing a button on her comm bracelet. She brought up a floating screen and gazed at the black rectangle, allowing her thoughts to settle in her head.

"I'm going to find you, Sam," she said to herself.

She immediately started creating programming symbols that allowed her to code a tracking bot. It would notify her any time Sam interacted with the Net. Tracking somebody without permission from the EGS was technically illegal. But she had a number of friends who existed in the gray areas of the law. They'd taught her how to trace people without leaving a footprint others could pursue.

Cora directed the bot to monitor the spaceport in Tymal and the spaceports in the neighboring cities. She linked her bot to Sam's last known address and the restaurants she had heard Hazel mention in the past. At the last minute, she instructed the bot to monitor the comings and goings of people at Pendleton Farm, and the main house where Evan Pendleton lived. She reasoned he'd done business with Sam in the past.

When she finished creating her bot, she released it onto the Net and then sighed.

"I just can't sit here and wait for the murderer to strike again," Cora said to no one. "I'm going to talk to everyone who was there the day Remy passed away. I know I missed something."

Glancing at the time, a few hours had gone by, and she thought of Brian. But he would be heading off to work now. She took a chance and sent him a hello message and asked if his family had come to any conclusions about the Cartwrights joining Albright Corporation.

Brian didn't respond, and this increased the heavy feeling in her chest. She knew he struggled to do Harold's old job, but she couldn't think of a way to help him without hurting his family.

Cora decided to get ready for her day. She jumped into the shower, changed into a powder blue blouse with matching blue and white pants. Then she wolfed down a slice of toast while sipping her coffee. She examined the in-

cident log from the Mystery Adventure players. This log displayed all the problems users
encountered while playing her game. Some required new code to fix, and others required
clearer instructions. For the first time in over
a year, there were no new incidents. She still
had many old corrections to implement on her
game, but for some reason, this lifted her spirits
a little.

It was now mid-morning, and she decided to
try to find out why she couldn't let Michael and
Remy's deaths go. She started a vidchat with
Hazel.

"Hey, Cora. Happy to hear from you," Hazel
said with a broad but forced smile. "Have you
heard anything about Sam?"

"Well, no. Sorry," Cora said. That smile usually
meant Winifred had done something. She mentally braced herself.

"Did something happen?" Cora asked.

"Well, yes and not really," Hazel said, shrugging. "I asked Mom if anybody had contacted
her like the EGS. She didn't answer at first—you
know how she is. We talked about other things,
but she eventually answered my question. Nobody from the EGS had talked to her. So I think

I'm in the clear. Even though you told them about the blackmail, they never contacted her."

Hazel's brightened face was the exact opposite of the heavy weight that settled in the pit of Cora's stomach.

What's wrong with Agent Lewis? she thought. *He's deliberately ignoring all the major clues.* But she decided not to say any of that.

"I want to have one last chat with everyone who was there when Remy passed away," Cora said. "If I don't discover anything else, I'm going to leave this all to the EGS. Something is still bugging me and I can't shake it."

Hazel's face fell, and she frowned.

"I don't see why you keep bringing this up," Hazel scoffed. "Nothing is wrong." She crossed her arms, staring at some point off the screen. After a moment, she lowered her arms and turned back to the screen. "Okay. If you want to talk to everybody, I'll help you. But I really think you're wasting everybody's time."

"I really hope you're right," Cora said with a frown.

"I'll gather everyone," Hazel said. "Well, I can't bring Sam, but I can contact Julia, Theo, and Delores. I don't know what to do about Ferna."

"I'll talk to Aunt Ferna," Cora said. "What about Kaye?"

"I'm not inviting her," Hazel said, peeved.

"I'll talk to her," Cora said. "Since this is last minute, she may not be able to make it, anyway."

"Should we try for some time this afternoon?" Hazel asked. "Maybe two or three? I think Delores might be trying to prepare for Remy's funeral. But I know Julia and Theo don't have anything planned."

"Sounds good," Cora said. "I'll let you know what time works for Aunt Ferna and Kaye."

Hazel rolled her eyes.

"Let's message later to firm up the time," Cora said, ignoring Hazel's behavior about Kaye.

Cora sighed, wondering again why she had this nagging feeling that wouldn't go away. She sent a quick message to Aunt Ferna, even though they were actually in the same house. Fortunately, Aunt Ferna replied she'd planned to visit Delores today anyway, and two in the afternoon was just fine.

Turning to Mystery Adventure's incident window, she selected one of the old incidents and began making corrections to her software.

Cora and Hazel sat on a traditional cream-colored sofa in the living room of Pendleton Farm. Placing her coffee cup on the table, Cora glanced at the others in the room with her. Usually, with so many people in the room, Cora had to remain shielded, but this time she took a chance reading everyone's emotions. She kept her shield partially raised.

Aunt Ferna and Delores sat opposite on a matching sofa. Aunt Ferna took a bite of a tiny pink and yellow cake, while Delores nursed a cup of tea.

Julia and Theo sat in two overstuffed floral print chairs. Julia stared at her untouched afternoon cake, while Theo read something on a private floating screen. Opposite them sat Kaye in a matching overstuffed chair. She turned her broad smile to Delores and then to Julia.

Sensing Kaye's unease and fear underneath her grin, an uneasy feeling settled in Cora's chest. She wondered what Kaye could be planning.

"I want to start off with a revelation," Cora said with a frown. "I have Hazel's permission to tell you that someone has been blackmailing her."

Hazel glanced at Cora with a stony face, but said nothing. Cora sensed her embarrassment that quickly dissipated into her usual sadness, tinged with despair.

Julia and Kaye smirked, while Delores shifted uncomfortably in her seat. Aunt Ferna exchanged glances with Delores. But Theo gasped.

Cora sensed surprise from everyone except Delores, Aunt Ferna, Kaye, and, of course, Hazel.

"Blackmail!" Theo said in a raised voice. "This is serious. If it's not too personal, what does the blackmailer want?"

Cora did her best to remain partially shielded, but she struggled with the new mix of emotions.

Unsurprisingly, Delores and Aunt Ferna knew about the blackmailer. Aunt Ferna somehow always knew what was going on, and those two didn't seem to have any secrets. But if Delores knew, why hadn't she told Julia?

"Delores, Aunt Ferna," Cora said. "How did you learn Hazel was being blackmailed?"

"Dedie and I happened to come upon Hazel and Sam." Aunt Ferna glanced at her friend. "They were having a disagreement because somebody was blackmailing Hazel. Sam wanted to go to the EGS, but Hazel refused."

"We weren't eavesdropping. We happened to be taking a stroll nearby," Delores said.

Cora sensed Delores's lie, but she chose not to pursue it right now.

"When I spoke to you a week ago," Cora continued. "You thought Michael's passing was an accident. What was the EGS's explanation about the antigrav safeties not working?"

"It was an unfortunate malfunction," Delores said. "They've released a preliminary report which states the same thing, but with more explanation."

"Yes, I read it," Cora said, reflecting on the weakly worded report.

"The person blackmailing Hazel said she somehow caused Michael's death," Cora said. "He or she never provided proof. After reading the EGS report, who do you think it could've been?"

"Ferna and I've been discussing this for a while," Delores said in an excited voice. "We think it was Oscar. Not because he'd any actual evidence, but because he desperately needed the funds."

Cora scrutinized her emotions. She was telling the truth.

"Julia, you initially tried to blackmail Hazel on your trip back from Mars," Cora said. "I know that didn't work out for you."

Julia turned a little pink and mumbled something under her breath.

"I'm sorry. I missed that," Cora said.

"It was a mistake," Julia said. "I was just desperate."

"Wait," Delores said. "Why were you trying to blackmail Hazel?" Julia grew quiet and stared down at the floor.

"Oh no, Julia," Delores frowned. "Don't tell me you're in debt again. I spent so many credits getting you out of debt last time. And now that Michael has passed away, there's nobody to help you. Evan won't give you a single credit.

"I know," Julia said in a low voice.

"On top of that, I'm still in debt from the last time I bailed you out," Delores said. "I get a very limited stipend from Evan. There's nobody left."

"Theo, did you know about Julia's debts?" Cora asked, trying to turn the discussion in a different direction.

"I knew Julia was in a lot of debt," Theo said. "I knew she tried to blackmail Hazel, but I also knew nothing came of it, so I left it alone. If she had gone further with blackmailing Hazel, I would have stepped in and either paid Julia's debts or supported Hazel to make sure she wasn't harmed."

Julia shifted uncomfortably in her chair.

Cora raised an eyebrow at Theo's words. She hadn't expected him to support Hazel instead of Julia.

"I would like to continue," Cora said, glancing from Theo, who returned a steadfast gaze, to Julia, whose eyes roamed the room and settled on nothing.

"I don't understand the point of all these questions," Kaye said. "What do you think happened to Michael?"

"I really don't know," Cora said with furrowed brows. "I'm asking questions to understand what a blackmailer might be thinking." She turned to Julia. "You said earlier that you didn't think there was anything unusual about Michael's passing. Right?"

"It was an accident," Julia said and glanced at Delores. "But Mom is right about Oscar. I thought he was a common thief. I didn't realize he was also a blackmailer. How much did he want?"

"The blackmailer wanted five thousand credits per month," Hazel said, interrupting Cora.

"But credits are traceable," Aunt Ferna said.

"Not if you pay the right people," Cora said. "It's possible to wash away the history of received credits. Of course, that's illegal, but so is blackmail."

"How did you respond?" Theo asked.

"I never replied," Hazel said. "I asked Cora for help, and then the blackmailer contacted my mom, who also didn't respond."

"The blackmailer sounds unlucky or stupid," Delores chuckled. "He chose the two people in the family who weren't going to give in."

A silence settled over the room.

"Kaye, did you know someone was blackmailing Hazel?" Cora asked, continuing with her investigation.

"Not until a few days ago," Kaye said. "I needed to talk to Delores about something related to the family when she hinted at the blackmail. I tried asking Delores more questions, but she either didn't know or wouldn't say."

"Who did you think the blackmailer was?" Cora asked.

"Oscar is the obvious suspect, given that he's left and nobody can find him," Kaye said. "Also Hazel is pretty much the only one in this family with enough funds to be blackmailed. She is more vulnerable because nobody likes her, which means no one's going to stand up for her."

Hazel shot to her feet, glaring at Kaye. Then she whipped around to face Cora.

"This is all your fault," Hazel growled. "You're exposing me to this horrible family for no good reason. I'm so glad that Mom cut them all off." She turned to everyone else in the living room. "You can all starve to death for all I care." She stormed out of the room.

Kaye chuckled.

"She's so excitable," Kaye said.

"My dear, that was uncalled for," Aunt Ferna scolded. "I understand you're grieving for Michael. But you don't need to attack someone who really can't defend herself. Not with her mother and not in this family."

Kaye twirled her red hair as her smile fell.

"Even though Oscar probably blackmailed Hazel," Kaye said, trying to divert attention. "Oscar is not the murderer. It's Sam. He killed Michael so that he could marry Hazel."

Delores and Aunt Ferna gasped.

"I don't believe it," Delores said.

"It's the truth," Kaye said in stronger, defiant words. "Sam would've had access to Hazel anyway if he'd just waited. Michael and I were planning to run away before he died. We were going to move to Lunar City and start a family."

Cora had to shield herself because the anger rolling off of Kaye was starting to overwhelm her.

Didn't she say Michael broke up with her? Cora thought. *I wish I could lower my shield again and sense her lie.*

At this point, Delores stood and crossed the room to sit in the overstuffed chair next to Kaye. She held one of Kaye's hands.

"Kaye, I love you like a daughter," Delores said in a gentle voice. "I've always felt that way about you, but there's something you should know. Michael would've never divorced Hazel, married you, nor had children with you."

"You're wrong," Kaye said with a catch in her throat. "In Lunar City, Uncle Evan couldn't bother us with my family's support." Kaye pulled her hand from Delores's.

"I know Michael loved you," Delores said. "But he still would've never gone against Evan."

Kaye shot to her feet and stalked around her chair and the neighboring sofa toward Cora.

"Do you know who alerted Michael to Oscar's theft?" Kaye asked. "Uncle Evan. The Spencers stole that mine while we were touring the Pendleton Mines. Once it was gone, the family's income had to be redistributed. Uncle's accountants performed an unscheduled review of Michael's accounts and discovered discrepancies. Then, they dug deeper and discovered Oscar had been stealing from Michael for about ten years. It amounted to hundreds of thousands of credits."

"My dear, come have a seat," Aunt Ferna said, patting a place on the sofa next to her.

"Uncle blamed Michael, who blamed Oscar," Kaye said, making her way to the sofa next to Aunt Ferna. "It was a mess. Uncle was so angry he demanded Michael send me away and start 'behaving.'" She glared at Delores. "I already know Michael would've never sided with me."

"Thank you, Kaye," Cora said, hoping to diffuse things. "I want to thank everyone for taking the time to answer my questions."

Aunt Ferna, Kaye, and Delores were the first through the door. They were followed by Julia and Theo.

I learned some things, but I didn't get any closer to understanding the blackmailer, she thought.

Later that evening, Cora sat in her home's dining room with Aunt Ferna. Cora toyed with the remains of her salmon and salad meal, lost in thought. Her aunt had moved on to a giant moist chocolate cake.

"Aunt, I'm confused about something," Cora said. "I heard the EGS discussing Remy being helpful with their investigations."

"Oh yes. Back in the day, he was actually almost a celebrity," Aunt Ferna said with a wistful smile. "He solved several high-profile crimes done by Askovian criminals. He pioneered several methods to test for the effects of a Mover's abilities on a body or a Reader's manipulation of a mind. The EGS used to rely on him heavily."

"Did he train anybody else at the EGS to take over for him?"

"Oh, I wouldn't know. That's a good question for Agent Lewis except..."

"I know. He's useless," Cora said. "I wonder if there's somebody at the EGS I could talk to."

Suddenly, Cora gasped.

"What is it, my dear?" Aunt Ferna asked around a mouth full of chocolate cake.

"I just remembered I have access to Remy's records from his room," Cora said in an excited voice.

"That's an active EGS investigation," Aunt Ferna said. "I don't want you to get into trouble."

"Don't worry, I won't be able to break into anything they've locked down," Cora said. "At least not without some help." She added under her breath.

CHAPTER 15

Cora's bracelet chimed repeatedly for about thirty seconds at three forty-seven am. Her eyelids drifted open, but it still took her several seconds before she realized where she was and what was happening. Once her brain worked through the sound and how it was connected with the time, she immediately sat up in bed.

In her darkened room, she reached for her dimly lit comm bracelet resting on the side table. Snapping it around her wrist, she pressed a button to create a floating screen, which winked into existence. The top of the screen displayed a location and immediately below a list of electronic files filled the screen.

"Pendleton Farm. Remy's file storage," she grinned. "Finally, it took that bot hours to crack into his storage. He must have had a pretty good security system."

She slowly scrolled through the files before coming across one that caught her attention. The title was a random mix of letters and numbers, but the date got her attention. It was the same day that Michael passed away. Eyeing the rest of the files revealed there were several of them.

Opening them one by one revealed Michael Pendleton's body scans. There must have been more than a hundred, and each one dated a day or two after Michael passed away.

Why does everything look fuzzy? she thought as she examined each scan.

"Haley, please examine the blurry body scans in Remy Pendleton's file folder," Cora said to her home's AI. "Is this an error with the medipad's scanner?"

"Negative," Haley said in a female, robotic voice. "The distortions are too regular to be a defect in the medipad performing the scan. Instead, the body scans indicate damage to the victim. Something crushed blood vessels, muscles, and internal organs. The pattern is focused on the center of the victim's back and radiating outward with lessening effect to his extremities. This level of damage would have resulted in immediate death."

She opened a new screen and retrieved Michael Pendleton's death report. Her eyebrows shot up.

"These scans aren't the same," Cora said as a heavy feeling settled in the pit of her stomach. "What were you up to, Remy?" she said, double checking the body scans in the death report, verifying they listed the correct date and time.

"Haley, please evaluate the body scans from Remy Pendleton's folder and the ones from the EGS report," Cora asked. "What is likely to have caused the damage?"

"Please wait for my examination," Haley said.

Cora's stomach rumbled, and she stood, pacing to the meal crafter on her dining table. She selected a cinnamon muffin with coffee. After a couple of gulps of coffee, she started munching on the muffin.

"I observe inconsistencies on all scans in the Pendleton folder," Haley said. "I have insufficient data to understand the cause of the injury pattern to Michael Pendleton."

"What are your recommendations to find the cause of these inconsistencies?" Cora asked, settling onto her sofa.

"I advise you to use a qualified forensic coroner," Haley said in a calm, detached voice.

Even though it was a few hours before the time Cora normally woke, she was too wired to even try to go to sleep at this point. Instead, she got on the Net to search for possible causes of scan distortions.

"Excuse me, Cora," Haley said in a quiet voice. "Incoming vidchat from Captain Donaldson at Earth Global Security."

Cora choked on her coffee.

"What! The EGS!" she blurted out. "What do they want?"

"They haven't included a notification," Haley said. "I don't know."

She promptly sat straighter on the sofa, wiping her mouth with the back of her hand. Pressing a button on her comm bracelet, she watched a middle-aged man with black and gray hair frowning at her.

"Coraline Brimble?" the middle-aged man said.

"Yes, how may I help you?" Cora replied.

"I'm Captain Donaldson," he said. "We've received a notification that you broke into Remy Pendleton's personal storage at Pendleton Farm,"

"Oh... Umm..." she said, her mind going blank.

"This offense is punishable with ten years in prison," Captain Donaldson said, grimacing. "However, I'm prepared to overlook it if you share your findings."

She paused, confused.

"Share my findings?" she asked. "What does that mean?"

"I followed your progress when you investigated Harold Albright's murder," he said. "I expected you to do the same for Michael Pendleton, but it seems you started working with Remy Pendleton's death."

Cora shifted uncomfortably on the sofa. She wondered if she should tell the truth or think up a lie.

"Do you deny you've broken into Remy Pendleton's private files?" he asked.

"Well... No, but I only made a copy of—" she started.

"No, don't tell me about it now," Captain Donaldson said while glancing off-screen. "Do you have time to meet today? I want to talk to you about your findings."

"Wait, why didn't the EGS look into Remy's private files?" she asked. "You'd have easily discovered—"

"Let me interrupt you right there," he said. "I don't have time to discuss this now. But I will have time later this morning or the middle of the afternoon."

Cora could feel anger bubbling from her stomach up to her chest.

Why won't he let me talk? she thought.

"How about three in the afternoon?" she asked.

"That's perfect," he said. "Please bring all the evidence you've gathered so far."

Cora nodded.

"Good, I'll see you this afternoon," he replied and the vidchat screen turned black.

What's going on? she thought.

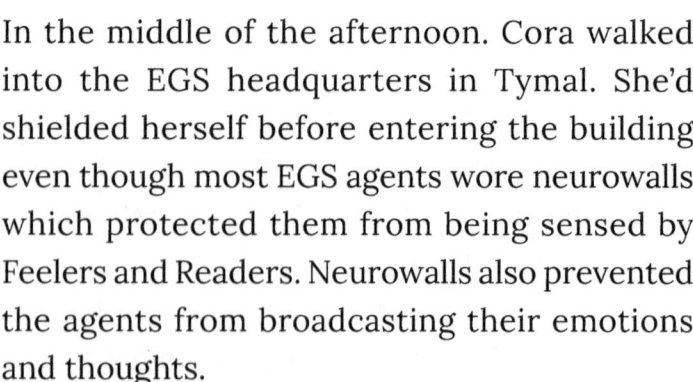

In the middle of the afternoon. Cora walked into the EGS headquarters in Tymal. She'd shielded herself before entering the building even though most EGS agents wore neurowalls which protected them from being sensed by Feelers and Readers. Neurowalls also prevented the agents from broadcasting their emotions and thoughts.

Approaching a floating screen that listed the EGS departments at the headquarters. She'd hoped to see Captain Donaldson's name. Instead, she peered at a long list of agencies, administrative units, and local stations.

"How may I help you?" the EGS AI asked in a friendly female voice.

"I have an appointment with Captain Donaldson," Cora said. "My name is Cora Brimble."

"Yes, of course," she replied. "Simply follow the lighting in the floor. It will take you to an antigrav lift to the fourth floor."

"Thanks," Cora said, turning to follow the softly blinking lighting.

The headquarters had a very crisp, impersonal feel, but it was surprisingly stylish and modern. On the ground floor, she walked past a large bank of windows that faced a busy street. She stepped into the antigrav lift.

Once inside of the lift, she surveyed the back wall of the lift, which was open to an atrium in the center of the building. Usually, plants had a calming effect on Cora, but this time it didn't work.

A moment later, the doors opened, and she stepped out onto the fourth floor. She followed the lighting again until she stood in front of an office and the door slid open. She paused, unsure if she should enter.

The same middle-aged man with black and gray hair she'd seen early in the morning lumbered to his feet. Captain Donaldson's slight paunch stretched his brown jumpsuit, the standard uniform for detectives. He limped toward her, reaching out to shake her hand.

"Ms. Brimble, it's a pleasure to finally meet you," Captain Donaldson said, smiling.

Cora blinked, surprised at the warm reception. She'd half expected the captain to lock her up like Agent Lewis had.

"I've heard a lot about you from Agent Lewis," he said.

She involuntarily wrinkled her nose.

"Well, try not to believe everything he says," she said.

Captain Donaldson chuckled.

"It's not really that bad," he said with a small smile. "I'm going to invite Agent Lewis in to join us in a few minutes, but first I would like to talk to you. Please have a seat." He gestured to one of two chairs at a large desk while he took the large chair opposite hers.

"Ms. Brimble, I know this morning I threatened to press charges due to your activities," he said with a sheepish smile. "I apologize for that. I really wanted to ensure you visited us today." He sighed and studied a screen on his desk. It was set to private and Cora couldn't see its contents.

"You know, I would have come if you'd asked politely," she frowned. "Agent Lewis always treated me like this, too."

"You're right, you're right," he said, raising both hands as if in surrender. "I've spent too much time listening to Agent Lewis and not enough time investigating this case for myself."

"So, why did you ask me here?" she asked.

"To be honest, we need you," he said in a quiet voice. "Basically, Evan Pendleton pressured Agent Lewis to investigate Michael Pendleton's death, Oscar Dalton's disappearance, and Remy Pendleton's death. I didn't check on Agent Lewis until a few days ago, and it turns out he's very behind schedule. Now I'm helping him."

"I see," Cora said.

Now, Evan's threatening legal action, and the EGS is finally taking things seriously, she thought.

"I want to ask you some questions about your investigations into these events," Captain Donaldson said. "Would you consent to be recorded?"

"Will I be charged with breaking any laws?" she asked.

"No... Unless you're the murderer, of course," he said with a small smile.

Cora agreed to be recorded. She explained about Hazel being blackmailed, Remy's strange body scans after Michael's death, and Remy's unexpected death. She also included information about her conversations with the other members of the Pendleton household.

"I'm very impressed, Ms. Brimble," he said with shock and respect. "You've done more work than..."

He mumbled under his breath as he scrolled through the screen built into his desk.

"I have a few follow-up questions," he said. "Would you send me the scans you accessed from Remy Pendleton's personal storage?"

"Yes, of course," she said. "But why do you need my copies instead of getting them directly from Remy's storage? I only ask because I didn't look through the entire drive, and there may be more information pertinent to your investigation."

"We are basically out of time," he said with a sigh. "If we don't produce some results this week..."

"Things will get ugly?" she asked. "I'm familiar with Evan Pendleton."

"Then you understand," he said with a grim smile.

Cora brought up a floating screen with her bracelet. She selected Michael's body scans and, waving a hand, sent them to Captain Donaldson.

"I've seen these distortions before," he said as he scrolled through a second screen built into his desk.

Even though she couldn't see the second screen's contents, she guessed he was referring to Michael's body scans.

"What does that fuzziness mean?" Cora asked.

"Just a moment," he said, creating a new floating screen over his desk. After a few hand gestures, he raised his eyebrows. "I thought so."

"You thought what?" she asked, leaning forward a little.

"You'll understand that I can't tell you everything," he said in a gentle voice. "This is an open investigation, but I can let you know a few things later on."

Cora leaned back into her chair with a frown.

"I'm truly sorry," he said. "But I'm extremely grateful for your help. I need to ask you a few more questions though."

"Sure," she sighed, letting her disappointment show.

"I want to know what you think," he said with an earnest face. "When you gathered members of the Pendleton Farm household, did you have a feeling that anyone there could have done either murder?"

"Either murder?" she said, sitting straighter. "The EGS is admitting Michael was murdered? How?"

"I'm sorry, I can't answer that," he said. "Please answer my question."

"I don't feel they could have killed anyone," Cora said. "Most of them have the impression Michael and Remy died accidentally, but most think Oscar blackmailed Hazel."

Captain Donaldson leaned back in his chair and gazed at the ceiling for a moment.

"Kaye thinks Sam murdered Michael and Remy," she said. "He benefited from Michael's death and was the first to reach Remy's body. She has no explanation for why he would have killed Remy."

"Just to be clear, we're talking about Kaye Stone and Sam Iverson," he asked.

Cora nodded.

"I somehow feel the blackmailer is at the center of everything," she said, feeling guilty about enjoying their conversation.

"Based on the evidence, I'm inclined to agree with you," he said. "But I want to keep an open mind." He frowned. "Now, I'm going to invite Agent Lewis in here because there're a few more things we need to discuss."

A heaviness settled over Cora—most conversations with Agent Lewis ended with him accusing her of something.

Captain Donaldson selected a button on his comm bracelet, and three minutes later, Agent Lewis slogged into the room looking grumpy. He grabbed one of the office chairs next to Cora, but he pointedly moved it farther away from her.

Cora smirked at his childish behavior.

"Lewis, I want you to explain what these scan distortions mean," Captain Donaldson said in a crisp voice as he turned his screen to face both Cora and Agent Lewis.

"This is against protocol," Agent Lewis said with raised eyebrows.

"Get started, now," Captain Donaldson said.

Agent Lewis glared at Cora before turning to the floating screen and surveying the images one by one.

"These distortions are significant," Agent Lewis said. "These are distortions you get when a Mover kills someone. It's rare for a Mover to actually kill because it's a little obvious. It's disturbing that the distortions are so widespread and go from his brain all the way to his feet. It makes me wonder what type of Mover would have done this. Why is the tissue damage so dispersed instead of focused?"

"You see, Lewis worked with Remy Pendleton the last year before he retired," Captain Donaldson said. "He was intended to be Pendleton's replacement, but it never worked out."

"This kind of damage can also be caused by military grade weapons," she said. "I searched the Net periodically while I was working."

"Those weapons are used mostly to guard mining operations," Captain Donaldson said. "And Interplanetary Security is not supposed to operate in our jurisdiction."

Agent Lewis snorted a laugh, causing the captain to glance at him.

"I know many mining operations also have their own weapons and don't stick to the rules all the time," Captain Donaldson said.

"So let me understand this," Cora said with furrowed eyebrows. "Remy hid those body scans, which means he was hiding the true cause of death." She glanced from Captain Donaldson to Agent Lewis. "He hid a Mover. Someone who probably killed Michael. Was it a family member?"

"Who was at the Gala?" Captain Donaldson asked.

"Everybody. The Cartwright family. The Pendleton clan," Cora said, staring at the ceiling, trying to recall Mover families. "Evan and his siblings, Remy, Lydia, and Paul. Remy's passed... Anyway, Lydia and Paul both have Mover abilities, and so do their children. But they live in Lunar City and left a day or two after the party with their children, many of whom are also gifted."

"Why would a Mover want to get rid of Michael, who had no Mover abilities?" Captain Donaldson asked.

"The mine," Cora said as dawning crept across her face. "Evan set aside one entire mine for

Michael's side of the family. When the Spencers stole it, that income went away."

"So, it'd financially cripple Michael's side of the family," Captain Donaldson said. "We should look into who benefitted from that."

"Yes. Also, there are the Cartwrights to consider," Cora said thoughtfully.

"You mean because they're Movers?" Captain Donaldson asked.

"Winifred and her sons have Mover abilities," Cora said. "Hazel and her dad have none."

"Since there's a chance this type of damage was done by a Mover," Agent Lewis said. "We should investigate members of the Pendleton and Cartwright families."

"Yes, we should, shouldn't we?" Captain Donaldson glared at Agent Lewis, who shifted uncomfortably in his seat because he'd done no work on the case.

Cora wondered why Agent Lewis hadn't done his job.

"Now, we have to go back and do the analysis that you should have done when Michael and Remy Pendleton passed away," Captain Donaldson said.

"There's a problem," Cora said. "The Pendletons, Cartwrights, and four other Mover families were present at the Spring Gala. But only the Cartwright family was present when Remy passed." Cora paused and gazed at Lewis and Donaldson. "They have no motive to kill Michael. They wanted Pendleton protection for their mine."

"Agreed. This case is not straightforward," Captain Donaldson said. "We've started this investigation over with a fresh pair of eyes," he glanced at Agent Lewis, who kept his head down.

"Ms. Brimble," Captain Donaldson stood. "Thank you so much for joining me today. I'd like to meet with you later in the week, after we've done more analysis. Would you be available?"

"Yes, of course," Cora said and rose to her feet. "I'll be happy to help."

She nodded at Captain Donaldson, ignored Agent Lewis, turned, and left his office. Cora never mentioned the trackers she'd created to find Sam and Oscar, as she didn't want to risk jail time.

CHAPTER 16

"Ding," a soft high-pitched chime sounded from the other side of the room where Cora sat in her home office, with her head buried among six floating screens.

Her fingers flew over the screens as she fixed a huge coding bug that prevented her from implementing several changes.

"Ding, ding," the muted high-pitched chimes sounded from somewhere nearby.

Times like these left a light, exhilarated feeling in her chest and was one of many reasons she really enjoyed programming.

"Ding, ding, ding," the high-pitched chimes sounded in her ear, interrupting her concentration.

"Ugh...," Cora frowned, glancing at her bracelet. She activated a floating screen.

"Zara Ingham!" she gasped at an image of the map of Tymal showing a neat, well-maintained neighborhood. "Oscar, you've been at your girlfriend's house all along? Why couldn't the EGS track you down?"

She glanced at her remaining screens filled with coding symbols.

Should I contact the EGS now? she thought. *Look for information on Zara Ingham? Wait 'til I've finished my code?*

She turned to her programming screens and, after a couple of seconds, figured out where she was in her code.

"Incoming vidchat from Captain Donaldson of EGS," Haley, her home's AI, said.

Cora's stomach squeezed as something dawned on her.

It's not a coincidence, she thought. *Two days in a row, Captain Donaldson has contacted me just after a bot has notified me.*

She pressed a button on her com bracelet, opening a new floating screen, and Captain Donaldson appeared with a friendly smile.

"Hello Ms. Brimble and how are you this fine morning," he said

"Why have you called?" she frowned. "Have you been tracking me?"

"Well... yes," he said and paused. "Technically, we're monitoring notifications your bots send to you."

"I thought I was a better programmer," she said with a grimace. "In order to observe my bots, you'd have to find them. That means you have your own bots watching my bots at my home and office."

"You're a very good programmer," he said in a lower voice. "We actually had to hire a professional to keep up with you. That was an embarrassing conversation I had to have with *my* boss."

"Okay, so what do you want?" she said, pride warming her chest in spite of herself.

"You received a notification from your bot monitoring Ms. Zara Ingham," he said, glancing at something off-screen and shifting uncomfortably. "What did it say?"

"My bot found proof that Oscar's in Zara's place," Cora said. "I don't understand why you'd pay someone to follow me on the Net, but not pay to trace Oscar's known whereabouts."

Captain Donaldson sighed and turned away from his screen for several seconds.

"I can't tell you everything," he said. "But Mr. Pendleton is putting a lot of pressure on my bosses, who are putting pressure on me. It's partially my fault—I didn't keep tabs on Lewis, who decided not to do any investigative work on the Pendleton murders." He sighed and seemed to age a few years in a few seconds. "Lewis is a good officer, but his hatred of Askovians has changed him. As of yesterday, he's on administrative leave."

"I see," she said as a light, contented feeling spread over her body. "I know you think he was a good officer, but I never experienced that."

"Yes, well... You're Askovian," he said. "He was a good cadet, and then management sent him to Lunar City, where he encountered your cousin Oliver Robertson. Lewis was never the same after that."

"Hmm... I can see how that would change him," she said, repressing a shudder at the mention of Oliver.

"Would you send me your bot's information?" he asked.

Cora used her bracelet to display a list of her messages on a floating screen. She searched for her bot's message and forwarded it to him.

"Thank you," Captain Donaldson said, looking down at his wrist. "Please don't contact Oscar

Dalton or do any more investigative work. I've dispatched some agents to pick him up."

Cora nodded.

"Also, I'd like to have you sit in during his questioning," he said. "I have to catch up on nearly three weeks' worth of work that was never done. Any help you can give me would be appreciated."

Cora stared down at the floor, thinking about lost time programming.

"Okay, what time should I be there?" she said as her curiosity won out over her urgent launch deadline.

"I'm not sure of the time," he said. "We have to process him first. I expect early afternoon. I'll message you when the time is set."

"That's fine," Cora said. "It'll give me time to finish something."

"Have a good morning," Captain Donaldson said, and his screen went black. Cora closed it.

She opened a new floating screen—the thought of the EGS tracking her bothered her. This time she started a new program, taking her time to create a super stealthy sniffer. The purpose of this sniffer was to find any nearby tracers. She hadn't programmed anything this advanced for a few months, but she decided to take her time and really be careful.

An hour later, she'd completed the sniffer and tested it. She examined the code one last time, and then she released it. The sniffer's notification appeared almost immediately, reporting three different EGS trackers locked on her two bots and her location.

"Three isn't too bad," Cora said, deciding to leave the EGS trackers in place.

Her mind turned back to her game, and the huge bug she'd found earlier in her program.

In the early afternoon, Cora walked into an observation room at EGS headquarters, her face tight with apprehension. Captain Donaldson met her in the white, stark room. He was sitting at a gray table and stood when she entered.

"Ms. Brimble," Captain Donaldson said with a warm smile. "Glad you could make it. Have you been to an observation room before?"

"Yes, Agent Lewis..." Cora said, pointing to a large window with a view to another room with a bland gray wall, one table, and four chairs.

"Sorry, I forgot..." he said, hurrying on as if he wanted to avoid any discussion about Lewis. "I'll be there with Mr. Dalton in a minute or two." He paused, as if collecting his thoughts. "I'm having you here to help me, but my bosses think you're here as a courtesy. Please keep that in mind if you run into any of them."

"This is so different from the last time I had to deal with the EGS," Cora chuckled, releasing her tension.

"Again, I'm sorry about that," he said. "But I'm grateful for your help.

"Well, I'm looking forward to the interview," Cora said. "I hope I can be helpful."

A robot floated into the interrogation room, followed by Oscar. It removed his restraints and retreated. A moment later, Captain Donaldson entered.

Oscar looked terrible. His red rimmed brown eyes and blotchy face made it look as if he'd been crying. Rumpled clothes and mussed brown hair made it seem as if he'd just woken up. His fingers trembled while waiting for Captain Donaldson to begin.

"Do you consent to being recorded?" Captain Donaldson asked.

Oscar nodded.

"You're going to have to say yes or no so that audio and visual are captured," Captain Donaldson said.

"Yes, I consent to be recorded," Oscar said in a wobbly voice.

"Would you verify your identification?" Captain Donaldson asked, pointing at a screen embedded in a table.

Oscar nodded.

"You're going to—" Captain Donaldson said.

"Yes, this is my identification," Oscar said, interrupting Captain Donaldson.

"Where have you been for the past ten days?" Captain Donaldson asked.

"My girlfriend's house," Oscar said.

"Is that Zara Ingham?" Captain Donaldson asked, pausing to survey Oscar.

"Yes, I was there because I received a message from Evan," Oscar said in a hoarse voice. "He promised to put me in jail, and I got scared and ran." Oscar wiped his eyes with shaky hands.

"What've you been doing at your girlfriend's house?" Captain Donaldson asked.

"Nothing much," Oscar shrugged. "I've been eating her food and watching Net entertainment. She was actually getting sick of me. I think she would've thrown me out in a few more days."

The room remained silent after he finished talking. This line of questioning reminded her of Harold Albright's negotiation tactics.

"Do you understand why you're here?" Captain Donaldson asked.

"Yes. I stole Michael's credits," Oscar said.

"You're referring to Michael Pendleton?" Captain Donaldson asked and waited.

"Yes, yes..." Oscar said, and fidgeted with his fingers. "You see, the thing is, I have a gambling problem. I have it under control most of the time, but sometimes things get out of hand. When that happens, I lose huge sums. A year ago, I got into more debt than usual and I borrowed from somebody who later threatened to hurt me. I needed more credits, and I took them from Michael's account. Normally, I fudge his account to hide the missing credits. Then, I pay him when I can, but this time..."

"Go on, Mr. Dalton," Captain Donaldson said.

"Someone was blackmailing me for stealing Michael's credits," Oscar said in an agitated voice. He wiped his eyes with the back of his hands again.

"Who was blackmailing you?" Captain Donaldson asked.

Oscar remained silent and examined the floor.

"Remy Pendleton," Oscar said in a hushed voice.

"Did you know Remy Pendleton's dead?" Captain Donaldson asked.

"Yes, Zara told me," Oscar said in a raised voice. "I didn't kill him. I promise it wasn't me."

"Of course, Mr. Dalton," Captain Donaldson said. "Let's back up a minute. What happened when Michael Pendleton found out about you stealing?"

"I tried to apologize and promised to pay him back," Oscar said in a flat voice. "He wouldn't listen and we got into a big fight."

"How did you leave things after the fight?" Captain Donaldson asked.

"Me, Michael, and Evan had a vidchat," Oscar said. "After Michael explained everything, Evan said he'd attend to the issue after the Gala. He said if I ran away, he'd call the EGS."

"Did you talk to Michael after that fight?" Captain Donaldson asked.

"Yes. The following morning," Oscar said. "I went to his room early in the morning and presented a plan to pay him back. But he didn't want to discuss it anymore and threw me out."

"That was the last time you discussed this with Mr. Pendleton," Captain Donaldson asked.

"Yes, the Spring Gala with the family was later that day," Oscar said. "So I decided to wait and try to talk to him again in a few days. But Michael passed away."

"Now to Remy Pendleton," Captain Donaldson said. "How long did he blackmail you?"

"Ten long months," Oscar said. "I tried to negotiate with him several times, because it was only a matter of time before Michael noticed the discrepancies, but Remy wouldn't back down."

"Why didn't you tell Michael about Remy Pendleton's blackmail?" Captain Donaldson asked.

"Remy forced me to continue stealing Michael's credits," Oscar said. "He said he'd turn me in to the EGS. He also wanted double the credits I'd been stealing before. I tried to tell him Michael would be more likely to catch the discrepancy, but he wouldn't listen."

"Were you on Pendleton Farm five days ago?" Captain Donaldson asked. "It's the day Remy passed."

"No," Oscar said, running his hands through his short brown hair. "Of course not. I've literally been in my girlfriend's apartment since I left Pendleton Farm. I didn't leave for anything."

Captain Donaldson looked down at the screen built into the desk and scrolled.

"Let's go back to the days after Michael Pendleton passed away," Captain Donaldson said. "What were you doing in the days before you disappeared?"

"The very next day, all of Michael's files were locked," Oscar said, furrowing his eyebrows. "No, that's not correct. I thought they were locked. Actually, Evan must have had them removed. Hazel said a robot came to the house and left with all the physical storage units."

"What was your plan with the storage units, anyway?" Captain Donaldson asked.

Oscar examined something on the ground and shifted in his seat.

"Mr. Dalton?" Captain Donaldson asked again.

"I had a plan, and I was going to pay Michael back," Oscar said in a pleading voice. "I just didn't need Evan to get angrier and then turn me into the EGS."

Oscar laughed.

"But I'm here anyway," Oscar's laughter died away. "I suppose Evan is going to press charges."

"Yes, he's pressing charges," Captain Donaldson said. "Let's continue." He looked down at the screen on the table and scrolled through something. "Did you kill Michael Pendleton?"

"No, never," Oscar said. "I'm a gambler and sometimes a thief, but I'd never kill anybody." He took a deep breath, as if trying to gather his thoughts. "Wait a minute, what are you talking about? Killed?" He straightened in his chair. "But he fell down the stairs by accident."

"No, there's evidence of foul play," Captain Donaldson said. "So, do you know who would want to kill him?"

"No," Oscar said with a quaver in his voice.

"Let's discuss Hazel Cartwright," Captain Donaldson said.

"Hazel? How's she mixed up in all of this?" Oscar asked.

"Did you blackmail Hazel Cartwright?" Captain Donaldson asked.

"Blackmail! Hazel?" Oscar asked. "Why would I do that?"

"Answer the question," Captain Donaldson said.

"No, I didn't blackmail Hazel," Oscar said. "What would I be blackmailing her about?"

"The blackmailer claimed Hazel killed Michael," Captain Donaldson said. "Do you think it's possible Hazel killed Michael?"

Oscar grabbed the sides of his head as if to stop his mind from spinning.

"What's going on here?" Oscar asked. "When I came in here, I thought Michael died by accident. Now I hear he was murdered, and Hazel might have murdered him?"

Oscar took several deep breaths, wiping his eyes.

"I've known Hazel for six years," Oscar said. "I can't even imagine her harming anyone."

Cora listened to the rest of Oscar's investigation, but it turned to things related to where he gambled and how often. It also included questions about who else he owed credits to, but Oscar declined to answer.

Half an hour later, Captain Donaldson stepped into the observation room with Cora.

"I understand you're under no obligation to help the EGS," Captain Donaldson said. "Do you have any questions or comments about his statement?"

"No, I thought your questions were thorough," Cora said. "But we now have confirmation that Remy was blackmailing Oscar. Based on Michael's body scans, I'd say he was blackmailing Hazel and Winifred."

"Why those two?" Captain Donaldson asked.

"Hazel has no Mover abilities," Cora said. "There wouldn't be a reason to assume she harmed Michael. But she always does what her mother says. I'm pretty sure he thought he'd rattle Hazel, which he did, and she'd pay up. That's what happened with Oscar."

"Now, how did you know about Remy blackmailing Winifred?" he asked.

"The blackmailer contacted Winifred," she said. "Her Mover skills are very advanced, and she could've harmed Michael. In the security vids, she stood the closest to him. But she doesn't really have a strong motive. I don't really have all the information."

"At least now I have enough information to satisfy Evan Pendleton," Captain Donaldson said. "But I still need to find the murderer. I'll start with the obvious suspects—Hazel and Winifred."

"Winifred hates the EGS," Cora said. "You're going to have a difficult time getting her statement."

"I'll approach carefully," he said with a half-smile. "Thank you for your time. If you need something in the future, let me know. I owe you one." He turned and left the room.

Cora stared at the empty interrogation room, wondering which Mover benefited from both Michael's and Remy's deaths.

In the evening, Cora curled up under a soft blue blanket on her sofa, watching a comedy on a floating screen and holding a forgotten cold cup of tea. Her comm bracelet chimed, and she glanced down at it. She paused the comedy, hurriedly placed her teacup on the coffee table and raked her fingers through her curly hair. Her bracelet chimed a second time, and she answered by launching a vidchat.

"Evening Brian," Cora said. "Haven't heard from you for a while."

"Yeah, it's been... difficult around here," he sighed.

"I suppose you're referring to the Cartwright family joining Albright," she said.

"Well, that's definitely not going to happen," he said. "Dad and Mom got into a huge screaming match. Mom accused him of trying to control her company. Dad got offended because, from his point of view, he's been trying to save her company from potential legal problems."

"Wow, that must've been hard to hear," she said. "I always hated it when my parents fought."

"Hmm... I don't know," he glanced at something off-screen. "I think Dad is right, but it doesn't matter. Mom got so annoyed that she refused to listen to him. In the end, he quit."

"What? Quit?" She leaned a little toward the floating screen.

"Well, technically, he was already retired," he said. "He was working as a contractor helping me, and it's the contractor placement he quit."

"You'll be by yourself," she said. "Is there something I can do?"

Brian paused, furrowing his eyebrows.

"I've basically been on my own since the Spencers started asking us to cover up their illegal activities," he said with sad, tired eyes.

"I'm so sorry, Brian," she said in a quiet voice.

"Eliza's been trying to help, but she's still in Lunar City," he said. "In any case, her 'help' feels more like commands. But she helped with one of our clients. What's making this even harder is Mom trying to give me really out-of-date advice. Mom worked in the business more than twenty years ago—it's been mostly Harold. Since she won't listen to me, I have to contact Eliza for every little thing before Mom will believe me."

"It seems the only solution is Eliza returning from Lunar City," Cora said.

"Yeah, and I can't wait," Brian said. "I'm just not suited for this job."

But what will happen to Albright Corp when Eliza takes over? she thought.

CHAPTER 17

Cora shielded herself before stepping into the Kelby Museum of Natural History. She'd picked a light yellow and white summer dress today and let her hair fall to her shoulders. She immediately spotted Hazel.

"Hello," Cora said with a gentle smile. When she received Hazel's summons early in the morning, she assumed Winifred and Hazel had fought.

"Cora!" Hazel greeted her with a big hug. "I'm so happy to see you." She grinned.

"When I got your message this morning, I thought something was wrong," Cora said with a raised eyebrow. "Is this only a friendly get together?"

"Yes and no," Hazel giggled as she linked arms with Cora and dragged her further into the museum. "I miss you, of course, but I also have some juicy gossip."

Cora raised an eyebrow at that. Even though she'd been to the Kelby many times as a child, she'd chosen this museum because of a traveling exhibit on extinct sea animals. The exhibit had received many good reviews, and she loved going to museums.

They made their way past the Modern Mammals, Ancient Reptiles, and Unusual Insects exhibits. This brought them to the entrance for Extinct Sea Creatures.

"Don't you find these things a little... unsettling?" Hazel asked, wrinkling her nose.

"No, it's interesting," Cora said, stepping into the room. "I've never been underwater and even if I did, I wouldn't see these animals."

"Okay, but if anything scary comes up, I'm leaving," Hazel said, wide-eyed as she stepped into the room.

The manatee was the first extinct animal they reached.

"Says it's called the 'Sea Cow,'" Cora said. "Interesting... It's related to elephants. Too bad they're extinct too."

"Yes, interesting," Hazel said, barely glancing at the manatee or the description beside it. "Ready for my gossip?" She bounced on her feet.

Cora sighed—she really didn't like mean gossip.

This is probably something that'll hurt Kaye, Julia, or both, she thought.

"What is it?" Cora said, turning to the next creature. "Oh, a Leatherback Turtle. I wonder how different it would feel from modern day turtles?"

"Ok, so you know Julia and Delores have to move out this week to Pendleton Manor in Heliton," Hazel said.

"I didn't know it was this week," Cora said. "That must be upsetting for both of them. I hope Aunt Ferna can continue visiting Delores even if she'll be so far away."

"I don't feel sorry for either one of them," Hazel said in a bitter voice. "They made my life miserable whenever Kaye was around."

Cora squeezed Hazel's hand.

"Anyway, Evan decided to run a background check on Julia and Delores," Hazel chuckled. "He didn't realize how much debt they both had, yelled at them, and cut off all access to their credits."

Cora stopped strolling and faced Hazel.

"A background check on his own family?" Cora asked.

"Oh, he does that routinely," Hazel said. "He claims family is always hiding things. Really, he's so intrusive, they're not comfortable sharing anything with him."

"Cutting off their credit isn't going to solve anything," Cora said. "They need to learn how to live within their budgets. They won't learn anything like that."

"Well... That's true," Hazel said in a contrite voice.

"Evan's always been a bully," Cora said, shaking her head. "I've heard so many stories from Aunt Ferna."

"Well, there's more to the story," Hazel said with glee.

"Okay," Cora stifled a sigh.

Nothing involving Evan is going to end well, she thought.

"Then, he ran a background check on Theo," Hazel could hardly contain her laughter. "Uncle Evan was so angry he paid us a visit yesterday."

A sinking feeling developed in the pit of Cora's stomach.

"Uncle and Theo got into a fight," Hazel said. "He revealed that Captain Theo Pike led the security team that took over the mine lost to Spencer Industries."

Cora's mouth fell open.

"That can't be true," Cora said with raised eyebrows. "Otherwise, why would he be dating Julia?"

"That's what Julia shouted at Theo," Hazel said, grinning. "It turns out, he fell in love with her, and he wants to marry her. He mentioned he had no idea taking control of that mine would affect her or he would've never done it."

"Oh, I feel sorry for Theo," Cora said in a low voice. "He really should have told Julia much earlier, but I could tell he really loved her."

"Your kind heart is getting in the way of my fun!" Hazel said with a lopsided grin.

"Come on, let's continue," Cora said, pulling Hazel along. "A whale shark. It's a beautiful creature." She silently read the plaque next to the shark replica.

"It's huge," Hazel said. "Was it dangerous?"

"No, it's a filter fish. It ate plankton, fish eggs, and generally small sea life," Cora said.

"Well, the fight continued, with Delores joining in," Hazel said. "It was three against one, but Theo held his ground. Eventually, Uncle stormed off. A few minutes later, Julia broke up with him and left. Delores gave him a proper dressing down before she left too."

"Wow, so unfortunate," Cora said. "It could've all been avoided if he'd been honest from the beginning."

"He says he didn't know when he first met Julia," Hazel said. "But I see your point. He should've said something as soon as he realized."

"Where is everyone now?" Cora asked.

"Theo left the house yesterday," Hazel said. "Julia and Delores will leave tomorrow."

"What about you?" Cora asked.

"I think I'm leaving at the end of the week," Hazel said. "Depends on Mom."

Cora sympathized with Hazel's levity—Julia and Delores had made her life difficult, but Cora still pitied them.

In the late afternoon, Cora arrived at her house and went to her room. She plopped down on her sofa and immediately began checking her tracker's notifications on a floating window.

She raised her eyebrows when she discovered Sam had been at an EGS substation at the edge of the city. He entered the building and left a few seconds later.

What does this mean? she thought. *Is he hiding from me? Hiding from the EGS?*

Suddenly, her bracelet chimed. Looking down, she realized it was an incoming vidchat from Captain Donaldson. She pressed a button on her bracelet, creating a new floating screen.

"Good afternoon, Miss Brimble," Captain Donaldson said. "I hope you are free right now. There's something I need to discuss with you."

Cora leaned forward, a little surprised he'd called her.

"Yes. How can I help you?" she asked.

"I've just sent you the preliminary version of Remy's autopsy," he said. "I want you to read it after we get off this call. But for now, there's something I want to discuss that is extremely important." He paused, looking down at something. "I've had this part of the report checked by three different doctors. There were crushed nanobot parts in Remy's blood."

"What?" she asked. "Crushed nanobots. Someone his age would've needed the nanobots to maintain his organs, but why crushed?"

"It's important," he said. "It takes a lot of force to overpower a nanobot due to how they're manufactured."

"What type of force could do that?" she asked.

"There're some military weapons," he said. "But those weapons would have to be cleared by the EGS. We've no records of any military weapons within city limits."

"Was there any tissue damage?" she asked.

"Yes," he said. "I think this is the work of another Mover."

"I don't understand how that could've happened," she said. "Nanobots are extremely resilient. Destroying them would've taken a sustained effort over several minutes."

"What's not clear is why destroy the nanobots," he said. "Why damage organ tissues?"

"Curious, isn't it?" she said. "I wonder if we're looking at two different Movers."

"Possibly," he said. "A trained Mover could cause that kind of injury."

"A Mover trying to commit a crime wouldn't cause such mass destruction," Cora said, furrowing her brows. "Instead, they'd do something like squeeze the heart, cut blood flow to the brain, or something similar."

"Winifred could've been angry about being blackmailed and lost control," Captain Donaldson said.

"Possibly, but that's not her personality," Cora paused, thinking. "She's cold and calculating. Not a hothead."

"Winifred was the only Mover at the Farm," Captain Donaldson said. "The only other people were Hazel Cartwright, Ferna Robertson, Delores Pendleton, Julia Pendleton, and Theo Pike. There are no more options. The rest of the Cartwrights traveled off-world a few days ago."

"Did you find anything from Winifred and Hazel's statements?" she asked.

"Not really," he said. "Today, I really only need clarification on a few things."

"Okay, what would you like to know?" she asked.

"What do you think about Winifred and her sons?" Captain Donaldson asked. "They could've committed both murders as they're very advanced. It would be nothing for her to crush nanobots."

"I understand, but I don't see what she gains by harming Michael or Remy," she said. "She needed Michael to attach Hazel to the family, whereas Remy would've been a good ally. Remy didn't get along with Evan."

"Except we know he was blackmailing Winifred," Captain Donaldson said. "You heard that from Hazel. Winifred had motive, and Remy knew it."

"True, but I still don't see her resorting to that," Cora said. "She's politically connected. There're many other ways she could've gotten rid of Remy. Based on what Hazel told me, her mom did nothing."

"That's because she didn't know who the blackmailer was at first," he said. "Anyway, that's only Hazel's story. I don't believe it's the complete truth."

"So, what do you intend to do?" she asked.

"I'm going to bring Winifred into EGS headquarters," he said. "I would like you to watch from the observation—"

Cora chuckled.

"I'm sorry. Apologies," she said between laughing spurts. "You'll never get Winifred into the EGS station. Not after what you did to her son. I wouldn't be surprised if she's amassing her own little private army around her house. You won't even gain access to her."

"We'll see about that," he said, setting his mouth in a grim line. "I'll start with a simple message requesting her presence and see if she chooses to cooperate."

"I think you should tread carefully," she said.

"I've already spoken to Evan Pendleton," he said. "He's satisfied with my work so far. I'm sure he'll support me when I go to talk to Winifred."

"Even if Evan supports you, I doubt you'll reach any Cartwrights," she said.

"I think you underestimate our resources," he said. "If she doesn't cooperate, I'll simply visit her."

"You have a limited window to even contact Hazel," she said, shaking her head. "Winifred won't allow any more government agencies to harm her children."

"It's not the EGS who harmed her son," he said with a pinched face. "It's her son who harmed another human being."

Cora raised both hands as if in surrender.

"I understand what happened," she said. "I'm explaining things from Winifred's point of view. The EGS took her son away, and she never saw him again. I don't believe she's going to allow that to happen again."

Captain Donaldson scowled at something off-screen.

"Well, I still have a job to do," he said. "Thank you for your time. I'll contact you tomorrow when we have Winifred."

"I'll wait to hear from you tomorrow," she said doubtfully.

The screen turned dark, and Cora closed it.

Her curiosity piqued, she wondered what Winifred would do if the EGS came for her. Thinking over some of Aunt Ferna's stories, she shuddered.

CHAPTER 18

Early the next morning, Cora's comm chimed several times before she rolled over and glared at the time floating above the bracelet.

At least it's close to when I'd normally wake up, she thought.

Flinging her legs over the side of the bed, she sat up, snatched her bracelet, and whipped it around her wrist. She rubbed her eyes and opened the message from Brian. Seeing his name made her smile.

Urgent message

Greetings to Albright Corporation Owners:

Urgent meeting at 10am. All owners must attend at Albright headquarters. Anyone who cannot physically attend, must appear by vidchat. This meeting is mandatory.

Brian Farris

Acting President

When Cora finished reading the message, her face fell. She had hoped for a more personal message. Then she thought about the meeting.

This is about Jessica Spencer and that mine, she thought.

Cora stood and paced to the window, looking at the backyard. She gazed out at the garden where sunlight began to brighten the beautiful blooming azaleas. Lost in thought, she jumped when her bracelet chimed again, as she hadn't expected another chime so fast. But when she pressed the button, a new window appeared showing Hazel in a vidchat.

"Hey, Hazel. What's going on?" Cora asked.

"Oh, it's Mom," Hazel said. "You won't believe what she did. She sent a robot early this morning to start packing my clothes. I don't know why she didn't tell me earlier. I could've packed last night."

Cora thought Captain Donaldson's attempt to interview Hazel had probably caused Winifred to accelerate Hazel's move.

"Does that mean you'll be at Cartwright Manor?" Cora asked.

"Yes. I hate being there—it's in the middle of nowhere," Hazel said.

"Pendleton Farm wasn't near Tymal's city center," Cora said.

"But it was a short hover car ride away," Hazel said. "The Manor is in Branvale, which isn't near anything." She pouted. "I think Mom just hates me." Branvale was a small town at the base of the Krega mountains where the Cartwrights maintained their family seat. It was four hours from Tymal.

"Actually, I think she loves you in her own way," Cora said, but didn't elaborate. She didn't have Captain Donaldson's permission to tell.

"You've always said that, but I don't see any proof," Hazel sighed. "Anyway, I'm letting you know where I'll be."

"So, who'll be left at Pendleton Farm?" Cora asked.

"As far as I can tell, nobody," Hazel said. "Julia and Delores are leaving later this morning. They're packing now. Uncle Evan will send a hover car around ten, I think." She paused, as if thinking. "On a brighter note, Kaye is leaving for Lunar City today, too. I only wish I could go to the spaceport for a good send off."

Cora strolled to her sofa as the floating screen followed her. She wasn't quite sure how to reply to that.

"Well, I suppose the good news is she'll be far away," Cora said. "She won't bother you anymore."

"Unfortunately, the damage is already done," Hazel said. "While she was with Michael, it was so difficult to get his attention. If I'd had a child..." She sighed. "Well, I say good riddance to her."

"You had a tough marriage," Cora said. "I hope you can later marry for love."

"Maybe. Anyway, looks like the bots are done packing my things," Hazel turned to something off-screen. "I think I need to go now. I'll invite you for a visit. Or maybe Mom'll let me come to visit you."

"You take good care of yourself, Hazel," Cora said, and the screen went dark. Cora closed the window.

Moving Hazel so quickly means Winifred has some kind of access to the EGS, she thought. *I don't think Captain Donaldson's going to have a good day.*

A couple of hours later, Cora stepped into Albright Corporation Headquarters. She hadn't been there since Harold passed away several months ago. She remembered Ruby, his assistant, sitting at the desk every time she entered the building, but now the desk was gone. And the only furniture filling the lobby area included several small tables, each with two complimentary chairs.

Cora felt emotions drifting from the conference room and shielded herself. She made her way there but paused, examining the door to Harold's office before opening the door opposite and entering the meeting room.

As she stepped in, Brian bounded to her with a happy grin. He leaned toward her and said, "So happy you're here," he whispered.

A happy, bubbly feeling filled her stomach as she beamed.

He turned to everybody else at the table.

"This is Coraline Brimble of Brimble mining," Brian said. "You of course know Dad, Mom, and Eliza." Brian and his sister had the same jet-black hair and blue-gray eyes, but Cora knew from experience they were very different people.

Benjamin stepped forward and gave her a quick hug. Eliza stepped forward and shook hands, but Nora merely exchanged a nod.

"You've met Jessica of Spencer Industries," Brian said. Cora had met her at several tea parties, mostly hosted by her sister Mabel. Jessica was an averaged height woman with brown and gray hair whose pinched face looked as if she never smiled. Cora nodded, but Jessica scowled.

Nora must have told her about my idea to bring in the Cartwrights, she thought.

Brian introduced Cora to four more families: the Meadcrofts, Uptons, Rowleys, and the Yarmouths. She'd met various members of their families, but never the heads of each Askov family. In most families, the heads had special abilities. Each of the owners she met were Readers, Movers, Viewers, and Listeners.

Cora felt Jessica was insecure because she was the lone exception with no special abilities. It would have been her sister Alice, who had been a reader, here today had she not passed.

Nora and Spencer Industries had the largest number of shares in Albright Corporation. In fact, this corporation existed because Harold Albright had come up with an idea to offer mining services to other Askov families. These services included tight security, replenishing mining equipment, trading ore, and other services. These were families who owned mines, but didn't really have the security to protect them from mine-jumpers. In the corporation, depending on their shares, they all received profits, paid expenses, and portioned the liabilities. That's what this meeting was about today.

Several more members joined by vidchat, but their shares were smaller than the four families Cora was introduced to, and many of them didn't live on Earth.

"Good morning," Brian said, getting everyone's attention. "Let's start with the first order of business. We have a new president and a distribution of new shares."

The families sitting at the table murmured to themselves.

"I've been acting president since Harold Albright..." Brian said. "But my family and I have decided to transfer the presidency to my sister, Eliza Albright."

"I want to add a few things before I step down," Brian said. "First, I've enjoyed working with so many of you. We've become very good friends, and I hope that'll continue through the coming years. I won't be available day-to-day.

But you all know how to reach me if you need to."

He turned to his sister and reached out a hand, which she placed in his.

"Second, Eliza has been managing our personal family mines in Albright Mining for 15 years, so she's more than capable. I'd like you all to stand behind her and give her your support."

Everybody clapped, and Eliza nodded to the crowd. Brian stepped away from the head of the table and took Eliza's seat.

"Hello, everyone," Eliza said with the efficiency of someone used to being in charge. "Although I know most of you, I look forward to getting to know you all, even better." She paused, looking at the Askovians sitting at the table. "As the new president of Albright Corporation, I want you all to feel comfortable coming to me if you have any questions. Shortly, I'll have an assistant so you can receive faster service."

She glanced at Jessica.

"Let's move on to an important matter that affects all of us," Eliza said. "Spencer Industries needed some legal work done for a mine they recently acquired. There was a little controversy due to the contested ownership of the mine, but that's settled now. We propose creating the necessary documents which will complete the legal process for Spencer Industries' ownership."

Eliza paused while some quiet conversations took place around the table.

"We're informing you all in case you have any issues with this. Are there any questions?"

"How was the ownership settled?" an Askovian from the Yarmouth family asked.

Jessica Spencer stood and seemed to force her face into a smile that didn't reach her eyes.

"Let me answer, Eliza," Jessica said as she strode to the head of the table while Eliza took a step back.

"We submitted the ownership paperwork a year ago," Jessica said with a wooden smile. "No one contested it. After one year, ownership is permanent."

"Sometimes ownership is contested after the one-year grace period," an Askovian from the Rowley clan said.

"I can't predict what others will do," Jessica said. "We've followed the law."

A heavy silence filled the room, as everyone knew there was very little legal about the way Spencer Industries had acquired their latest mine.

"I only wonder about the security of our mines," Cora said. "Once all the legal stuff is settled, how will our mines be protected?"

Eliza stepped forward.

"I don't understand," she said.

"Protection for our mines is organized through Albright Corp," Cora said. "The Spencer's recent mine was obtained with their security forces. I watched the number of guards decrease from the Rowley and Meadcroft mines while the fighting ensued. This means Albright Security really prioritizes Spencer mines. How can we ensure the safety of our mines, especially during the next skirmish?"

Several people at the table mumbled amongst themselves. Eliza waited until they quieted down. Jessica glowered at her, but Cora was relieved she had shielded herself ahead of time.

Unable to shield herself very well, Nora's face contorted in pain as her husband helped her out of the room. Eliza and Brian gazed at her with worried expressions.

"You've asked a very good question," Eliza said after a moment's distraction. "We should all be worried about the security of our mines. They're our livelihood, and we literally wouldn't be able to exist without them. But think of it this way: Spencer Industries' goals align with Albright Corp. We both want protection and maximum profits."

The room clapped after Eliza spoke, but Cora knew she hadn't answered her question.

"Spencer Industries has a large percentage of Albright Corp to keep us safe," Eliza said. "That's why we have meetings where we discuss all of our needs, and how we can accommodate them. Our common goals will allow us to keep trusting each other and keep us safe from mine jumpers."

"I understand Spencer Industries had some legal issues that are now resolved," an Askovian from the Upton family said. "Now Albright is proposing to create some legal documents showing past management. Is all of Albright Corporation now liable if the Pendletons contest this mine?"

Jessica glared at Brian before turning to Upton.

"There are no legal ramifications for any of you," Jessica said. "The Pendleton family never contested ownership."

That wasn't exactly true, Cora thought. *If the Pendletons went to court and won, every owner would have to pay. Realistically, Evan Pendleton isn't likely to go to court, but he is going to retaliate.*

The meeting took a turn as Jessica continued to speak.

"Spencer Industries has most of the risk," Jessica said. "Albright Corp's security is almost entirely funded by us. In our last battle, it became obvious that we needed more ownership points so we could properly fund our guards."

For some reason, Captain Pike flashed across Cora's mind.

The Spencer's funded mercenaries, and that's why they needed more credits? she thought.

A long conversation followed as they discussed ownership points. After a vote, Spencer Industries gained four percent more ownership of Albright Corporation.

Cora shuddered. A few more votes like this, and her mine would essentially be controlled by Spencer Industries.

Soon after, Eliza closed the meeting and everyone trickled out. One of the last to leave, Cora made her way out the door. A moment later, Brian caught up with her.

"Would you like lunch?" Brian asked.

"We haven't had lunch together in a long time," Cora said as the happy, bubbly feeling filled her chest again.

"What do you say about the Flying Noodle Bowl?" he asked.

"An old favorite," Cora chuckled. "I'd love to—let's go."

Later at lunch, Cora and Brian leaned over a table in a cozy corner of the Flying Noodle Bowl. He slurped up some noodles while she munched on some synthetic shrimp.

"I'm happy to see that being fired has brightened your day," Cora said with amusement on her face.

Brian chuckled, and it looked as if he'd regained years of his life. He looked like his old self, which left Cora lighthearted.

"I've never been so happy to be fired," he said. "It was the best thing that could've happened to me.

Cora chortled.

"What do you think about Eliza taking over?" she asked. "Do you feel that she's competent?"

"Absolutely," he said. "She's way more capable than I'll ever be. Dealing with the day-to-day messes of a management company was so stressful. But Eliza seems to live for that stuff. So more power to her. Also, she, Mom, and Jessica seem to have formed a little trio and were already making decisions behind my back."

"I'm concerned about Jessica's influence over Albright Corp," Cora said. "I think your mom is eventually going to lose her company."

"I don't think so," Brian said. "The Corps by-laws protect the family. In any case, I don't have to worry about it anymore. Now I can go and live my life."

"What about your personal ownership interests?" she asked. "Aren't you worried?"

"There's only ten percent which stays with the presidency," he said. "I've passed that to Eliza. Instead, I'm one quarter owner of Albright Mining, our family mines."

"I'm sorry it was so difficult for you," she said. "At the same time, I'm glad you've escaped."

"I'm happier," he said. "I was wondering if I should do what I was doing before—work as an attorney helping mining investors. But I had a chance to talk to Sam Iverson."

"What? When did you talk to him?" she asked.

"Oh, a couple of days ago," he said. "We happened to run into each other at the same restaurant and struck up a conversation." He reached for a sip of water. "He asked about you and Hazel, but I explained I've been so busy with the Spencer Industries mine seizure that I hadn't spoken to you."

"I've been looking everywhere for him," Cora said. "I must be losing my touch, but I couldn't put trackers on every restaurant in town. I've probably missed my chance."

"Well, I had the impression he was planning to hang around for several more weeks at least," Brian said. "He's got several projects lined up."

"I don't suppose you know where he's staying?" she asked.

Brian shook his head.

"So anyway, what did you two discuss?" she asked.

"Oh, his life as an investor," he said. "It requires lots of interplanetary travel to survey mines, monitor miners, track traders, and more. It was really fascinating. After his detailed analysis, he makes a comprehensive report that several Askovs happily pay for. He also charges for private consultations."

"Is this something you're thinking of doing?" she asked.

"Maybe," he shrugged. "I liked traveling and evaluating mines, but I'm not sure I'd want to advise Askovs. I had enough of them at Albright."

"Sounds interesting," she said. "I wouldn't mind occasionally traveling with you."

"I was thinking of some combination of working as an attorney and investor," he said. "I don't know if I want to travel that much. Not sure."

Cora finished her meal and placed the empty bowl in the recycling.

"So what about you?" Brian asked. "Where are you with the case?"

"Oh yes," she said. "There's been so much." She caught him up on Michael and Remy's death report, Oscar's theft, Captain Donaldson's suspicions of the Cartwright family, and the blackmail.

"Wow, you've been busy?" he said, placing his empty bowl in the reclamation receptacle

"Yeah, it's mostly because I've been working with Captain Donaldson," she said.

"Who's Captain Donaldson?" he asked. "I thought you were working with Agent Lewis."

"No, thank goodness," she grimaced. "He's on administrative leave. Instead, I've been working with his boss."

"What's he like?" he asked.

"A bit more reasonable than Agent Lewis," she paused to think. "Unfortunately, right now, he thinks the primary suspect is Winifred. So his plan is to get her into an interrogation room."

"What? Winifred? I've heard stories about her..." he shivered. "The captain will never get near her, especially not after the EGS took one of her sons away. Didn't you tell him not to bother her?"

"Multiple times," she said. "He wouldn't listen. In that way, he's similar to Agent Lewis."

"So he plans to approach her today?" he asked.

"Yes. I'm a little scared for him," she said.

"Well, you can't save people from themselves," he shrugged. "How are things going with your game?"

"Very well," she said. "If I had to launch tomorrow, I'd feel confident I could release something that I wouldn't be ashamed of. It won't have all the bells and whistles, but it will work properly."

"What about the feature to work in groups?" he asked.

"The first phase of that's done," she said. "It works with all the major options, and I've clearly marked the features that aren't compatible."

"Sounds good," he said, paying for lunch.

"With a bit more time, I could squeeze in a few more features, but I think I'm going to focus on testing. Launch is in a few weeks, anyway."

"Good for you," Brian said. "You can release it into the wild and start getting feedback from everybody."

A contented joy filled Cora's chest as she sighed with pleasure.

CHAPTER 19

"Come along, Ben," Aunt Ferna said, pulling Benjamin through the sunroom and out into the back garden of her home. "This way and don't give me that face. I know you'll enjoy it."

"I don't see why we have to go into the garden," Benjamin said. "This is boring."

"Oh, you sound like a petulant child," Aunt Ferna said.

"Anyway, what are we going to do out here?" Benjamin asked.

"What we're going to do is talk," Aunt Ferna said while she hooked one arm around Benjamin's. "Also, it's a beautiful morning, and we can get a little exercise."

Cora and Brian exchanged glances as they stifled their laughter. They followed Aunt Ferna and Benjamin out into a beautiful, sunny day, walking the path to Cora's favorite garden feature, a statue of Askae—the goddess of meaningful gifts.

Cora sensed Aunt Ferna's safe, familial radiated emotions as well as Brian and Benjamin's broadcast comforting, friendly feelings.

Aunt Ferna didn't stop at the fountain, and instead continued further into the garden. She strolled under an arbor among the cool trees, and after a few steps, she turned to Cora and Brian, causing her floral dress to fan out around her.

"So you two are quiet," Aunt Ferna said. "What's going on with you?"

Cora and Brian exchanged glances.

"I've been catching up on some sleep," Brian said. "This is the first time I've had a break since Uncle passed."

"I see, I see," Aunt Ferna said. "Have you made plans for your future yet?"

"No nothing firm," Brian said. "I definitely want to go back to being an attorney. But I also want to learn more about mine investing."

"Investing?" Aunt Ferna asked. "How did you become interested in investing? I only ask because you already own Albright Mining."

"A few days ago, I ran into Sam Iverson," Brian said. "He's Hazel's... friend. He raved about the life of an investor, studying mining operations, writing reports, and getting paid for all that research. He seemed to particularly enjoy all the travel that comes with it."

"Remember, let me know if you see him again," Cora said. "I've got a few questions for him."

"What are you going to ask him?" Aunt Ferna asked.

Cora hesitated, sensing her aunt's rising fear, but she had to be honest.

"I only want to ask what happened when Remy passed away," Cora said. "Agent Lewis didn't really get a proper statement from him. Also, I'm not sure if Captain Donaldson has thought to interview him again."

"Cora my dear," Aunt Ferna said. "Leave well enough alone. Let the EGS do their job. Otherwise, they'll blame you for the murders of both Michael and Remy Pendleton."

"I have to agree," Benjamin said. "The EGS is not really on the side of truth or justice. They're exactly like IPS. They're also owned by the two largest Askov families. And they don't enforce the law for the Pendleton and Spencer families—they do exactly as they please."

Cora sensed their increasing anxiety and wracked her brain to think of something to change the direction of the conversation. But Aunt Ferna inadvertently helped her.

"Now, now, Ben," Aunt Ferna said. "Not everybody's corrupt. Some families are kind and helpful."

"Oh, yes," Benjamin asked. "Which families are you talking about?"

"Well, the Farris family, for one," Aunt Ferna said.

Benjamin chuckled.

"Oh, you know what I mean, Ferna," Benjamin said.

"You and Brian have been fired for going against corruption," Aunt Ferna said. "I'm sure there are more families who would've done the same."

Benjamin harrumphed and turned a little pink at the compliment.

"So what about you, Ben?" Aunt Ferna asked. "What are your plans for the future?"

Cora breathed a sigh of relief at the change in the conversation.

"Before my brother-in-law passed away, Nora and I planned to travel," Benjamin said. "We were going to take a long jaunt to Lunar City and then to Anteros on Mars. We hadn't quite decided on Ganymede, but we probably would have made it. You see, we were checking on mines controlled by Albright, but we'd get to spend time together."

"Oh, that sounds like fun," Aunt Ferna said with a gentle smile. "But are you sure you *can't* take Nora with you?"

"No, she's not coming," Benjamin said matter-of-factly. "She's worried about Albright Corp, and I've been told to stay out of it. So I've decided to continue with my retirement plans."

"I don't understand," Aunt Ferna said. "If Nora's not going with you, are you really going to travel that long distance by yourself?"

"If I have to, yes," Benjamin said. "But I have two backup plans." He glanced at Brian. "I asked Brian to consider going with me at least part of the way."

Brian coughed and glanced at Cora, who raised a questioning eyebrow.

"My second option is my old friend Omar," Benjamin said.

"Do you mean Omar Washington?" Cora asked.

"Yes," Benjamin said. "Do you remember, Cora, when you came to visit us a few days ago for lunch and I showed up late?"

Cora nodded

"Nora and I were visiting Omar and his new girlfriend," Benjamin said. "They mentioned they'd like to join us for a trip to Mars, but they're not interested in Ganymede. So I thought I could also go with them."

"That should be fun," Aunt Ferna said. "I've known Omar since we were children. If Omar goes with you, I think I might like to go." She turned and glanced at Cora. "What do you think?"

"Well, I'd be a little worried about running Brimble Mining," Cora said. "While on board a ship, communication is intermittent."

"True," Aunt Ferna said. "It'd be more difficult for you. But maybe you could take a shorter trip to Lunar City. Have you been there before?"

"Yes, as a child," Cora said. "But I don't remember much."

"Oh, it just came to me," Aunt Ferna said. "It was for a wedding. One of the youngest Yarmouth sisters got married. I met so many great friends."

Benjamin chuckled.

"Actually, you're great friends with every-body," he said. "You even know Winifred Cartwright. How's that possible?"

"I don't know," Aunt Ferna grinned. "Some-how, people tend to gravitate toward me. We exchange confidences and become friends."

Cora and Brian also chuckled.

"Now Benjamin," Aunt Ferna said. "If you trav-el that long distance away from Nora, what will happen to your marriage?"

Cora sensed Brian's unease and thought of trying to change the conversation again.

"We both feel we need a small break from each other," Benjamin said. "We've been married a long time, and we'll weather this storm too. Also, I'm at the age where I really want to relax and enjoy my life."

"Don't you think Nora wants that too?" Aunt Ferna asked.

"She's worried about our income," Benjamin said. "But I don't understand her. We actually have most of our income from Albright Mining. The Corp is only a management company."

"I'm sorry it's all come to this," Aunt Ferna said. "Have you tried talking to her?"

"Many times," Benjamin said. "But I just can't reason with her anymore. And I don't want to wait to start living—I want to go now."

This time, Cora sensed Brian's broadcast distress.

How can I change this discussion? she thought.

"Maybe Nora will come to her senses," Aunt Ferna said.

The four of them wound their way through the copse of trees, eventually stepping into bright sunlight. It was part of the garden easily visible from Cora's window, and she loved this view. It was as if somebody had taken a million flowers and jammed them as close as possible together to create a huge cacophony of color. From her bedroom window, it was beautiful, but standing in the flower patch, it was stunning.

Her face transformed into a huge grin. Aunt Ferna, Brian, and Benjamin stopped along the trail, delighting in the view. Then Benjamin turned back to Cora.

"Now, young lady," he said. "I want you to tell me about your investigations."

"It's been difficult to understand," Cora said. "The first issue is Michael and Remy's autopsies show evidence that a Mover actually murdered them. Next, there are two Mover families involved, the Pendletons and Cartwrights. The only one with Mover abilities when Remy passed was Winifred, but what's not clear is motive. It turns out Remy was blackmailing her."

"Sorry. Did you say Remy was blackmailing Winifred," Benjamin asked.

"Yes, and Hazel, too," Cora said. "But he never presented them with any evidence."

"I've known Remy since he was a boy," Aunt Ferna said. "I find that very hard to believe."

"Unfortunately, it's true," Cora said. "Captain Donaldson had a chance to look through his finances. It seems Remy retired with an average pension. But it wasn't enough to live the way he was accustomed to. Like Julia, since he came from an Askov family, he had to keep up appearances."

"Oh, poor Remy," Aunt Ferna said. "I understand not being able to attend required functions."

Cora sensed her aunt's sadness, but wondered which Askov events were truly required.

"Initially, Remy blackmailed Oscar to have access to Michael's credits," Cora said. "Later he moved on to Hazel, then Winifred. But Hazel and Winifred never replied. Shortly after that, he died."

"This all sounds so dangerous, dear," Aunt Ferna said. "I wish you would leave this to the EGS."

"I don't have any options now," Cora said. "I'm out of ideas."

"When Winifred ignored Remy, what did he do?" Benjamin asked.

"As far as the captain can tell, nothing," Cora said. "There's no evidence he received any credits from either of them, and now he's dead."

"Can't help feeling sorry for Remy," Aunt Ferna said. "Knowing how miserly Evan is, I can see why he'd be suffering."

Benjamin turned to Brian with one raised eyebrow.

"So, my boy," Benjamin said, changing the subject. "What do you think about a short trip to Lunar City?"

"I liked the idea, Dad," Brian said. "Since we're clearly both free, when do you think we should go?"

"How about in a couple of weeks?" Benjamin said. "I need to tie up some loose ends with Albright to hand it over to Eliza. Then I'll really be free."

"Great," Brian said. "I think we should all take the trip to Lunar City."

"I think so too," Aunt Ferna said. "Sounds like fun."

"I can't go now," Cora said. "Maybe I can catch up with everyone after I launch my game."

"I think that's fine," Benjamin said. "Brian and I aren't in a big hurry. We'll start planning to leave for Lunar City in about two weeks. You and Aunt Ferna can join us a few weeks after that."

Later in the afternoon, Cora flew the family hover car to EGS Headquarters, as Captain Donaldson had requested a meeting with her. While her car descended onto a parking space, a notification popped up on a floating screen she'd used to make last-minute changes to her game. The automatic message came from one of her trackers stating there had been a brief sighting of Sam Iverson at a hotel, but he'd already checked out.

Sam must be evading her trackers, she thought. *I'm going to ask him how he does that when I find him.*

After the hover car landed, she stepped out and walked to the front entrance of the headquarters. A few minutes later, she stood at the captain's office door as it slid open.

"Hello," Cora said.

The captain shot to his feet, stepping around his desk to greet her with a welcoming smile.

"Come in, come in," Captain Donaldson said. "Have a seat." He led her to the pair of soft, comfortable chairs resting on one side of his desk, while he took his larger chair on the other side.

"And have you had a good day?" he asked in a cheerful tone.

Why's he stalling? she thought, while nodding her head.

"Good, good," he said with a nervous grin. "Umm, I need to talk to you about something." He scratched his head, thinking. "Yesterday, I took some EGS agents with me and we flew to Pendleton Farm. It was empty. We discovered Julia and Delores Pendleton moved to Pendleton Manor in Heliton. And Hazel had gone to her mother's house in Branvale."

"Yes, that sounds about right," Cora said. "Hazel called me before she left and told me Julia and Delores were going to leave as well."

"What? Hazel called you?" he said in a raised voice. "Why didn't you make her stay?"

"I thought you didn't want me to tell her about your investigation," Cora said as she felt her chest beginning to constrict with anger.

"Of course, I didn't want you to tell her," he said irritably. "But you should have made up something to make sure that she stayed."

"Just make something up on the fly," she said with a sarcastic snort. "I don't know if you're aware of this, captain, but I don't work for the EGS. I thought I was doing you a favor by not telling Hazel that you plan to interview her."

"Well, yes," he said. "But then, if you knew she was leaving, you should have contacted me."

"Again, I don't work for the EGS," she said. "I don't know anything about how the EGS operates. There was no reason for me to assume that you'd even need help. The EGS has way more resources than I do."

Captain Donaldson grumbled something under his breath.

"I'll be honest with you," he said. "My boss and her boss are furious right now. We feel some member of the Cartwright family is responsible for the deaths of both Michael and Remy Pendleton. After all, Winifred was present at both deaths. Now we've lost our chance to interview them."

"How have you lost your chance?" she asked. "All you have to do is fly to Branvale and talk to them."

"It's not that simple," he said. "Winifred Cartwright called an attorney, who put an injunction on us. We can't come within a kilometer of her home."

"I've heard of Askovians invoking that in the past," she said. "It's used for the safety of the EGS agents, as well as the safety of the Askovian."

"In this case, it's an abuse of justice," he said, slapping a hand on his desk.

"I can see where she's coming from," Cora said. "After her experience with the EGS taking Zach, she probably remembers the EGS's abuse of power."

"That was a different case," Captain Donaldson said. "A little boy died!"

"And another little boy was locked away for the rest of his life," she said with prudence.

"We'll have to agree to disagree," he said with a frustrated look.

"Well, I don't know how you're going to get around the restraining order," she said. "They are a family of Movers, and your agents could actually be in danger."

Captain Donaldson scoffed, climbed to his feet, and paced to the window behind his chair. It faced the center of the building, a large atrium filled with hundreds of hanging plants and several seating areas.

"The EGS could've been more lenient with Zach," he said with his back to Cora. "I've reviewed that case and many others like it. I'm not sure why the EGS was so strict with Zach Cartwright."

"I wonder if it was politically motivated," she said. "Maybe Winifred made the wrong Askovian mad."

"Several days ago, I located her two sons," he said. "I thought they'd be easy to find. But they're not even on Earth anymore. They've left for Mars."

"I'm not sure, but I think that was a planned trip," she said.

"Now, it's a case for the Interplanetary Security," he said. "But those idiots only do what they're told by either the Spencer or Pendleton families. I suppose we'll never find out what really happened to Michael and Remy.

Captain Donaldson paced in a circle from the window to the entrance of his office and then back to the window to face the atrium.

"I suppose you can check if Evan Pendleton is willing to pressure Winifred to cooperate," she said.

"He'll never do that," he said. "Evan provided the attorney that protected Winifred and her family."

"Except those were Evan's relatives who were murdered," she said. "He may be willing to force her to make a statement."

Captain Donaldson slowly turned to face her and she could almost see the wheels turning in his mind.

"Do you know that might work?" he said with a grim smile. "He should be interested in finding out who murdered his brother and his nephew. That might cause him to turn on Winifred Cartwright. Not a bad idea." He scratched his chin, examining the floor.

Cora reflected for a moment. Evan wasn't really fond of his brother, but based on Hazel's words, he valued Michael. On the other hand, he received a lot of credits from the Cartwright mine because they had to pay him for protection. Being a larger mine, the payments were big, too. Since Evan didn't retaliate when Jessica stole one of his mines, Cora realized it was possible he couldn't afford a battle.

"I don't think Evan will turn on Winifred, but I could be wrong," she said. "Do you have any plans to investigate any Pendleton family members?"

"No," he said. "None of the Movers were around when Remy passed away. Only the Cartwrights have been in both places, and I think it's Winifred."

"Winifred doesn't have an alibi for the time of his murder," Cora said shrewdly. "But her control of her abilities is flawless. I don't think she would've done that kind of damage."

"Still, it won't hurt to talk to her," he said, turning to Cora. "Thank you for your help, Ms. Brimble. You've provided some much-needed insight."

Cora stood, and he walked her to the door.

I don't think his talk with Evan will go very well, she thought.

CHAPTER 20

After an evening full of programming to implement changes and fix bugs on Mystery Adventures, one by one she closed her floating screens. Once they were all closed, she stood from her desk in her bedroom and made her way to the bathroom. She cleaned her teeth by inserting a sonic cap over them. The high frequency vibrations removed food residue in a few seconds, and afterwards, she rinsed her mouth. She washed her face and headed toward her closet for pajamas when her comm bracelet chimed.

She paused, glancing at it when she realized it was a notification from her tracker. A heavy feeling settled on her shoulders because these bulletins always apprised her of Sam's location after he left.

She created a floating notification screen, and a slow smile spread across her face. This time, the alert stated Sam's current position.

A giddy feeling shot through her as she rushed out of her bedroom, sprinted the length of the hall, flew over the stairs, and burst through the front door of her home. Cold rain immediately washed over her but didn't dampen her spirits.

The city of Tymal existed under a weather bubble, which maintained a pleasant temperature during the day, and allowed needed rain during some evenings. These evenings varied, but the city officials always posted them. Unfortunately, Cora almost never took the time to look up the forecast for the evening.

"Ugh..." she said in a tense voice and pressed a button on the door of the car.

She dove in immediately, turned on the heater and dehumidifier. Breathing a sigh of relief as her body warmed, she inputted the hover car's destination, and it climbed into the sky. She glanced at her sleepy neighborhood where one or two lights were still on in some houses. After rising into the air, the car headed away from the town's center.

Within minutes, she floated over dark fields with the hover car emitting the only light. Off in the distance, she saw bright lights and the outline of three enormous space shuttles. In a few more minutes, her hover car slowed, and she saw the outline of the spaceport. A wide road divided the grounds, resulting in a smaller grassy parking lot on one side and a large terminal building on the other. The terminal building served as a lobby for passengers waiting to board the shuttles to space. Cora gazed at the three space shuttles parked on the other side of the terminal. She noticed the shuttle crew working inside and around one of the three shuttles, while the remaining two were dark.

Oh, I hope I haven't missed him, she thought.

Her hover car came to rest about a meter above the close-cropped grass of the lot. She jumped out before its steps reached the ground and got soaked again. Dashing across the empty road, she began to shiver. The door slid open as warm, whooshing air calmed her trembling. Cora relaxed with the warmth and stepped into the lobby.

She raised her shield to shut out others' emotions as she paused and glanced at the three main lobbies. Only one contained a handful of seated people waiting to go to Lunar City. Sam turned to her and their eyes locked. His features fell, but a lopsided grin spread across her face. He climbed to his feet, waiting for her while she strolled past a large mural depicting the lunar landscape. Cora entered the lobby area, passing a sleeping child on his dad's lap, and came to a stop in front of her quarry.

"Hello, Sam," Cora said in a low voice, trying not to disturb the sleeping passengers.

"Cora, I should've known it was you trying to track me," Sam said in a dejected voice.

She ignored his lack of enthusiasm, assuming he expected to see Hazel.

"How've you been?" she asked with a small smile.

"I knew once I took off my Tracking Armor someone'd find me," he said. "I thought it'd be the EGS. Why did you put a tracer on me?"

"Why were you hiding?" she asked. "If you thought the EGS was trying to reach you, why not talk to them and get it over with?"

Sam sighed and surveyed the minute details of the carpeted floor.

"I've been thinking about it for the past few days," he said as his face drooped with sadness.

"But I resolved to talk to someone and stop running from this."

Cora gestured to one of the empty lounges and they both stepped away.

"So you've been avoiding me," she said. "How did you do it?"

Sam pulled a tiny wire loop resting over his right ear and showed it to her.

"This is Tracking Armor," he said. "It blocks most devices from monitoring my comm bracelet and prevents the EGS's facial recognition from finding me. It's technically illegal, but after dealing with that buffoon, Agent Lewis, I knew I could get away with this."

"No one from the EGS has contacted you?" she asked.

Sam shook his head.

"Agent Lewis is off the case," she said. "I thought Captain Donaldson would find you."

"He might be on his way," he said with a dry chuckle.

They reached the waiting area furthest from everyone else.

"What did you want to talk about?" he asked.

"What I've been doing is talking to everybody who was there the day Remy died," she said.

"I know. I briefly spoke to Julia," he said. "You know, you're doing Lewis's job."

Cora nodded.

"I think the captain is overwhelmed right now," she said. "He had to take over suddenly from Lewis. Would you tell me what you saw the day that Remy passed away?"

"Oh, it's fairly straightforward," he said, pacing methodically between the chairs. "I made my way from the barn to the house. But before I rounded the corner, I heard Remy calling for help. When I rounded the corner, I saw Hazel step into the house—she never saw me. And I also saw Remy collapse. I ran toward him and turned him over. But he was already dead. His eyes were wide open, and he was not breathing. I... I shouted for help."

Sam stopped talking as his voice became thick. Cora waited and watched his changing emotions on his face. She wished she could lower her shield and sense his emotions, but with so many people, she would become overwhelmed.

"You and Hazel showed up first," he said in a strained voice. "Sorry, now that I'm talking about this, it's all coming back to me."

"It's okay," she said in a gentle voice. "Take your time."

"Well, I think Hazel brought a medipad," he said. "It was too late."

"What I don't understand is why you were hiding this," she said.

Sam stared at the ground for a long time, and Cora thought he wasn't going to respond. Eventually, he gazed at her with a bleak, defeated look in his eyes.

"I really loved Hazel," he said with a wobble in his voice. "I would've married her months ago if I could. But when I saw her leave a dying man in the yard and never come back, even after he called for help. I knew I could never marry somebody that heartless. I'd never seen that side of her. I'd always viewed her as the victim."

"I ran into Hazel in the corridor," she said. "I think she was heading back toward you."

"Maybe..." he said with furrowed eyebrows. "In any case, Lewis showed up, and I started to explain what happened. He cut me off many times—he didn't want to hear anything. So I gave up trying to explain, even though it was clear Hazel was the last person to be with Remy."

"That may not be true," she said. "I haven't seen it yet, but the surveillance vid shows Winifred exiting the garden and stepping onto the gaming field after Hazel and I arrived."

"What are you saying?" he asked. "Remy died of a heart attack."

"Is that what you really think?" she asked, tilting her head. "These days, most people above fifty have medical nanobots that keep them healthy. Remy also had them. So, why is he dead?"

Sam stared, nonplussed.

"Did Hazel…" he said as his eyes moistened.

"I don't think so," she said. "I really don't know. Captain Donaldson seems to think it's Winifred, but her motive seems shaky. We know a Mover killed him—"

"What?" he said in a raised voice, interrupting Cora. "How do you know?"

Cora guided him to a nearby seat that included four chairs around a table. The table featured one lonely meal crafter, but neither of them drank anything. She explained her investigation starting from Michael's death, including the blackmail, and ending with Remy passing away.

Cora waited in silence for Sam to grasp everything she'd explained. When he turned toward her, she continued.

"Captain Donaldson is in charge of the investigation now," she said. "And he's much more competent than Lewis and very sympathetic to Askovians. He's interested in actually finding Michael and Remy's murderers."

"Wait, the captain is looking for a Mover," he said. "So, it can't be Hazel. She doesn't have any powers."

"I agree," she said. "And Winifred was on the property—she seemed to come out of nowhere after Remy passed away."

"You haven't seen the surveillance vids?" he asked.

"True," she said. "The captain described what he saw. He's very set on Winifred being the murderer."

"Why doesn't he arrest Winifred?" he asked.

Cora chuckled.

"I thought you knew Winifred Cartwright," she said. "Winifred is powerful, politically connected, and extremely wealthy. She's a very strong Mover and nobody's going to *just* arrest her."

Sam laughed without mirth as well, nodding. "That's fair."

"Since you removed your armor," she said. "Can you talk to Captain Donaldson?"

"I don't see the point in talking to him," he said. "If I give him my statement and Winifred finds out. I'll never sell another report to an Askovian. She's very connected and will tank my business."

"I understand that," Cora said. "But at the same time, I think you should try. Your testimony could at least help keep the captain's focus away from Hazel."

"It doesn't sound like he's going after her, anyway."

"I still think it'll be helpful for him to know your story."

Sam climbed to his feet and resumed his earlier pacing. He wove his way between tables, thinking while Cora waited.

Cora wracked her brain as her eyes slid over a brightly colored mural filled with a kaleidoscope of colorful geometric shapes. She needed a way to convince Sam to talk to the captain.

"Think about it the other way," she said. "If word gets out that the EGS could've arrested Winifred, who murdered two members of an

Askov family, but you chose not to help, that won't look good." She leaned her elbows onto her knees. "If she could kill Askovs, nobody's safe."

"I think your argument is weak," he said. "But I'll talk to him." He stopped pacing as a resigned expression came over his face. "What should I do? Show up in the morning?"

"No, while you're here, let me contact the captain," she said, raising her left arm. She started a new floating screen and displayed her contact list. When she found the captain, she started a vidchat.

"Cora," Captain Donaldson said. "This is a little late for you, isn't it?"

"Yes, it is," she said. "I thought you should know I'm at the spaceport talking to Sam Iverson."

Sam leaned toward Cora and waved at the captain.

"Don't go anywhere," Captain Donaldson said. "I've been looking for you for four days. I'll be there in ten minutes, and you'd better be there."

The floating window turned dark and Cora closed it.

Almost exactly ten minutes later, the captain strode toward them, looking surly. His dark brown jumpsuit hadn't wrinkled after a full workday.

"Mr. Iverson. Ms. Brimble," Captain Donaldson said. "It's good to see you both here. Is there some place private we can talk? He looked around for a private room."

"I sometimes meet clients here," Sam said. "But I always have to create a privacy bubble. Otherwise, the terminal's surveillance will read our lips."

"I can create that privacy bubble now," Captain Donaldson said, activating his comm and creating a new floating screen. He did something on the floating screen that Cora couldn't see and a moment later the entire screen transformed into a giant half dome that covered the three of them.

"Whoa, I haven't seen those in years," Cora said, studying the faintly glowing pale blue dome.

"Where can we sit?" Captain Donaldson asked.

Cora gestured to the nearby table with four chairs and a lone meal crafter, and all three took their seats. The dome expanded automatically to accommodate their chairs.

The captain used his bracelet to create another floating screen. He arranged something on his screen, but it was also a privacy window and Cora couldn't see anything on it.

"Do you consent to be recorded?" Captain Donaldson asked.

"Yes," Sam said.

"Since Remy Pendleton's death, where have you been?" Captain Donaldson asked.

"Oh, here and there," Sam said. "I had some business to take care of. Cora convinced me to talk to you."

"What happened when Remy Pendleton died?" Captain Donaldson asked.

Sam explained the same story he had told Cora about how he found Remy and heard him calling for help. He ran to help Remy, but he was already dead.

"Why didn't you bring this up earlier?" Captain Donaldson asked.

"I tried to talk to Agent Lewis," Sam said. "But he barely took my statement. He stated surveillance vids are more accurate than eyewitness accounts."

Captain Donaldson shifted uncomfortably in his seat.

"I was available the entire day," Sam said. "He knew how to find me, but after a day, I realized he was never going to contact me. So I continued with my business meetings."

Captain Donaldson sighed and rubbed his face.

"Lewis again. All right," he said. "Yours and Ms. Brimble's story don't completely explain Pendleton Farm's surveillance vids. Let me show you."

Using his comm, he launched a new floating screen. This time, Cora watched him scroll through a list and select an item—it wasn't private. Sam, Cora, and the captain leaned toward the screen as the vid played.

Hazel stepped into view from a trail flanked by several trees and small shrubs. She hurried across the gaming lawn, carpeted with shortcut grass. A few seconds later, Hazel stepped out of view in the direction of the house. Remy stumbled from the path with a sweaty, contorted face, and Winifred followed with furrowed eyebrows.

"Please. Stop. Help me," Remy said in a distressed voice. He fell to the ground.

Winifred darted back into the garden and disappeared.

Sam appeared a few seconds later from the right side of the vid, which was consistent with walking from the barn to the house.

"Help. Somebody help me," Sam yelled.

Less than a minute later, Cora and Hazel appeared, racing to Remy and Sam. Seconds later, Hazel ran off-camera in the direction of the house and returned with the medipad. At the same time, Winifred emerged from the lane onto the games field and blended into the chaos of Remy's death.

The captain stopped the vid and turned to Sam and Cora.

"Neither one of you mentioned Winifred. Why?" Captain Donaldson asked.

"I didn't notice her," Cora said. "What about you?"

"Same," Sam said. "Now that I see this vid, it's clear Winifred had access to Remy long before he stepped out of the garden onto the playing field."

"Also, I think he's asking for Hazel's help," Cora said. "Remy didn't think she was a danger to him."

"That's not completely clear," Captain Donaldson said. "But it seems the real danger was from Winifred."

"What was her official alibi?" Sam asked.

"She has no alibi," Captain Donaldson said. "She was taking a walk around the garden."

"I still don't understand why she'd murder Remy," she said. "She was never really in danger from him."

"Maybe Remy's blackmail attempts really bothered her," Captain Donaldson said.

"Perhaps," she said. "But this sheds a new light on things."

"What do you mean?" Sam asked.

"I ran into Hazel in the hall leading to the patio," Cora said in a serious tone. "I assumed she'd come down from her bedroom, but Aunt Ferna and Delores didn't see her descending the steps. This supports the vids showing her entering the house a second time from the patio. How'd she get out the first time?"

"Winifred and Hazel must have worked together," Captain Donaldson said.

"Why would Winifred need Hazel's help?" Sam asked.

"I don't know, but Hazel's involved somehow," Cora said thoughtfully. "Think about it. Hazel walked into the house while Remy called for her help and didn't return. That means she knew what her mother was doing."

"That sounds so much worse than what I'd been thinking," Sam said.

"And it's conspiracy to commit murder," Captain Donaldson said. "It'd explain why Winifred moved Hazel so swiftly." He sighed. "I really need to get both of their statements."

"I had several conversations with Hazel about the extortion," Sam said. "I wanted them to go to the EGS, but Hazel and Winifred ignored the blackmailer. I thought their strategy was working."

"I don't know," Cora said. "Something feels off about this whole mess."

Captain Donaldson continued Sam's interview with other questions about the Pendleton family, Hazel, Winifred, and his business dealings. Sam answered, occasionally glancing at the time on his bracelet.

Cora glanced at the lobby of people waiting for the last shuttle to Lunar City tonight. Three times as many people now filled the waiting area, including several parents with kids. She wondered if the captain would obtain a complete statement before Sam needed to leave.

"Thank you for your time, Mr. Iverson," Captain Donaldson said, closing his floating window and removing the privacy dome. "You're free to go to Lunar City, but make sure I can still reach you if I have follow-up questions.

"Of course," Sam said. "I'll be back in two or three days, anyway."

They all stood. Sam nodded to Cora and Captain Donaldson, then left to join the other passengers preparing to board for Lunar City.

He never asked about Hazel, she thought, feeling sad for her.

"Ms. Brimble, as usual, your insights have been invaluable," Captain Donaldson said with a small smile. "But please, for your safety, do not involve yourself further with this investigation. The EGS will decide on the best way to approach the Cartwrights. Understand?"

Cora nodded, and the captain strode toward the exit. But she couldn't leave these murders alone.

CHAPTER 21

Early the next morning, Cora flew in her hover car, out of Tymal and down a major slope of the Krega mountains. She drifted over boulders, sparse clumps of bushes, and the occasional lone pine tree. Reflecting over everything, the events of the past few weeks made her review Michael and Remy's deaths and what they had in common.

A deep sadness settled into the pit of her stomach. She loved Hazel like a real sister. Now she realized all of that might be lost. She squeezed her hands tightly together, like an ancient prayer, hoping she was wrong.

Her bracelet chimed, and she answered the vidchat to see Brian's grinning face.

"Cora. What's going on?" he asked, glancing behind her. "Where are you going?"

"I'm visiting Hazel in Branvale," she said. "I should be back in the afternoon. The trip's a few hours."

"Is that a good idea?" he asked, frowning. "What if Winifred's the murderer? You'll be closer to her."

"I know. It could be Winifred," she said. "And... Hazel may have helped."

"Hazel? How could she help?" he asked as his worried expression deepened.

"I don't know... I'm grasping at straws," she said as the sadness expanded in her stomach.

"Look, why don't you stop where you are," he said. "I'll join you, but we'll fly in separate cars. When you get there, I'll wait outside to make sure you're safe."

"No, no. I'm not in danger from either of them," she said. "I've known them both since Hazel and I were kids. I don't always agree with Winifred, but she wouldn't hurt me." She sighed. "If I thought I was in danger, I wouldn't be going."

"But why chance it?" He asked.

"Look, I only want to have a conversation with both of them," she said as irritability began to replace her sadness. "I want to find out what really happened to Michael and Remy."

"You think they're just going to tell you?" he said, crossing his arms. "I'm still not okay with this. I think you should turn around and come back."

"I'm completely safe," she said, forcing a smile. "And in any case, you can monitor my trip. I'll send you my coordinates." She pressed the bottom of the floating screen, bringing up a new window, and sent her coordinates. "Now, you can tell where I am and you also have some biometric data, heart and respiratory rates. Okay?"

At that moment, Cora's bracelet chimed again.

"Look, Brian, I really have to go," she said. "I have an incoming vidchat."

"Okay," he said. "But I really don't like this." His window went dark, and she closed it and a new floating window popped up with Hazel's smiling face.

"Cora, your message was a pleasant surprise," Hazel said. "When do you think you'll be here?"

"It looks like I've another hour to go," Cora said. "I left as soon as I sent you the first message."

"Excellent. I look forward to seeing you," Hazel said. "Oh, Mom programmed the meal crafter with a new dessert recipe. I think you'll like it."

"I'm always open to trying new desserts." Cora smirked.

"I'll see you soon," Hazel said, and her screen went dark.

Cora closed the window and sighed. The thought of losing a friend weighed on her, but she just couldn't let a murderer go free.

As Cora approached the small town of Branvale, patches of wild grasses and bushes appeared below the hover car. The landscape turned greener and denser, and before long, she was flying over a thick forest. She continued to her destination for another thirty minutes.

An immense mansion glimmered in the distance and grew larger as the hover car neared the reflective gold colored gilding on the fence and the towers. The sun shined brighter here at the foot of the mountains, causing her to lower the shading inside the car.

She'd only visited a handful of times, but the mansion never failed to impress. The only downside was the mansion was extremely traditional and formal. Its white marble, boxy shape, and ornate decorations around every window made it seem like a relic from her grandparents' era. She noticed the backyard, even though significantly larger than her own, had much fewer plants. Instead, it was filled with small temples, towers, and offering tables that were popular two or three generations ago. Huge gravel walkways connected each of these outdoor structures. The idea was that the more places you had to honor Askae, the more powers she would grant to you.

Cora sent a message to Hazel, letting her know that she'd arrived as she maneuvered the hover car to a flat, grassy front yard. The hover car came to rest, floating about a meter above the grass while steps extended to the ground.

Cora stepped out with her hair in a ponytail. She checked her casual pink long sleeve shirt and smoothed out her blue pants. She had dressed warmly because Tymal, even with its controlled weather, was usually kept a little cooler than the bottom of the mountain in Branvale. As she made her way down the stairs, she immediately began to sweat.

"Cora, Cora," Hazel called, running toward her with bouncing blonde curls. She gave Cora a tight hug. "I'm so happy you're here. I've been desperately lonely."

Hazel spoke dramatically, like she had when they were in school, and Cora grinned at the familiarity of it. She loved being the big sister and taking care of Hazel. The two of them linked arms and walked away from Cora's hover car, but didn't enter the house.

Cora felt a fresh spike of Hazel's excitement.

"I want you to see something back here," Hazel said with a broad smile. "I've prepared a feast for the both of us."

Hazel giggled and Cora allowed herself to be swept away and chuckled. They strolled to the back of the large mansion and paced to one of the marble offering tables. Hazel created a little mid-morning snack. Two chairs sat across from each other while two pieces of pink fluffy cake filled two plates, two empty teacups, and silverware that sat on either side of each plate.

"Oh, this looks lovely," Cora said. "Is this the recipe you were talking about?"

Hazel nodded. "You won't believe it," she said. "So yummy."

The two women sat down, and Hazel pressed a button from the meal crafter, which filled both cups with tea. They both sipped tea and ate the cake in silence.

Hazel sighed with a small smile as she placed her empty teacup on the table.

"I got word from Mom," she said. "She and Dad have picked out my new husband."

Cora felt her deep stream of sadness, which contrasted with her smile.

How have I never noticed this difference before? she thought. *When facial expressions don't match broadcast emotions, something's wrong.*

"I'm so sorry, Hazel," Cora said. "I know this isn't what you want, and I wish I had the power to change it."

Deciding to address her projected emotions instead of her facial expressions, Cora hoped to get Hazel to trust her more.

"It's okay," she said, shrugging a shoulder. "I was expecting it, and Mom is determined. The only downside is I'm going to be distantly related to Kaye."

Cora wrinkled her nose, and Hazel laughed.

"Seriously, I'm sorry to hear about that," Cora said.

"I don't know why I can never get away from that woman," Hazel smirked. "Umm... Have you heard from Sam?" she asked in a low voice.

Cora hesitated, looking down at her empty plate.

"Well, yes," she said. "I met him yesterday with Captain Donaldson."

"Captain Donaldson? Why?" Hazel asked.

Cora repeated Sam's statement, explaining what he'd seen during Remy's death and why he was not interested in seeing her.

As tears began to fill her eyes, Hazel wiped quickly.

"I see," she said. "It's really over then."

"I'm so sorry, Hazel," Cora said. "But now that we're on the subject of the two Pendleton deaths, can I ask you a few questions?"

Cora hesitated as her courage drained away.

"What?" Hazel asked. "What's going on?"

Cora took a deep breath and plowed on.

"Are you a Mover?" Cora asked.

Hazel gazed at Cora for a long moment with an expressionless face. She studied the surrounding garden flowers, rocks, and trees. Before turning back to Cora.

"How did you know?" Hazel asked.

Something inside Cora died. She couldn't believe somebody she had loved as dearly as a sister could do something so heinous. She'd hoped Sam had been overreacting yesterday when he explained he couldn't stay with her anymore.

Sam thought she'd *left* Remy to die, but now Cora knew Hazel had *caused* Remy to die.

Hazel stood and stepped away from the offering table. She took a few steps and gestured to Cora, who joined her. Trying to ignore the heavy, devastating emotional storm slowly engulfing Hazel, she pressed on, as she had a mission to fulfill.

"Michael and Remy's murders struck me as sloppy," Cora said. "Did you know I could frequently sense your emotions? I could tell you were trying to mask your sadness or anger, but your shield didn't completely protect you. It's sloppy." Hazel stopped and glared at Cora. "Last night, as I thought over all the evidence, I kept thinking of you. This morning when I woke up, I was sure."

Hazel turned and continued ambling along a gravel path. Cora kept pace and listened to a warbler.

"I didn't know my shield leaked," Hazel said with a stony face. "I paid someone a lot of credits to teach me."

They strolled toward a mini-temple full of yellow and white wildflowers. It looked like a sun, rising from the middle of the structure. Cora couldn't enjoy the sight with so much weighing on her.

"Okay, I don't have as much control," Hazel said, her lips in a grim line. "But my timing was impeccable. There were several Movers at the Spring Gala. That's how I knew I could get away with murder—too many suspects."

"Yes, but every Mover at the Gala would've had training," Cora said. "At the Spring Gala, your mom expertly delivered gifts and even made them do a little dance before they landed in front of everyone at the head table. Precise. I didn't realize what Michael's scans meant until the captain explained the damage to several of Michael's and Remy's organs and bones. Not Precise."

"Doesn't change the fact that I got away with it," Hazel said with a smirk.

"In Remy's case, it would've been safer for you if you'd made it seem like an accident," Cora said. "As it turns out, Sam saw you kill Remy, although he didn't understand at the time."

"So, you think you have this all figured out?" Hazel said with a dry chuckle.

Cora shook her head.

"How long have you known you're a Mover?" Cora asked.

Hazel sighed, but didn't answer for several seconds.

"Do you remember Pearl?" Hazel asked.

"She used to bully you, but I made her stop," Cora said as a light perfume of flowers wafted past her.

"Well, after you graduated, she started bullying me again," Hazel said. "We were the same age and taking many of the same classes—I couldn't get away from her."

"Why didn't you tell me?" Cora asked. "I spoke to you several times a week."

"I know..." Hazel said in a low voice. "I was embarrassed that you had to stop her before, and I still couldn't defend myself."

"Did she do the same stunts to you as before?" Cora asked.

"Yeah," Hazel said. "She'd dump water on me at the dining hall, sprinkle crumbs in my hair, and trip and push me. Claiming everything was an accident made the instructors ignore her behavior."

"Oh, Hazel... I wish you'd told me," Cora said, gazing at her. "You didn't need to endure that constant harassment. Did anyone see what she was doing?"

"Yeah," Hazel said. "Her gang of friends laughed along with her."

Cora felt Hazel's radiated anger washing over her in waves.

"What happened after that?" Cora asked, trying to distract Hazel and lower her broadcast animosity.

"One day," Hazel said, "I'd failed a test in a class I never wanted to take. I knew Mom and I were going to have an argument in a few hours. I was furious. I stomped out of class, down the hall, and headed for the stairs at the back of the building; the ones no one ever used."

Hazel grew quiet, and the warbler continued its song for several seconds.

"Pearl cornered me on the landing at the top of the stairs. She sneaked behind me and pushed. I wasn't expecting her attack and smacked my face into a wall. After that, I saw red. Pearl squealed with laughter and headed to the top step. Something came over me. I've never felt that kind of power—it came from deep inside me. When I flung my hands toward Pearl, her eyes grew wide and I pushed as hard as I could. I felt the antigrav safeties trying to stop me, but I was stronger. She slammed onto the steps three times as she tumbled backwards.

Each time she broke a bone—I felt them crack. First her left arm, next her right, and finally her right leg."

"Wow, was that the first time you used your Mover abilities?" Cora asked.

Hazel nodded.

"Heliton has surveillance everywhere," Cora said. "Why didn't anyone see you?"

A mirthless laugh escaped Hazel's lips.

"Because Pearl pushed me against a wall," Hazel said. "I ended up in a dead zone between two surveillance monitors. Too bad for her." She smirked. "On the vids, it seemed I'd stepped back from the stairs while Pearl appeared to trip on the stairs."

"But Pearl bounced hard enough to break bones," Cora said. "They should have been questioning your abilities."

"Oh, they did," Hazel chuckled. "But I show up as non-Askovian in every test. I have to be enraged to pass their tests. Pearl claimed I was a Mover, but no one believed her. She never bothered me again."

They strolled past a mini-tower replica. Cora barely noticed as she struggled to digest Hazel's words. She'd thought they were best friends for more than two decades, but now she wondered if she really knew Hazel.

"So, what happened with Michael?" Cora asked. "Why did you have to kill him?"

"I really hated him and Kaye," Hazel said. "Michael took every opportunity to humiliate me in public. Or he let Kaye do it. At the Spring Gala, she told me about the children they planned to have. For me, it was the last straw, and I vowed to find a way to make them both pay."

Cora felt Hazel's rising rage wash over her.

I'll need to distract her soon, she thought. *It's too much.*

"When I questioned Kaye after Remy's death, she admitted she'd lied," Cora said. "Evan had asked Michael to send her back to Lunar City. He'd also demanded he start a family with you immediately. If you'd waited one or two days, you would've had your family."

"I *never* wanted a family with Michael," Hazel said, holding her trembling fingers in front of her as her anger increased. "I enjoyed hurting him."

Cora considered shielding herself, but held on a little longer.

"I can see it now. Michael hooked his arm around Kaye's," Hazel said. "He whispered something to her, and they started toward the stairs. I followed."

"That feeling from deep inside started rising again," Hazel said. "In an instant, I had a plan. I was going to push them both down the stairs."

Hazel made two fists with her hands. Cora could feel the barely controlled anger.

"Then something odd happened," Hazel said in a shaky voice. "Delores called Kaye away to chat with Julia. This change slowed me down and I considered waiting until later, but Michael continued to the top of the stairs. Suddenly everyone parted, and I could see him clearly. When he turned around, I saw Pearl all over again. I closed my eyes and this time only pushed with my mind. I saw Pearl tumble backward down the stairs while I pounded her into the steps three times."

"No," Cora's throat squeezed out.

"Just like last time, I felt the antigrav safeties trying to activate," Hazel said with a grim smile. "I was as surprised as anyone when he died. I thought he'd only have broken bones like Pearl, but he broke his neck. Maybe that's because I kept my eyes closed."

"I sat beside you for most of the Gala," Cora said. "Why didn't you talk to me?"

"I really wasn't trying to kill him," Hazel said. "I wanted to teach him a lesson."

"I wish I could have stayed and protected you," Cora said in a quiet voice. "You know, I love you. You were the sister I always wanted."

Both women stopped walking. Hazel reached for Cora, who backed away.

"I've disappointed you, haven't I?" Hazel said in a low voice.

"As much as I love you, I can't cover up your murder," Cora said, blinking back tears. "I can't do it."

Hazel glared at her.

"What are you saying?" Hazel asked. "Are you going to turn me in?"

Cora detected something she'd never sensed before. Something that surpassed rage. Venom? She shivered, trying to control her own rising panic.

"No, I'm not going to turn you in," Cora said, taking a steadying breath. "You're my sister, and I can't do that. I want you to turn yourself in."

Hazel scoffed and laughed bitterly.

"No thanks," Hazel smirked. "I don't want to disappear like Zach."

"I understand that," Cora said. "I'm not expecting you to agree with me right now. But we can't continue like this."

"Well, you're going to have to get used to it," Hazel said with an edge to her voice. "Because I'm not turning myself in."

Both of them jumped when Winifred suddenly appeared on the gravel path.

CHAPTER 22

"Hello, Cora," Winifred said with a small smile. "I didn't realize you were coming here today."

Cora took a moment to gather her thoughts. She detected nothing from Winifred, which meant she'd shielded her emotions well.

"Early this morning I woke, realizing Hazel must be a Mover," Cora said with a slight waver in her voice. She clenched her hands together to stop them from shaking. "I also realized you know your only daughter has Mover abilities."

"Yes, Hazel is a Mover," Winifred said. "But she doesn't have very much control—she's never been trained. I didn't know about her abilities until Remy passed away."

"Michael's body scan shows diffuse energy use," Cora said. "It reminded me of the way young Movers use their abilities—scattered and chaotic."

"Diffuse energy use," Winifred said with a smile that didn't reach her eyes. "Is that even admissible in court?"

"I don't know," Cora said. "Remy was the expert on Askovian forensics, but he's dead and his replacement isn't ready. Hazel's probably safe." She turned to Hazel. "That's why you have to turn yourself in."

"I told you to keep your distance from her," Winifred said to Hazel. "She's always been smarter than you."

Cora's knees nearly buckled as Hazel beamed fresh waves of hatred. She raised her shield in self-defense.

"Hazel can't control her powers enough for any testing," Winifred said, addressing Cora. "Like you said, Hazel's safe."

"Is there anything else you'd like to know?" Hazel asked in a hostile tone.

Cora steeled herself to continue questioning Hazel.

"What happened with Remy?" Cora asked. "I saw the same signature as Michael—damage distributed throughout the body. But I also

saw pulverized nanobots floating in his blood-
stream."

Hazel glanced at Winifred.

"I tricked Remy into meeting me in the garden," Hazel said, crossing her arms defiantly. "I
sneaked down the back stairs. But when I found
him in the garden, he was talking to Mom."

"I ran into Remy in the garden. He was quite
drunk," Winifred said, taking up the story. "He
admitted to blackmailing Hazel and tried to
taunt me, saying I couldn't do anything about it.
His evidence would be sent to the EGS if anything happened to him." She chuckled. "But I've
done enough negotiations to tell when someone is lying to me."

"That's when I stumbled on the two of them,"
Hazel said. "I didn't know who the blackmailer
was until I heard their conversation."

"I asked him to stop blackmailing Hazel,"
Winifred said.

"You mean you and Hazel," Cora said.

"No," Winifred said with a sarcastic smile.
"Hazel assumed Remy blackmailed me, but he
seemed to always know it was Hazel and nobody else. Maybe it was his years working for
the EGS and hunting down Askovians."

"When it looked like Mom wouldn't give him any credits, he became upset," Hazel said. "Suddenly, he turned and took the garden trail in the direction of the front lawn. I kept pace with him and asked him again to leave us alone, but he wouldn't listen to anything I had to say."

"I decided to remain in the garden," Winifred said, "to give Hazel a chance to change his mind."

"Before we stepped onto the lawn, Remy smirked," Hazel said, as her eyes narrowed. "I know he thought he'd won, but it made me furious to think he could ruin my life over a few credits. I turned, stepped onto the lawn toward the house while I pushed him with as much force as I could gather."

"I realized a little too late that Hazel was going to kill Remy," Winifred said with a sigh. "I rushed to catch up with them. But stepping onto the lawn, I heard Remy calling for help. Too late, I remembered the home's surveillance and ducked back into the garden."

"I may not have much control, but I have a lot of power," Hazel said in a tense voice. "I destroyed the nanobots with the amount of force I was using, making sure he couldn't talk to the EGS."

"What happened to you?" Cora asked as a heavy feeling settled in her heart.

Hazel crossed her arms and glared.

"What do you plan to do now?" Winifred asked. "Are you going to turn Hazel in?"

"No, I don't have hard evidence," Cora said. "You need to turn yourself in, Hazel."

Winifred laughed, and Hazel chuckled softly.

"I've already lost a son to the EGS," Winifred said. "I'm not going to lose my only daughter. On top of that, once we're away from Earth, we'll be out of EGS jurisdiction. Nobody will be able to touch us."

"I can't stop you from leaving," Cora said. "But have you thought of the legacy you're leaving for your children?"

"Of course, I know the legacy I'm leaving for them," Winifred said in a soft, menacing tone. "That legacy is life. I never saw Zach once the EGS took him away. I don't know if he's alive or dead. Maybe he's part of some government experiment. All I know is he's gone."

Hazel's bracelet chimed.

"I think we're going to have company in about forty-five minutes," Hazel said in a tense voice.

"It's fine," Winifred said. "The EGS will need time to break through our home's defenses."

Cora sighed as a new numbness settled over her. She'd hoped Hazel was still the girl she'd left behind at school, but she had died a long time ago.

"Any more questions?" Winifred asked. "We're going to have to leave soon."

"When you asked to meet Remy in the garden," Cora said. "Were you going to kill him?"

"Not at first," Hazel said, turning slightly to continue their stroll. "I wasn't completely sure who the blackmailer was."

They passed an enormous statue of Askae carved in a shiny white metal. It was an old, wrinkled woman draped in robes, holding a walking staff with a crystal on one end.

"You gave me the idea to ask for evidence," Hazel chortled. "I'd hoped the evidence would hint at the blackmailer. Imagine my surprise when I stumbled across Mom and Remy. He'd assumed Mom had asked him to meet there in my place. With slurred words, he actually threatened to contact Uncle Evan if Mom didn't give him any credits."

She sensed Hazel's broadcast glee, but this only made Cora sad.

"That's when I *knew* I had to kill him," Hazel said.

"So he contacted you first because he figured out you were the Mover who'd murdered Michael?" Cora said, turning to Hazel.

"But I didn't respond," Hazel said, crossing her arms. "I didn't fold because I'm not weak." She said the last to Winifred through gritted teeth.

"Then he contacted you," Cora said, turning to Winifred. "I suppose he thought you'd pay, but he was also afraid of you." She peered at both Winifred and Hazel. "He must've been terrified when you both showed up in the garden."

"Yes, he left shortly after Hazel joined us," Winifred frowned. "I let Hazel go with him, but that was a mistake."

"He thought he was safe walking with me," Hazel chuckled. "But I had a plan. I knew his blackmailing would never stop. So, I destroyed him knowing the surveillance monitors wouldn't detect my Mover abilities. It looked as if I simply walked into the house."

Cora stopped along the path, her mouth gaping. This forced Hazel and Winifred to stop and turn to face her.

"You planned his murder," Cora said in a hoarse voice.

"I worked out how much of the games' yard the home's surveillance could see." Hazel smirked. "I set my trap to lure the blackmailer to the gardens. Then making them feel at ease, encouraged them to follow me back to the house."

"Hazel did the right thing," Winifred said. "My only regret is she got caught."

Cora gawked at the two of them, nonplussed.

Is this real? she thought. *You'd have thought of something less public?*

"At that point, you had options," Cora said. "Remy had body scans, but he had nothing connecting them with you."

"You haven't dealt with Evan too much, have you?" Winifred scoffed. "If you catch him on a good day, he might believe you, and if it's a bad day, he probably won't. Evan disliked Remy, but it's not clear if he'd trust Remy's decades of experience or ignore it."

Hazel's bracelet chimed again.

"They'll be here in thirty-five minutes," she said with urgency.

"I still want to encourage you to go to the EGS with the truth," Cora said. "With Remy's blackmailing, you should get a lighter sentence."

"We're never going to the EGS," Hazel spat.

"We don't need to get angry, Hazel," Winifred said.

"You've been telling me for years that you love me like a sister," Hazel said with an edge to her voice. "That you'd do anything to protect me. Well, you didn't. Bad things still happen to me. Mom, Pearl, her friends, Michael, Julia, Kaye, the list goes on."

Cora glanced at Winifred, who grimaced.

Cora gaped and then inched open her shield. Perceiving a tidal wave of Hazel's beamed venom, she hurriedly raised it again.

"What are you talking about?" Cora said in a soft voice. "I couldn't protect you from Pearl—I wasn't there. Just like I couldn't protect you from your mom, Michael, or the rest of the people on your list."

"Hazel, dear, I think we need to continue this conversation later," Winifred said with urgency. "Right now, we really should go."

Hazel glared at Cora, who suddenly felt a wall of intense energy coursing through her body. The sharp, deep pain made her cry out.

"Stop, Hazel! Stop!" Winifred yelled.

Cora's pain only intensified, and her knees buckled. Her throat began to close, and her own panic drowned out rational thoughts. She couldn't breathe and her world dimmed, and as she lost consciousness, it suddenly stopped.

She coughed repeatedly, trying to take in air that simultaneously filled her aching lungs and irritated her throat. The hacking cough made her convulse, and she vomited. The bile stung her throat, and sucking in fresh air for her lungs also stung. She lay on her back, trying to steady her breath. That's when she saw Winifred repeating a hand over hand gesture to form a circle, focusing on a spot above the walking lane.

Seeing this gesture again reminded Cora of the Spring Gala. She followed Winifred's gaze and peered at Hazel floating in a shiny silver bubble. Hazel beat against the sides of the bubble with both fists while yelling something no one could hear.

Changing her hand motions to two flat palms caused the bubble to sail down the path around the corner and toward the house.

Winifred turned to Cora and helped her to stand.

"Are you all right, Cora?" Winifred asked. "Do I need to call the medipad?

Cora shook her head, but continued coughing. "Why..." She wheezed but her throat wouldn't cooperate.

"Why did I help you?" Winifred asked, helping Cora to the house. "I didn't want Hazel to kill you." She wrapped an arm around Cora, supporting her weight as they stepped along the path.

"Just to be clear, I don't like you," Winifred said. "But Captain Donaldson is on his way here now, and if you die with so much evidence, even the IPS won't shelter us."

Cora glared at Winifred, wishing she could yell at her for terrifying Hazel her whole life.

"I know you don't think too much of me either," Winifred said. "Evan could still come after us, but I'm gambling he won't do anything about Remy's death. He might care about Michael's death, but I'm still not sure if he'd pursue anything. If you die with the EGS on its way, well... Nobody would help Hazel."

After a minute or two, they reached the patio.

"My daughter is in the house, and I've locked her in her room," Winifred said.

How did she lock Hazel in her room? she thought.

"I can see your wheels turning," Winifred smirked. "We Movers have a lot of tricks up our sleeves."

She activated the medipad, which unfolded from the wall, floated toward Cora, creating a padded bed and extending medical instruments. Winifred helped her onto the bed, and the medipad scanned Cora. Her coughing decreased, but the searing pain still etched her throat.

A beam of white light scanned her entire body, and a gradual, warm feeling surrounded her throat. The stinging and burning sensation melted as the medipad repaired the abrasions in her trachea, esophagus, and strained neck muscles.

Winifred watched the screen, monitoring Cora's progress.

"It looks like you've suffered a lot of tissue damage," Winifred said matter-of-factly. "Not surprising, of course. Your throat had the most damage, but there's tissue damage throughout your body. You have no broken bones." She turned to Cora. "I've had a message from Brian and Captain Donaldson. They'll be here in about fifteen minutes. I want you to tell them everything that happened to you here. Tell them everything you know. They'll also have access to the surveillance vids. Tell them that you urged us to turn ourselves in."

"Why?" Cora asked in a shaky voice. The medipad still worked on her throat.

"Because we're not going to be here," Winifred said. "I'm taking Hazel with me, and we'll be off-world in a couple of hours. Once we leave low-earth-orbit, the EGS will have no jurisdiction. It's the IPS in charge and we all know how useful they are."

"What's going to happen to Hazel?" Cora asked in a steady voice.

"Hazel is engaged to be married," Winifred said. "He knows all about her, and he's a powerful Mover—he can defend himself. He's related to the Stone family, which can also offer additional protection for our mine. The Stones and Pendletons are allies."

Winifred's bracelet chimed at the same time the medipad chimed.

"The medipad has completed its repairs," she said. "The EGS will be here in less than fifteen minutes."

She turned and entered the house, leaving Cora alone on the patio, feeling more drained than ever before.

Chapter 23

Cora placed her empty teacup on the table and relaxed into her chair with a satisfied sigh. Her floral green and pink dress was the standard for afternoon teas.

"The sandwiches were refreshing," Aunt Ferna said, as she dabbed her mouth with a napkin. Her blue and white striped dress wasn't exactly fitting for the occasion, but nobody at the table cared.

"I love eating out here," Cora said, taking in the warm breeze rustling the yellow-green leaves.

"Brimble Manor has a lot to offer," Brian said with a straight face. He brushed a few crumbs from his tan short-sleeved top and matching tan pants. His dad, Benjamin, and Aunt Ferna burst out laughing. A true manor would be about three times larger than Brimble House, the home's official name. The real attraction to the home was their extensive gardens.

"Did you know we lived in a manor house?" Aunt Ferna asked with a grin.

"No," Cora said with a chuckle.

"So Cora, explain it to me again," Benjamin asked. He wore a formal jumpsuit suitable for a business meeting. Cora thought he may not have any casual clothes. "What happened with Winifred and Hazel yesterday?"

Cora described the events of the day with Winifred and Hazel and provided more details when he asked.

"Oh, the whole thing is despicable," Aunt Ferna said. "I can't believe someone can kill two people and nothing can be done about it. I think we need to do something about the IPS."

"The IPS, ha," Benjamin exclaimed. "Everyone knows they have no teeth."

"I know," Aunt Ferna said in a sharp tone. "The result is that Askovs do whatever they want."

Cora didn't reply. She'd heard this complaint a million times.

"I agree with Ferna," Benjamin said in a surly tone. "If I ever come across either one of those two, I'm going to give them a piece of my mind."

"I don't think that's a good idea," Brian said. "One is a powerful Mover, and the other is a wild card. Based on what Cora described, Hazel could end up killing you by mistake."

"It just bothers me," Benjamin grumbled.

"Besides, Ben, you're meant to be on vacation when you go to Mars," Aunt Ferna said in a softer voice. "You don't need to act like the EGS."

A moment of silence settled over the four.

"I've been thinking about Oliver," Aunt Ferna said in a quiet voice. "What happens when an Askovian gets locked up for breaking the law? I only heard from him before and during his trial. After he lost, I heard nothing. I can't even visit him."

"Winifred wondered the same thing," Cora said. "That's why she absolutely refused to turn Hazel in. And she's got a valid point. After her son's trial, she never saw him again."

"Oh yes, Zach," Aunt Ferna said. "In his case, it seemed a simple accident, but the EGS didn't take it that way."

"Sometimes I wonder what's worse," Brian said. "The IPS, which has no power, or the EGS, which has too much power."

"Well, it's true." Benjamin said. "The EGS has a lot of explaining to do, but we still need them.

Otherwise, Askovians and their families would run around committing all sorts of crimes and the rest of us wouldn't be safe."

"I see what you mean, Dad," Brian said. "But Aunt Ferna's point is, what are they doing with the imprisoned Askovians? How are they even holding them?"

"I know Oliver would've been treated differently if he hadn't been Askovian," Cora said, leaning forward a little. "You would've been able to see him on a regular basis, Aunt. That's what happens to everybody else."

"Well, that makes sense to me," Benjamin said in a stern voice. "Askovians are dangerous. Can you imagine trying to have a visitation with a Mover?"

"They installed a neurowall on Oliver," Cora said. "Since it was blocking his powers, Aunt Ferna was safe around him."

"Those things don't work on all Askovians," Benjamin scoffed. "I still think the EGS should lock up the bad ones."

"You just don't understand," Aunt Ferna said in a wobbly voice.

"Yes, Ferna, I do understand that you love your son," Benjamin replied. "But your Oliver was a holy terror. I've heard rumors of other

EGS agents who needed to be hospitalized after crossing paths with him."

"On a different note," Brian said, turning to Cora. "Have you had a chance to think about my offer?"

Cora met his expectant eyes and could feel her face warming. She hadn't expected to have this conversation in front of Aunt Ferna and Benjamin.

"Yes, I have," Cora said and turned toward the garden.

"Well... don't keep me waiting," Brian said playfully.

"Don't tease the boy," Aunt Ferna said with a chuckle.

"Does that mean you're coming with us?" Brian asked with a broad smile.

"Aunt Ferna and I will join you and your dad in Lunar City," Cora said, glancing at three sets of eyes.

"When do you think we should all leave?" Brian said, glancing at his dad.

"I can be ready in about two weeks," Aunt Ferna grinned.

"I need one or two months to launch my game," Cora said, and frowned. "Also, I can't stay there for a whole month. I'm thinking about two or three weeks because I have one of those mandatory meetings your mom scheduled."

"She's already started working?" Benjamin frowned. "Mark my words, nothing good will come of this."

"We don't know that yet," Brian said. "Maybe between Mom and Eliza, they'll manage the company just fine."

"Well, I don't think so," Benjamin said. "In one or two years, the company will completely unravel. Nora's made a mistake."

"Okay, so back to pleasant topics. How about you, Dad?" Brian asked. "I know you have a longer journey to Mars."

"I've been ready to leave for a few weeks now," Benjamin said. "Ever since the Spencers dropped that awful mine on us."

"In a strange way, the Spencers stealing that mine seems to have been a blessing," Cora said. "It's allowed you two to travel. I wish I could go all the way to Mars with you both, but I'm the only one here representing Brimble mining."

"Well, I don't wish to go to Mars," Aunt Ferna said. "I prefer my home life with my family and friends. I don't mind the occasional excursion to Lunar City. But all the way to Mars means we'd be gone for three or more years."

Cora smiled gently at Aunt Ferna and reached out to squeeze her hand. "I feel the exact same way. I'd rather stay here with my family."

***

To enjoy more cozy mystery science fiction, pick up Lunar Justice(https://katherinesbook s.com/lunarjustice).

Please Leave an Honest Review

Authors thrive on reviews. These reviews help other readers decide whether to buy the book. To write a review, simply go back to the website where you purchased this book, provide a star rating, and add a couple of sentences explaining why you liked the book. Thank you for your review.

Review Link (https://katherinesbooks.com/movers-review)

WOULD YOU LIKE ANOTHER SCI-FI WHODUNIT?

Want to know how it all began? Dive into *Short Stories from the Feeler Universe* (https://katherinesbooks.com/sci-fi-short-story/), and once you join my newsletter, read this thrilling short story from *The Feeler* series! This prequel takes you to the very beginning, where Cora uses her unique Feeler abilities to unravel a gripping whodunit.

Books

Standalone Books

The Puzzle Safe Mystery
https://katherinesbooks.com/psmamz
The Runaway Martian
https://katherinesbooks.com/runawaymartia
namz
***

The Feeler Series Books

The Feeler (Book 1)
katherinesbooks.com/feeler
Movers, Mines, and Murder (Book 2)
katherinesbooks.com/movers
Lunar Justice (Book 3)
katherinesbooks.com/lunarjustice
Spencer Legacy (Book 4)

katherinesbooks.com/spencerlegacy

ABOUT THE AUTHOR

Katherine is a science fiction author who spent nearly thirty years working as an engineer before retiring and turning to her life-long love of storytelling. She grew up devouring classic sci-fi, especially the works of Isaac Asimov, Arthur C. Clarke, and Ray Bradbury. As much as she adored those stories, she often felt something was missing.

Over time, her reading tastes broadened to include cozy mysteries, thrillers, and fantasy. Eventually she realized her ideal book would be a blend of the genres she loved most. The solution was obvious: write cross-genre stories that fuse the wonder of science fiction with the charm and puzzle-solving of cozy mystery.

Katherine lives in New England, where she spends her days writing, reading, and enjoying time with her family.